D1412445

# V

## IS FOR
## VICTORINE

### Anne Nesbet

CANDLEWICK PRESS

Copyright © 2023 by Anne Nesbet
Epigraphs and quotes from *How to Write for the "Movies"*
by Louella O. Parsons (Chicago: McClurg, 1915)

First edition 2023

Library of Congress Catalog Card Number 2022923579
ISBN 978-1-5362-2828-1

23 24 25 26 27 28 APS 10 9 8 7 6 5 4 3 2 1

Printed in Humen, Dongguan, China

This book was typeset in Hightower.

Candlewick Press
99 Dover Street
Somerville, Massachusetts 02144

www.candlewick.com

MIX
Paper | Supporting
responsible forestry
FSC® C144853

A JUNIOR LIBRARY GUILD SELECTION

For Linda Williams,
with whom I have laughed and cried
at the movies for so many years

# Chapter 1

## The Vanishing of Victorine

*I have prepared a series of photoplay lessons for the beginner,*
*which I have endeavored to make as simple as possible.*
—How to Write for the "Movies" (*1915*), *by Louella O. Parsons*

It is a truth only rarely acknowledged that most people of the age of twelve or thirteen travel this world in some degree of disguise: their insides and their outsides do not always exactly match.

The girl now traveling through life as Bella Mae Goodwin had learned this lesson very well. She had had to leave behind the name she was most accustomed to in order to escape from villains and the system that kept young, orphaned heiresses in constant peril.

For now we can call her Vee, as her friend Darleen liked to do.

Vee and her dear friend Darleen were both at this very moment *in disguise*, trying their best to look like two absolutely ordinary girls of twelve or thirteen, out buying tickets for today's absolutely ordinary moving picture matinee.

It was quite an adventure to be in disguise, actually: to be pushing toward the theater in a crowd that paid no attention to the two of them at all, dressed up as they were in simple sailor dresses, their hair unpretentious in brown waves (Vee) or ordinary-little-girl braids (Darleen). The man who sold the tickets did give Darleen a wink and a tip of the cap and start to say something about how pleased he was to see her here again, Miss Darleen—but she shook her head at him and put a finger to her lips, and he hushed right up like a good fellow.

He had recognized her, you see: Darleen Darling, star of the photoplays, known to the world as Daring Darleen.

But today Darleen was simply here, like everyone else, to watch the new picture, while remaining pleasantly incognito.

Vee did not enjoy disguises quite as much as her friend did, and yet she had already managed to accumulate a number of names and aliases over the past year or so, despite being the sort of person who would really prefer to have one solid name—to be one single, solid, consistent sort of person.

At the moment, Vee was digging some dimes out of a secret pocket, of which (pockets, not dimes) she had an exceedingly great number, since it is practical and convenient (as her Grandmama had always reminded her) to be able to carry the various necessities of life with you, wherever you go. She had coins tucked into one pocket, her trusty pocketknife (inherited from her father) hidden in a second, and an excellent book she had begun to study waiting for her in yet a third. Oh, and a roll of butterscotch candies! She never traveled far without a bit of butterscotch at hand, in case of emergencies.

*Because,* as her Grandmama used to say, *you never know what may happen in this world.*

Vee knew all too well how true that was. Things had happened in her world—many things—and as a result here she was, in layer upon layer of disguise, all secrets and hidden pockets, when it was the longing of her heart to be simply and openly herself, whoever that was.

"There we go!" she said, putting the necessary number of dimes on the counter.

"And that makes two for *The Vanishing of Victorine,* Episode Thirteen," said the ticket man, and he handed over the little tickets. "Enjoy the picture, my dears! I hear there's plenty of excitement for the poor Berryman heiress this time 'round. Maybe even a touch of romance!"

"Oh, dear—*romance,*" said Vee, and she said that so forlornly that Darleen really couldn't help laughing.

"Now, now!" said Darleen, squeezing her friend's hand. "It's just a picture. You know that. All make-believe!"

"Enjoy the show, girls," said the ticket man, and the eager crowd had already pushed the girls in through the doors.

They nabbed two seats and waited for the darkness to fall, for the clattering whir of the projector to start up, and for the pianist to begin his accompaniment with a few stirring chords.

The piano, by the way, was quite out of tune. In a former life, Vee—the girl with too many pockets—had lived in a world where a man came regularly to tune the mansion's pianoforte. But that was all quite long ago already. That home and that piano were truly, as they say, lost in the past.

As soon as the title of the serial appeared—*THE VANISHING OF VICTORINE*—Vee felt the usual glow of awkwardness and shame creep up from her cheeks to the tips of her ears. Thirteen episodes in, and it still felt so strange every time she saw those words!

Darleen gave her friend's hand an understanding squeeze and then whispered into Vee's glowing ear, "But it's funny, Vee, isn't it, when you think about it? Here I am, watching a photoplay with someone who is famous for having disappeared!"

Oh, Vee did see the irony of the situation, of course. But it didn't make her want to laugh. It made her feel most peculiar inside.

Here's the thing: once upon a time, she herself had been Victorine Berryman.

And then—alas!—Victorine Berryman had had to *vanish*.

# Chapter 2

# The Story
of Her Life

*The first and most essential point in learning
any art is concentration.*
—How to Write for the "Movies"

Most people will never have to wrestle with the strange feeling that comes from watching movies—or, in this case, a whole multi-chapter serial ("new episode every Monday!")—about their own private lives. But then again, most people aren't orphans kidnapped at a young age by evildoers posing as distant relatives to get their hands on the Berryman fortune.

And even fewer people, having been kidnapped by villainous "cousins," have found themselves escaping captivity thanks to the nimble arms and quick mind of a young photoplay actress.

And really, probably just about nobody since the

beginning of time can have had the especially complicated experience of being kidnapped, escaping with the help of an actress in the movies, and then taking on a new name (Bella Mae Goodwin) and hiding out for the long term in the little photoplay-producing town of Fort Lee, New Jersey, while loved and protected by a moviemaking family, the Darlings of Matchless Photoplay.

This extremely unlikely series of events was, however, the story of our Victorine's life, as it had dramatically unfolded a little more than a year ago now.

As far as the world knew, the Berryman heiress had disappeared, had been lost, had "vanished." It was a mystery, and like all mysteries that involve young orphans, dastardly criminals, and a huge fortune (that would eventually come to the missing heiress when she turned twenty-one, years and years from now), it could be counted on to pop back up in the public imagination from time to time.

Especially over the last twelve weeks, when that rival Fort Lee movie studio Phoenix Photoplay had started running its serial adventure *The Vanishing of Victorine*, in which a story "plucked from the headlines" had been spun into an epic adventure and fantasy, complete with chases through the icy Alps and a scene or two in the deserts of Arizona, plus an assortment of absolutely terrible and very entertaining perils for their version of Victorine, played by a blond-haired actress who was *at least* twenty-five years of age and perhaps a few more years on than that. This was absolutely ridiculous, considering that the real Victorine had hair that could perhaps best be described as "anonymous brown" and was still only thirteen.

And the ticket man had been right: the episode this week ended with a sickening hint of romance—that young detective and would-be suitor of the vanished Victorine, Jim Brown (entirely fictional, of course), finding the lost heiress's emerald brooch in the sand of that oceanside cave and turning to the camera with tears in his eyes . . .

*Ugh*, thought the real Victorine, several times over. *Ugh, ugh, ugh.*

It was all the most dreadful bunkum and hogwash!

But Victorine wasn't here to count the ways her actual life had been mangled as it was turned into motion picture material. No. She was here with an agenda. More precisely, with that secret guide cleverly tucked into one of her pockets: the little book called *How to Write for the "Movies,"* by Miss Louella Parsons.

It was time (Victorine had decided) for her to prove that even a person who had had to *vanish* could eventually find her own way forward. Learn something new. Stand on her own two feet, as it were. Become a contributing part of this motion picture business—of the serious work of the Matchless studios—where she had found a haven last year, in her time of utmost need.

In her first weeks in Fort Lee, she had first been preoccupied by the anxious thrill that comes with having to escape from villains and hide oneself safely away. She had not had much time in those hectic days to worry about *future plans*! And in the months that followed, she had found herself strangely immobilized, almost as if under a spell, by the pang of having lost so much, so fast: her Grandmama, her childhood home, her name—really, *everything*.

But at some point a girl, even one who has been through a great deal of trouble, has to begin thinking about what she wants to do next. It was time to wake up. It was time to come up with a long-term plan. But what should that be?

Victorine Berryman was a very honest person when it came to reckoning up her skills and weaknesses. She knew she wasn't really cut out for an acting career, even though over the past year she had wandered or waltzed in the background of a number of Matchless photoplays as an extra. She had been wondering for some months now: *What should I do, under these odd new circumstances I find myself in, here in Fort Lee? What can I do?*

Then, some weeks ago, a special announcement had appeared in the closing title cards of the bunkum-and-hogwash-filled *Vanishing of Victorine*.

It was the opening salvo of a contest—oh, and here was that title card again! Just like every other week!

How Should Victorine's Story End?
The Writers Of This Serial Turn
To YOU For The Answer.
$750 Prize For The Best Proposal—
And The Chance To See Your Story
Brought To Life On The Screen!

"You'll do it, won't you?" Darleen had said that first time—and she was squeezing Victorine's hand now to remind her. "You *have* to do it, Vee! You simply have to! It's only fair, if it's supposed to be the story of your life! And words are your talent, Vee, they really are."

And Victorine had thought: *Well, why not?*

After all, writing stories for the motion pictures was surely something one could *learn*, and Victorine had a lot of enthusiasm for anything that involved learning and studying. So she had gone out and spent a precious dollar on Miss Louella Parsons's helpful and encouraging and pocket-size book, *How to Write for the "Movies."* Miss Parsons had given Victorine's plans an immediate boost, because right at the start of her book she said, "The first and most essential point in learning any art is concentration"—and Victorine (again only being honest) knew that her powers of concentration were outstanding.

Surely if she concentrated very, very hard, her

efforts and Miss Parsons's little book could transform her into a plausible *photoplaywright*.

(A photoplaywright was someone who wrote the scenarios for photoplays.)

"Wouldn't seven hundred and fifty dollars be simply lovely, Vee?" Darleen was whispering now. "Maybe we could get a whole new camera for Matchless! Or a set of fancy lights! Or replace that broken boiler Aunt Shirley is so worried about!"

But the contest meant more than money to Victorine. She closed her eyes for a moment to savor her most secret hope: if she could become enough of a genuine photoplaywright to win this contest, it would mean she really deserved a place in this moviemaking world she lived in now.

It would mean, in this life where so much was always so uncertain, that she was *here to stay*.

And that was when Darleen, next to her, gave a little gasp of surprise that made Victorine jump in her seat, while her heart threw in an extra quick beat or two.

"Vee!" said her friend. "What in heaven's name is THAT?"

Another title had come onto the screen. Darleen wasn't the only one taken by surprise—there was a general stir in the room.

And here is what this new title card was shouting (by means of large letters and bold type, since the photoplays themselves, of course, were silent):

ONE MORE CHALLENGE
FOR OUR LOYAL VIEWERS!
WE KNOW YOU HAVE LOVED THIS STORY:
BUT WHERE, OH WHERE IS
THE REAL VICTORINE BERRYMAN?
IF YOU CAN FIND HER—
OR PROVIDE PROOF OF
HER UNFORTUNATE DEMISE—
PLEASE CONTACT
THE LAW OFFICES OF
RIDGE & WATTLE,
NEW YORK CITY!
$1,000 REWARD FOR INFORMATION
LEADING US TO THE LOST GIRL!

"A thousand dollars!" said voices all around them. "A *thousand!*"

But Darleen leaned close and said, with both worry and concern, "What can this mean, Vee? What can this *mean?*"

Victorine trembled, because of course it was clear enough what it meant: it meant they were *looking for her* again. There are many unpleasant things in this life, but the feeling you have when ruthless people announce they are looking for you must surely (thought Victorine) be one of the absolute worst.

# Chapter 3

# Vee!

*You must now visualize your story. Close your eyes and work
it out mentally. Don't rush for paper and pencil until you have placed
each character and each scene in your mind's eye.*
—How to Write for the "Movies"

Once that audience had spilled onto the paved walk-
way outside the little theater, there was a ritual they
seemed to have to go through, each and every one of
them. Everyone paused, took a breath of outside air,
and blinked.

Victorine blinked too.

She could tell that all those eyes around her weren't
seeing the trees, the street, the streetcar rattling by,
not yet. The light outside here was still far too bright
and far too real. Everyone was dazed—by the sun, by
unexpected twists in the plot of their lives (if they
were Victorine)—but they stumbled forward anyway.
They imagined the path ahead of them. They made

it up when their ordinary eyes had failed. That must be what Miss Parsons's book called the "mind's eye," then, hard at work.

"Vee?"

Darleen was pulling on her sleeve—and smiling.

"Oh, sorry!" said Victorine, coming back to the present moment as quick as she could. "I started thinking about eyes, you know. Whether we see with our eyes or with our mind—that sort of thing."

"Well, never you *mind* about *eyes*, Vee," said Darleen, who was used to Victorine getting caught up in her own thoughts. "Why are law offices suddenly looking for you? That's what I want to know."

A new thought made Victorine blink again.

"Not just any law offices: the title card said Ridge & Wattle, didn't it? Do you think—oh, I'm pretty sure it must be—my Grandmama's old attorney, Mr. Ridge! But why would he do such a thing? And why now?"

The girls looked at each other: they had no idea. Mr. Ridge had been—well, the truth was the truth— *unimpressive* as a defender of young Victorine's rights and safety, after the death of her Grandmama had left him the executor of the Berryman estate. He had actually allowed Victorine to fall into the hands of unscrupulous impostors posing as Victorine Berryman's distant family. And really, if Darleen hadn't caused a ruckus by standing in his office window and threatening to climb all the way up that very tall building, who knew where

Victorine might be today? But that is another story . . .

They had not seen him in person since that fateful day. He had, however, dutifully fulfilled the terms of the amended will, leaving a few hundred dollars every six months in the Berryman safety deposit box at the American Bank.

That money had been a real help, by the way, to Victorine herself, and to Matchless Photoplay. Aunt Shirley didn't know that "Bella Mae Goodwin" was actually (or had been) the famous lost heiress Victorine Berryman, but she certainly did appreciate the way Bella Mae's benefactor—"some old uncle of yours, I suppose"—sent along some money from time to time, money that Bella Mae was quick to share. That had helped with the rising price of coal this past winter. A photoplay studio has so many bills to pay!

Victorine didn't spend much time thinking about Mr. Ridge anymore, but this was a strange turn of events: cautious and hidebound *Mr. Ridge* paying to have that odd contest—a kind of "wanted" poster for Victorine Berryman, if you thought about it—posted at the end of a motion picture. It was strange. It didn't sound like something he would do. Why not just leave her a note in the safety deposit box, for instance?

"I don't understand it," said Victorine.

"Well, it's only going to cause trouble," said Darleen. "Can you hear what those people over there are saying?"

Victorine had just opened her mouth to say "No" when a trio of men strode by, their voices so loud and excited that the girls could not help eavesdropping on their conversation.

"I know! I know! She's got to be dead and gone! She was drowned in that lake from Episode Three, I bet!" said the first of them, a man with unruly red hair.

"Nah," said Number Two. "She's hiding somewhere. Why would they ask if they didn't think she might be alive and tucked away somewhere? And I've been thinking about where. That house the wild horse rode by in the picture today? I know where that is! That house is right near here—in Fort Lee!"

He had paused to puff up his chest a bit, he was so proud of his shiny theory.

"Oh, yeah?" said Number Three. "Show me then. I could sure use a thousand dollars!"

"Guess we all could," said Number One. "Steak every night, boys!"

The streetcar came then to take the excited young men away. The girls weren't interested in the streetcar—they were saving their pennies after the indulgence of the photoplay.

"How silly those fellows are," said Darleen. "That house is only in Fort Lee because *Phoenix Photoplay* is in Fort Lee, so that's where they filmed that episode. What nonsense!"

"Well, yes, nonsense," said Victorine more soberly. "But Dar, I'm in Fort Lee too. Seems like people will be buzzing around curiously, doesn't it? That can't be good."

"It's true, I suppose, they might be. But don't you worry," said Dar with total conviction. "We'll keep you VERY safe, *Bella Mae*! Oh, but look at the time! Dinner's at Aunt Shirley's today—we had better trot a bit faster. Nobody's truly safe if they're late for dinner at Aunt Shirley's."

That woke Victorine all the way up. Her own beloved Grandmama had also been very impatient with anyone who dared show up late for dinner.

"And anyway," panted Darleen, as they walked very briskly up the hill. "At least—that silly actress they have playing you—in the pictures—is a fluffy-haired blonde. Very pretty, but—she doesn't look—a stitch—like you, not really."

But then they passed another little knot of movie-goers, and they were also full of talk about the contest:

"I've got a cousin in the police—maybe he can give me a hint or two—"

"Well, my theory is—the people making that moving picture must know the truth. Maybe that girl playing Victorine really IS Victorine! Hidden in plain sight, you know!"

"You think they're hiding the lost girl in a movie studio? Sam, you brilliant rascal! And, jiminy, what if you're right? Worth some in-ves-ti-gation, I'd say! A thousand dollars, boys! . . ."

The voices trailed off a bit as Dar and Victorine scooted by, keeping their faces turned toward the dirt of the road so as not to attract any extra attention.

"Oh, dear," said Darleen once they were safely by. "All those wild theories running through everybody's heads! That's not good at all, is it? People get so fired up sometimes. But I'm sure it will wear off. We'll just have to be a little extra cautious for a while . . ."

And then they practically ran right into two older women who were so caught up in their conversation that they had stopped suddenly, right in their tracks, at the side of the road.

"I'll tell you what I think," one was saying to the other, as Darleen dodged to the right to avoid knocking her over. "Careful now, you girls! Watch where you're going, mind! I think they chose that actress, pretty as she is, just to lead us all astray. Mark my words, the real Victorine won't be graceful and blond—she'll be a scrawny little thing—you know, like one of these girls pushing by us so rudely right now. Listen, girls!" And the woman actually *giggled*, right in the middle of her own rather striking rudeness. "Is one of you Miss Victorine Berryman, by any chance, dearies?"

Victorine opened her mouth and then clamped it shut again, while Darleen (who knew all about Victorine's awkward tendency to spill the truth, even when the truth wasn't what was called for under the circumstances at all) rushed in to distract everybody, as loudly as she could manage, by spouting who-knows-what—"Oh, goodness gracious, we were at that movie too! But now we're late, aren't we, *Bella*?"—while she pulled Victorine past the danger.

Then she didn't stop pulling until the top of the hill, and then Darleen had to breathe very hard for a moment to catch her breath.

"Don't you scare me that way, Vee," she said.

"They did ask *directly*," said Victorine. "It's very hard not to answer with the truth when a person is asked *directly*."

"But the answer is no, for now, right?" said Darleen. "Dear Vee! If someone asks you—and it looks like they will be asking all of us for a while, because one thousand dollars is so awfully much money—if someone asks you, *are you Victorine Berryman*, please do remember the answer right now has to be NO."

It was such a great weight on Victorine's heart. She actually had to clasp her hands very tightly together for a moment to keep herself properly calm.

The unsettling thing was that she did not even really know anymore who she was. At least not with complete confidence. She couldn't yet feel that she was Bella Mae Goodwin, not all the way through. So was she still Victorine Berryman? But she was no longer part of that Berryman world of marble floors, featherbeds, and fine peppercorn sauces—no, she had been forced by circumstances, by villainous kidnappers and arsonists and all those people trying to steal her fortune, to leave that world behind.

If her own much loved and lamented Grandmama were suddenly to reappear, visiting from the Better Life Beyond, would she even recognize her loving, lamenting granddaughter anymore?

And if she was no longer Victorine Berryman and not yet really Bella Mae Goodwin, then who even was she? The name "Vee"—though Darleen filled that little syllable with a good bit of friendly warmth—was perilously close to being no name at all. The tiniest tip of an iceberg! No, "Vee" did not solve the larger problem of who Victorine was.

She bit her lip.

There are, apparently, some people who don't need to know who they really, truly are, but Victorine was not one of those people.

She needed solid ground under her feet. She needed to be one thing, all the way through. She needed—

"Oh, dear, we're so, so, *so* late!" said Darleen now. "Come on, Vee—we need to run!"

# Chapter 4

# Trouble

*Cast.—List of players who take part in the play. . . .*
*These characters are real to you; they live and breathe*
*and have all the other attributes of a human being.*
—How to Write for the "Movies"

## CAST OF CHARACTERS

VICTORINE BERRYMAN, ALSO KNOWN AS BELLA
MAE GOODWIN, *a girl trying to figure out who*
*she is going to be in this hard world. She will come*
*into the Berryman fortune when she turns twenty-*
*one, but until then her identity must remain a*
*secret from all but her very dearest friends.* (Lead)
DARLEEN DARLING, *who has spent her life act-*
*ing in the new art of moving pictures. You may*
*know her as the star of the adventure serial* THE
DANGERS OF DARLEEN, *and last year she*
*rescued Victorine Berryman from a dreadful*
*gang of kidnappers. But now that the Darlings'*

*Matchless Photoplay is struggling, what can she do to keep her beloved Papa and her whole family safe, healthy, and employed?* (Lead)

BILL DARLING, *Darleen's Papa, who runs the studio's laboratory and has a nagging cough and a heart of gold.*

SHIRLEY DARLING, *aunt of Darleen and sister of Bill, who takes care of all the practical challenges involved in running Matchless Photoplay and who tolerates no nonsense from anyone.*

CHARLIE DARLING, *uncle of Darleen and brother of Bill and Shirley, who works as director at Matchless Photoplay.*

DAN DARLING, *uncle of Darleen and brother of Bill and Shirley and Charlie, who works as cameraman and is an inventive genius who far prefers machines to words.*

The girls were five minutes late, in the end—but when they slipped through Aunt Shirley's door, they found the whole family (Aunt Shirley, Uncle Charlie, Uncle Dan, and Darleen's own Papa, Bill Darling) sitting gloomily in the padded chairs of "the Birdcage," as the room was called by the uncles when Aunt Shirley wasn't around to give them silencing looks.

Aunt Shirley's half-gray hair, curling back in two well-controlled waves over her ears to the equally well-organized bun in back, gave the accurate impression that this head must belong to a sensible and effective person, which indeed Aunt Shirley was: skilled at keeping the account books and cooking plain but tasty food and arranging for necessary repairs to the Matchless Photoplay building at very reasonable prices. The walls of that front parlor, however, told secrets on her: that despite her generally practical nature, Aunt Shirley had a soft spot for pretty things and fancy wallpaper, in this case a gazebo motif amply supplied with vines, blossoms, and birds, in colors that surely once had been shining emeralds and amethysts, before the long years and the fireplace smoke calmed them down. Those walls were still greener and purpler than walls had any right to be.

Even though the girls were five whole minutes late, as it happened, no eyes were on the clock, not even Aunt Shirley's.

"Oh, good heavens, what's wrong?" asked Dar, and Victorine could feel her hand tighten in hers.

Something *was* clearly wrong.

After all, Aunt Shirley not watching the clock? That was very strange.

And for a second strange thing, the grown people in the Birdcage were looking up at the girls almost guiltily, as if they had been caught out in the middle of a conspiracy. There was a slightly extended pause, long enough and quiet enough that the girls could almost hear everyone thinking, *What do we tell them?*

It was quite vexing, really, to be surrounded by people (people you trusted) who were clearly trying to think of how to keep you in the dark.

"Hello there, Darleen," said Uncle Charlie eventually. As the chief director for Matchless, he tended to take responsibility for maintaining the forward flow of any conversation he might be part of. "And there's our Bella Mae with you too. Hello, girls. Hope you have been having a nice afternoon."

"Yes, thank you, Mr. Darling. It has been very nice," said Victorine. (She was Bella Mae everywhere, apart from those hours she spent at home with Darleen and Darleen's Papa, Bill Darling, the only two Darlings who knew the truth about her dramatic, eventful, and almost aristocratic past.)

"We went to a matinee performance at the movie theater!" added Darleen.

"And there we have it. Frittering away another fifty cents!" said Aunt Shirley, who was the family accountant and organizer and executive and, honestly, general boss. "What were you thinking of, you foolish girls? If you want to watch a photoplay for some reason, have Bill run one of ours for you at the studio, for goodness' sake."

Bill Darling, Darleen's Papa, worked in the Matchless studios' laboratory, making long ribbons of film emerge like miracles out of chemical baths.

Darleen was shaking her head. Sometimes she found herself getting impatient with her family these days when they tried keeping secrets from her, forgetting she was older now than she used to be.

"But Aunt Shirley, what's wrong?" said Darleen. "Why is everyone looking so sad? Whatever has happened?"

(And Victorine felt something tighten inside her: Had the Darlings heard about the contest? Had they figured out who she really was? Were they thinking of turning her over to the Law Offices of Ridge & Wattle for that appealing prize of *one thousand dollars*?)

"Now, now, Darleeny, don't you go worrying yourself this way," said Mr. Bill Darling. He never wanted Darleen worrying about anything, certainly not about the nagging cough that the laboratory had given him, the cough that never quite faded entirely away.

Darleen ran over to kiss her Papa on the head, while Victorine hung back—still a bit shy about inserting herself into Darling family politics, and still a bit fretful about the contest—although the fact that the Darlings weren't paying much attention to her, Victorine, suggested whatever was up, it wasn't *that*.

"Is there a problem with the new photoplay, perhaps, Papa?" Darleen was asking.

They were supposed to start filming this picture in a few days, some ambitious story about a flood and a heroic girl (to be played by Darleen, naturally) caught on a rocky island in the middle of a rising river. It was going to be terribly dramatic and exciting, if they could just get it filmed before the next round of autumn rainstorms. (Real rainstorms can be counted on to mess up pretend floods most dreadfully.)

Victorine found every part of the process of creating moving pictures quite fascinating, even if she had decided that *acting* was probably not, in the long term, for her; indeed, she was working hard on acquiring a complete and thorough education in moviemaking. And so she had been very much looking forward to learning from the Darlings how to create a convincing flood for a photoplay.

Aunt Shirley pressed her lips together in impatience. She did not approve of young people asking unnecessary or probing questions. But the other grown-up Darlings responded anyway, and all at once:

"I guess you might say so," said Darleen's Papa

—at the very same time that Uncle Charlie said, far too brightly to be telling the truth,

"Why do you ask? Why ever would you think something like that?"

—at the very same time that Uncle Dan cleared his throat and remarked in his plain, no-wasted-words way,

"Money troubles, girls."

And from the hollow sound of Uncle's Dan three words, both Dar and Victorine instantly understood the truth of the matter. A serious lack of money was, to be honest, a regular state of affairs at Matchless studios.

"What are we going to do about it this time?" said Darleen. "Sell the shiny black Ford?"

That was a motorcar they liked to use in car chases. Uncle Charlie was always joking that it was worth a pretty penny—and thus not to be scratched or marred in any way at all, please.

"Don't be absurd, Darleen," said Aunt Shirley, while most of the other people in that room heaved sighs of one size or another.

"I'm afraid it's not a one-motorcar problem we're facing," said Uncle Charlie, exchanging his previous false brightness all at once for a more realistic gloom. "This time the hole's much deeper than any single car can fill, no matter how shiny."

The last few photoplays put out by Matchless had not done as well as the Darlings had hoped. In addition, a couple of cameras had broken down, and rainwater had gotten in through the glass roof of the studio, so there had been some expensive repairs there too.

"Cost of everything's going up," said Darleen's Papa. "Chemicals, film stock, you name it. And coal. Shirley's always very worried about the coal."

"Winter's always coming," said Uncle Dan.

"Costs a fortune and a half to keep that place

heated," said Aunt Shirley. "I can stretch a penny pretty far, you all know that. But I'm being asked to stretch pennies as if they were taffy candy, and that just can't be done."

"So what are we going to do?" said Darleen.

"Cut our expenses," said Aunt Shirley, with a voice so full of icy determination that you'd think expenses would hear her and simply shrink in terror.

"We can hire ourselves out to other studios," said Uncle Charlie, with a sigh.

"Or we could rent it out, the studio itself," said Darleen's Papa.

"Oh, no!" said Darleen. This sounded very serious indeed.

"Or . . . !" said Uncle Dan, who seemed, for some reason, less glum than the rest of the family.

Darleen clapped her hands and asked, "Or what, Uncle Dan? Do you have a clever idea of some kind up your sleeve?"

"Possibly, possibly!" said Uncle Dan. "Tell them, Bill."

Darleen's Papa took a deep breath and folded and unfolded his much-weathered, half-pickled (as he liked to claim) hands.

"You see, Dan and I have been working on something very exciting—we've got a real treasure, we think."

A treasure! That sounded good!

"What do you mean, Papa?" said Darleen. "What kind of treasure?"

"Not saying a word more about it until we make something out of it," said Bill Darling. "But it's absolutely chock-full of potential, Darleeny."

And Uncle Dan put a finger to his lips—he wasn't a chatty sort under the best of circumstances, which probably gave him something of an advantage when it came to keeping secrets.

"Very nice," said Aunt Shirley. "But if you aren't willing to tell the rest of us about it, it's no more than a twilight dream, as far as I'm concerned."

"It's a secret, Shirley!" said Darleen's Papa, radiant with delight. "We just need to get our treasure into the right hands and then you'll hear about it for sure."

"Whose hands are the right ones, I'd like to know," said Aunt Shirley.

"We do have some ideas about that," said Bill Darling.

"I'm sure you do," said Aunt Shirley. "Those hands are nearby, I trust?"

"Um," said Uncle Dan.

"Not exactly *near*," said Darleen's Papa. "But we are operating on really excellent advice, don't you worry. In short, Shirley, we're thinking—"

"California!" said Uncle Dan.

There was certainly some commotion in the Birdcage then! Aunt Shirley snorted, Uncle Charlie clapped his hands and laughed, Darleen said "Oh, *California!*" and to Victorine's startled eyes, even the birds on the walls seemed to be stretching their wings and widening their eyes in surprise.

"California?" said Victorine to those birds, and to the room generally, and then added for Uncle Dan specifically: "Are you really saying you want to take your secret whatever-it-may-be to California?"

"A nice cozy sort of place called Hollywood," said Bill Darling, on behalf of his not very chatty brother. A chuckle rumbled through the Darlings—they had certainly heard about *Hollywood!* Warm weather and film studios popping up like mushrooms after a rain, only not actually like that at all, because from what they heard, it didn't rain very much out in sunny California. "Tell them about the letter, Dan," said Bill Darling.

"Ahem," said Uncle Dan, and he pulled what did indeed look like a letter right out of his pocket, with a bit of a showman's flourish.

"What's that now, Dan?" said Aunt Shirley with some suspicion.

"A letter," he said.

"I see that," said Aunt Shirley. "What can it possibly have to do with the rising cost of coal, though?"

"From *Lois Weber,*" said Uncle Dan.

Victorine's feet jumped a little in surprise: Lois Weber, the famous director and photoplaywright?

"Lois Weber wrote to *you*?" said his sister, evidently impressed. "From California? How'd that happen?"

"She's the sort of person who's interested in new things, see," said Darleen's Papa. "Always has been too. Got her start working with the Blachés, right around hereabouts. So Madame Blaché recommended—"

"Hmm," said Aunt Shirley, perhaps without actually meaning to make a sound. Madame Alice Guy Blaché was an eminent director who had come over from France and until recently had been in charge of the Solax studios, and Aunt Shirley couldn't help thinking of her as something of a rival. Especially since last year, when Madame Blaché had taken a warm interest in the futures of Darleen Darling and that new ward of Bill's, "Bella Mae."

"Lois Weber knows the Blachés from way back, of course. Why, she worked for Gaumont on those peculiar speaking pictures," said Bill, pausing to cough a little into his handkerchief.

"Chronophotographs," said Uncle Dan.

"Fancy name, isn't it?" said Bill. "And the machinery's still too fancy for ordinary, everyday photoplays. They won't be silent forever, though, our movies! I'm quite certain of that!"

"Yes, yes, yes, yes, I'm sure," said Aunt Shirley. "Well, then, do tell us: What did *Mrs. Smalley* have to say to you, Dan, in this letter of yours?"

Mrs. Smalley was Lois Weber's name in private

life, as Aunt Shirley knew well. Aunt Shirley was acquainted with a great many of the residents of movie land. She also read the gossip magazines faithfully. She knew—they all knew—that Mr. Phillips Smalley, Lois Weber's husband, also worked in the photoplays. They were an outstanding team, said all of the photoplay magazines. Imagine, a man and a woman functioning as equals, at home and in their work! Victorine and Darleen had read those articles together—and looked at each other with awe in their eyes.

"She invites me to visit," said Uncle Dan. "Three p.m., September eighth, her house in Hollywood. There."

"A chance to get our treasure into the best possible hands," said Darleen's Papa, by way of filling up the gaps Uncle Dan was always leaving in his explanations.

"Ha!" said Aunt Shirley. "That's very kind of her, I'm sure, but Hollywood is surely a bit far from Fort Lee. Could you find yourselves a pair of 'best possible hands' a bit closer to home? Seems foolish, dreaming about California—"

"But perhaps I *will* go, though, Shirley," said Uncle Dan calmly.

There was a sudden hush in the Birdcage.

All the Darlings looked back and forth at one another, wondering what the sudden tension in that room's atmosphere would lead to. And Victorine looked at all those faces, too, and then over at Darleen, who was beginning to rise up on her toes in excitement, as if some invisible lighter-than-air balloon had suddenly started pulling her up toward the ceiling or perhaps even the sky. It was the word *California* that had done it, probably.

And then Uncle Charlie made Darleen's invisible balloon pull a dozen times harder. He said: "Well, then, fine. Maybe we should all go off to California. No, really, I hear the weather's very nice there. Would be good for our Bill's lungs, wouldn't it? And then there's the hope of filming right through the winter without worrying about the price of coal. Everyone's moving west, Shirl, and you know it. Reckon we will all be following Biograph and Rex and the others out there eventually."

It was true that other studios had been trickling away westward recently. Some, like Biograph, had started out by going for the winter and then returning like the birds in the spring. Others were packing up shop and moving away for good.

The West: that was where the future of the motion picture business almost certainly lay!

That light in Darleen's eyes just glowed brighter and brighter, Victorine saw. She knew from many evening conversations that Dar had a true longing in her heart for *California*, for a magical place where you could reach right up and pick an orange off a tree, and where the weather was gentle and balmy practically all of the time, and a whole different ocean lapped at the shore . . . Victorine, for her part, had seen the Pacific Ocean long ago, on her childhood travels with her Grandmama. (Those happy childhood days!) She had learned very young that the world has many fine and beautiful places.

"We can't just pull up our stakes all of a sudden and go waltzing out West," said Aunt Shirley. "At the moment, just to remind us all of the FACTS, there's a studio building to keep up here in Fort Lee, and per-haps, yes, to rent out for some needed cash. Travel requires money, in case you had forgotten. Renting the studio isn't easy, mind: it will take some time and arranging. And the old boiler's been acting up so wick-edly recently! Rude of it, I say, after Bella Mae's old uncle helped out so nicely last winter."

"Oh!" said Victorine, since "Bella Mae's old uncle" was actually, of course, that safety deposit box in New York City, into which, following the rules set up by Victorine's Grandmama's will, a few hundred dollars were left for her every six months. Aunt Shirley did not know about the safety deposit box. Aunt Shirley thought there was a post office in the city, where "Bella Mae" occasionally received letters from a mysterious and generous uncle.

And *those* thoughts instantly brought back to Victorine all those other uncomfortable concerns she'd been having this afternoon about Mr. Ridge, of Ridge

& Wattle. Fortunately, Aunt Shirley had too much to say to notice Victorine's nervous twitch.

"But Charlie," continued Aunt Shirley, "if you think a move is really, eventually inevitable—"

"What's that word mean, Vee?" whispered Darleen.

"Fated, unavoidable, going to happen," Victorine whispered back. She did know a lot of words. When she was younger, she had dreamed of growing up to become a World-Wandering Librarian.

"Are you saying, Vee, that us going to California is actually *going to happen?*" said Darleen in wonder.

"Girls!" said Aunt Shirley from across the room. "Please. Were you raised by wolves?"

Another thing she didn't approve of was young people whispering to each other when surrounded by their elders and betters.

"So perhaps that should be our plan, then," Aunt Shirley said once she had finished glaring at Dar and Victorine. "If our Bill and Dan are willing, perhaps they will go on ahead to California and examine the possibilities out there for the rest of us. By way of establishing an outpost for the future efforts of the Darlings, you know."

That was a shock.

Everyone in the Birdcage turned to stare at Aunt Shirley. Was she really admitting that a great move and change was probably in their future? Was she *really*?

"You heard me," said Aunt Shirley to all those

bright eyes. "Stop sitting there with your mouths dangling open. High time those mouths came to eat their supper before it gets cold."

In short: change must definitely be coming—if even Aunt Shirley said it was!

The girls were the last to filter (or flitter) their way from Birdcage to dining room table. They hung back briefly to share their astonishment and wonder.

"California!" whispered Darleen, in awe. "Oh, Vee!"

And Vee thought, *Could perhaps my make-believe Victorine—the one for the contest—could she maybe really go traveling somewhere?*

Then she gave a more practically minded sigh. "I'd better go into the city and visit my Grandmama's safety deposit box again, then, if big changes are afoot," she said. "You heard what your Aunt Shirley said: traveling is always expensive. And perhaps I should go and—inquire—at the offices of Mr. Ridge? To see what seems to be going on there?"

She wasn't sure about that. Darleen evidently wasn't, either.

"Oh, dear," said Darleen. "I'd be careful about that Mr. Ridge of yours, Vee. After all, there are some very basic things we might want answers for before we go trusting him. Like, for instance, *why* is he looking for you? And why *now*?"

Chapter 5

# The Bank!

*Remember, a scene is where*
*the action takes place in one location.*
—How to Write for the "Movies"

Two days later the girls were standing in front of the huge brass doors of the American Bank of New York, in New York City.

They had decided to be cautious, considering the suddenly inexplicable actions of Mr. Ridge. As Darleen put it, rather dramatically: "What if he suddenly pounced on you and dragged you away?"

Which was unlikely, of course. If you had seen the elderly Mr. Ridge looking at you in confusion and perplexity over the tops of his glasses, you would understand just how funny the idea of him *pouncing* on anyone or anything actually was.

But the fact remained that something was up. The

Law Offices of Ridge & Wattle were searching very hard for Victorine, for reasons unknown, and so caution seemed warranted.

"I'll simply dash in, pick up my money as quickly as can be, and then we'll be done," said Victorine, reaching a hand toward the door.

"And I'll wait for you by the desk in front," said Darleen. "With all my ears and eyes wide open, you can be sure!"

The bank was very grand. Banks like to look grand; apparently all that brass and marble boosts their confidence.

Victorine had to ask to be escorted back into the vault, and then the woman at the front desk guided her through the fancy metal gate that kept the secret parts of the bank safe and separate from the front areas. When she glanced back, Darleen gave her an encouraging little wave and settled onto an uncomfortable but expensive-looking sofa in the lobby to wait.

Victorine had her hand on the little key at her neck all the way to the vault. She was always nervous back here, in this room that felt so closed off from everywhere else in the world.

"Here you are, miss," said the lady from reception. She pulled the metal box with the proper number on it right out of the wall, as if it were a drawer, and plopped it onto the small wooden desk left in the vault for the convenience of those paying visits to their safety deposit boxes.

"Thank you very much," said Victorine with her usual politeness.

"Do take your time," said the bank lady. Did she seem a bit nervous? Or was Victorine just letting her own nervousness spill out and color the world?

"In fact, take as long as you like," said the woman. "I'll be right on the other side of the gate, you know, if you need me."

Fortunately, the bank lady did not close the door to the vault or the gate beyond it as she left, because Victorine's insides might have tied themselves right into claustrophobic knots if she had.

Victorine's hand fumbled a bit with the little key, but then the door of that metal box recognized the key and sprang open willingly, and she looked in.

"Oh!" she said.

The contents of that box had changed! In the past there had always been the folder holding a copy of her Grandmama's will, and then, of course, and in accordance with that will, the small packet of banknotes, refreshed every six months, which was the only money Victorine—once known as "the richest little girl in the world"—could touch until she came into the full Berryman fortune at the age of twenty-one.

But today: a letter, on top of another letter, on top

of a sealed packet—and no sign of the will itself or of any money.

The first letter was brief and formal, and it was typed up on official stationery of the Law Offices of Ridge & Wattle:

"To the Owner of the Other Key to the Safety Deposit Box #3476 Held at the American Bank of New York—"

*Goodness, that's a very long-winded way of addressing me,* thought Victorine. *When Mr. Ridge could easily say "Miss Berryman," and be done with it!*

"It is my duty to inform you that the recent demise of Mr. Ridge, Senior, one of the esteemed founders of the firm of Ridge & Wattle—"

*Oh, my!* thought Victorine. *But that means—poor old Mr. Ridge is gone!*

Even if he had been terribly ineffective as an executor, still it was always sad when a human life came to its natural end.

But the letter went on:

"—the recent demise of Mr. Ridge, Senior . . . has led to a reexamination of records and practices, and we are in the process of clarifying and rectifying any irregularities—"

*Irregularities?* thought Victorine.

"—such as the cash payments made in the past year to this Safety Deposit Box #3476 at the American Bank of New York—"

*Oh, dear!* thought Victorine.

"—cash payments which seem to have been inspired by contradictory and illogical precepts of the Will of Mrs. Hugo Berryman, deceased in 1914—"

*Grandmama!* thought Victorine (with a true pang). How much she had loved and appreciated the presence of her Grandmama! How much she missed her still!

"We note in particular the contradictory demands in sections two (2) and three (3) of the will's Addendum. In section two (2), the will states the Berryman fortune is to be transferred to a third party (the New York Public Library), in the case of Miss Victorine Berryman's disappearance or death, and there is a line clearly stating, and we quote, 'no money or material good may be transferred to any person, company, or entity until the date that would have been Victorine Berryman's twenty-first birthday.' This evidently contradicts the demand in section three (3) that 'a sum of money, not less than five hundred dollars, shall be deposited every half year in the safety deposit box of Mrs. Hugo Berryman at the American Bank of New York.' The deposit of any further money into the safety deposit box is therefore, in our judgment, an unacceptable irregularity, and will cease immediately."

*Oh, rats!* thought Victorine, who instantly saw that the phrasing of the will's addendum should have been clearer, to avoid this very inconvenient twist. *No more money!*

"Moreover," continued the letter, as Victorine's stomach grew tighter and sourer, "we note that it is highly irregular that Miss Victorine Berryman, should she still be alive, is not in custody of a guardian properly selected and monitored by the Law Offices of Ridge & Wattle, as the official agent in charge of the Berryman estate. Let this letter serve as official notice that we have indeed selected a suitable guardian, who, if Miss Berryman is found alive, will closely and reliably control the actions, location, and fortune of the missing person in question until she comes of age."

*No*, thought Victorine, with perfect, simple stubbornness. She had no interest in being "closely and reliably controlled" by a representative of the Law Offices of Ridge & Wattle, whoever that guardian might be.

"And that carefully selected guardian, furthermore, is Mr. Ridge, Junior, signatory of this letter and new partner in the Law Offices of Ridge & Wattle."

*So Mr. Ridge has—I mean, had—a son!* thought Victorine.

Well, good for him. But Victorine had no interest in being remanded to the custody of anyone by the name of Ridge. Not after the terrible misadventures of last year! No!

"So let this be a warning to whoever has been taking advantage of the irregularities in the Berryman will by taking (under false pretenses, and in violation of the law) money from the American Bank safety deposit box. Impersonating Miss Victorine Berryman is legally and morally unacceptable. The Law Offices of Ridge & Wattle will see to it that all such irregularities cease."

*So they think I have been impersonating Miss Victorine Berryman?* thought Victorine, and shook her head. That certainly wasn't true. That seemed to her to be the exact opposite of the truth, frankly. But there was one more line in this rather awful letter:

"In the effects of Mr. Ridge, Senior, were also the two letters addressed to Miss Victorine Berryman, which we have deposited here, in order, we must specify, to comply with the specific wishes of the late Mrs. Hugo Berryman."

*WHAT?* thought Victorine. She dropped the letter she had been reading as if it had suddenly started to burn her hand, and plucked up instead the other letters that had been stacked underneath it, the smaller one and the larger packet.

Oh! She knew the handwriting on these envelopes! She knew it so very well. Her Grandmama had addressed those letters:

*TO BE DELIVERED*
*TO MY DEAREST VICTORINE,*
*WITHOUT DELAY—*

Oh! *Oh!* Victorine's eyes blurred with tears. She clasped those letters close to her chest. She couldn't think in words. For a moment she couldn't think at all. She could only *feel*.

And that was when the shouting began, from outside that cave of a vault.

"Bella Mae! Bella Mae! Come quickly, please!" she heard—that was Darleen's voice, of course. And then also, still definitely Darleen speaking, but as if to someone else: "*Oh, no, no, no! You will NOT close that door!*"

Victorine jumped up from that desk; she grabbed all the letters from the box (and, being Victorine, she did pause just long enough to lock the box back up with her little key), and then she *ran*, back out the vault door, back to the brass gate—where Darleen was for some reason spread out like a spider, arms wide, blocking someone's way—oh, the woman at the front desk, who was (everything was becoming stranger and stranger) sobbing.

"Darleen?" said Victorine. "What's happening?"

"Oh, you're out! Thank goodness!" said Darleen. "Imagine! This person here was going to shut you—an innocent child—in that vault!"

"It was the special orders," sobbed the woman from the bank. "For Box #3476. To call the lawyers. And then they said close up the vault so the suspect couldn't get away—"

"Oh, how could you even think of doing such a

thing?" said Darleen with great feeling, while the woman wept into her handkerchief, and Victorine slipped back out through the gate. "Locking up a *child*? In a closed vault where she might simply *smother*? How could you? Because I'm sure you must generally be a kind person, miss. I'm sure that when you are surrounded by your family, when you are at home, you would surely not be capable of smothering an innocent child."

"Special orders!" wailed the woman, her face buried in her hands. "It's awful, I know. But I'm sure the lawyers will sort it out when they come—"

"Shall we run?" said Darleen to Vee, under her breath, and also, it must be said, in an entirely different sort of voice than she had been using with the poor, sobbing (but apparently treacherous) bank employee.

Victorine nodded, and they did not wait another moment. They RAN!

And only once they were safely several blocks away did Victorine pause, gasping for air, and say to Darleen, "That woman—was she really going to trap me in there? Simply because Ridge and Wattle told her to?"

"She called them up on her fancy telephone! So I knew something was up! She even said, 'Lock her in?!'—almost as if she couldn't quite believe what she was hearing. And then she stood up to go toward the gate—"

"Oh, dreadful! But you stopped her, Darleen. Goodness! You told her what she was doing was wrong—you appealed to her conscience—you made her cry!"

"Oh, pshaw," said Darleen with a shrug. "That was nothing—that was only *acting!*"

# Chapter 6

## A Voice from Very Far Away

*The summer is the delight of the producer's heart.*
*He has the big outdoors to stage his play.*
—How to Write for the "Movies"

A few hours later—after a nervous ferry ride to carry them away from New York City and a long, steep walk uphill from the ferry to the quiet houses and bustling photoplay studios of Fort Lee—Darleen and Victorine were safely ensconced under one of Darleen's favorite trees.

Darleen was someone who took great delight in the climbing of a good tree. And in the summer, both girls had a deep appreciation for the way the right tree could create a haven of cool shadow.

The tree they had retreated to now was a black willow, all long dark leaves hanging gracefully down. They sat on its roots, leaning their backs against its trunk, and had the comfortable confidence that comes from knowing that nobody was likely to spot them there, whether from the street or from the windows of Darleen's home, which was quite nearby.

Darleen had brought glasses of cool ginger water, as well as a little heap of brown sugar cookies wrapped up in a tea towel. Victorine came with the letters she had just carried away from the New York City safety deposit box.

"How could the old Mr. Ridge have kept these from me?" said Victorine, with her fingertips gently resting on the smaller of the two envelopes, the one that bore those sweetest words from her own beloved Grandmama: "To be delivered to my dearest Victorine, without delay . . ."

"Almost a year and a half after your poor grand-mother passed away! I'd call that a DELAY, all right," said Darleen, her voice warm with sympathy and indignation. "And accusing you of being an impostor! Goodness, have a cookie."

The cookies were crunchy, heartening, and sweet, just as cookies ought to be.

"None of this makes a lick of sense, though," said Darleen. "Why would the younger Mr. Ridge put your grandmother's letters into the safety deposit box if he thought you weren't really Miss Berryman?"

"I think it's that overgrown fear of 'irregulari-ties,' honestly," said Victorine. "It must have seemed exceedingly *irregular*, you know, for the elder Mr. Ridge not to give me those letters all that time. So the best that Mr. Ridge, Junior, could think to do was to pop these letters into the safety deposit box *now*, even if it is a year later."

She brought that letter up to her heart.

She hadn't opened it yet. Such a momentous thing could not be done in a public place, on a ferry crossing the Hudson, or on the noisy, rattling elevated train that had brought them up to the ferry building on 120th Street. It needed the comfort, the shade, and the safety of a kind old tree.

"And how strange it is," added Darleen, between sips of ginger water, "that your grandmother tells you NOT to open the other package!"

To be precise, the message on the outside of the larger envelope was this: "For my beloved Victorine, to have at hand once I am gone, but not yet to be opened."

Victorine set that one aside for the moment, as a mystery.

The smaller letter fit so nicely into her hands! And the stationery was very lovely—you could tell from the feel of it. There was even a faint aroma of lavender clinging to that envelope, which reminded Victorine very much of her Grandmama.

"Have one more cookie, Vee, before you open that," said Darleen, full of sympathy. "I'm sure it will make you feel more courageous."

Darleen understood that courage was involved when it came to reading letters from a grandmother whom you missed with all your heart.

"Here I go," Victorine said to Darleen at last, and she slipped her fingernail carefully along the top of the letter, not wanting to risk doing any damage to her Grandmama's message.

The letter unfolded in her hands (which were shaking a little—but who could blame them?), and while Darleen turned her head tactfully away, Victorine let the words of that letter sink very directly into her soul, like water on parched earth.

*My dear Victorine,*

*As I come to the end of my journey here in this world we have explored together with such joy in recent years, my thoughts are entirely with you, my darling girl. I have loved every moment of being your Grandmama. I remember when you were just a tiny baby, deposited by your father into my arms—how extraordinarily bright your eyes were, how they followed any person passing through the room with such interest and curiosity! I knew then what I know with even more certainty today: that you, my darling Victorine, are a light in dark places. From the day you first came to live with me, I have felt that darkness could have no real power over me ever again. I hope you know how much joy you brought then to an old and grieving woman—and how you continue to bring joy into my life, every single day.*

*My child, you deserve to be happy. When I am gone, I hope with all my heart—and have charged our attorney, Mr. Ridge, most solemnly with the responsibility to make this hope real—that you will always find yourself in the care of people who love you and respect you as you deserve to be loved and respected. You are so young still, dear Victorine, and so honest, and sometimes perhaps even a touch too serious for your own good, so you need true friends to support you, to wipe your tears, to smile with you, and to help you grow into your true Self.*

*I wish I could travel with you many more years, my dear one! But I will have to wait for you beyond that curtain that separates this world from the next. Until we meet again, darling Victorine, know that you carry all my love wherever you go and whatever you become.*

*(signed)*
*Your loving Grandmama*

Victorine was not a weepy sort of person by nature, but as you can imagine, she cried quietly all through the reading of this letter. And Darleen, who wasn't even trying to read over her shoulder, who was just there to provide support, patted her arm and made comforting sounds and generally just joined the old willow in being affectionately, undemandingly present.

Soon, however, Victorine looked up with shining eyes and said, "Oh, Darleen! Somehow she knew—she guessed—about you!" She showed her the line about needing "true friends to support you," et cetera—at which point Darleen burst (understandably) into tears herself, and for some minutes the friends cried together, sad about the people they had lost in their lives and glad for the ones they had somehow miraculously found.

Some restorative sips of ginger water and nibbles of cookie later, Darleen pointed at the back of Victorine's Grandmama's letter.

"There's more here, Vee—what does that say?"

"Goodness, you're right. There's a *postscriptum*!"

It was written in a more faded, wobbly hand, as if the person forming those words had already traveled quite far on that hard last journey of hers.

And it said:

*P.S. I am writing you another letter, for you to read when you are older. My dear, you will probably be tempted to read that letter earlier than you should, out of sheer curiosity. But I appeal to your basic honesty, dear Victorine: do not open it until you are quite grown up, independent and mature and ready for things that are more complicated than any child should face. While you are a child, dear, be a child—be, I hope, for many more years, a happy child!*

Victorine read that aloud, twice over. She hardly knew what to think. Then she looked at Darleen, who was staring back at her with an equally puzzled expression.

"This is so strange," said Darleen. "Do you have any idea what your grandmother might possibly have hidden away in an envelope like this one?"

"No idea at all," said Victorine. "And Dar—how do I decide?"

"Decide what?" asked Darleen.

"How do I decide whether I'm old enough to open this other letter? Whether I count as 'independent and mature,' you know? Or whether I'm still just a—"

And here her expression became rather gloomy, despite her best efforts.

"—a 'happy child'?"

Darleen actually laughed a little at that (but in a sympathetic way).

"You make that sound so dreadful! But your grandmother wanted you to be happy, Vee—of course she did. She would have been so upset to know how those fake cousins tried to take advantage of you after she passed away. Or how that old Mr. Ridge failed to protect you—"

"Which is why I will NEVER agree to put myself into the hands of any Mr. Ridge, Junior!" said Victorine with some fervor.

"Absolutely not," agreed Darleen. "You are ours

now, and the Darlings won't let any Ridges make you miserable, ever again!"

"Unless your Aunt Shirley learns who I really am, and decides the studio really needs a nice, fat reward." Victorine blushed a little as she said that, but she did wonder, sometimes, about how solid the ground was she rested on, here at the Matchless studios. (It is only human to wonder about such things.)

"Vee!" said Darleen. "Don't say that! You know Aunt Shirley loves you."

And then Darleen thought for another moment and added, more cautiously (and, alas, perhaps more realistically), "And anyway, we don't have to tell her about any rewards, do we?"

Victorine took a steadying breath. "No, I suppose not," she said. "I guess that's not the question just at the moment. The real question is, how do I know whether I am ready to open my Grandmama's letter? She said to wait until I'm 'quite grown up,' but I've been through so much the past year, perhaps I count as nearly grown now, you know?"

There was a pause.

"I suppose you could ask someone wise for advice?" said Darleen. "We mustn't bother Papa, of course, but someone else? Perhaps Madame Blaché?"

Oh, yes! It was as if a light went right on in Victorine's head! Madame Blaché was the French director who had helped Victorine wriggle out of the clutches of those dreadful impostor cousins last year. Victorine was filled for a moment with clear purpose and determination: she should just gather up these puzzling letters of hers and run directly to Madame Blaché's house in Fort Lee, run up those steps and ring the bell and ask her *what she should do*—

And then another, brighter light went on in that same crowded room in her brain, and she put her head in her hands.

"Oh, dear," said Victorine, and she was amused at herself and quite disappointed, both at once. "Why am I so foolish so much of the time?"

"*Foolish?*" said Darleen. "Why would you say that? I'm sure I'm foolisher than you. And anyway, don't you think Madame Blaché is a trustworthy sort of person?"

"Oh, she's lovely!" said Victorine. "But think about it, Dar: running to ask her whether I'm 'independent and mature' enough to open a letter from my Grandmama is just *proof* that I'm not nearly as 'independent and mature' as I might think. Oh, Vee, she would just look at me, you know, and raise her elegant eyebrows, and I would simply SEE her thinking that very thing—*Why is this child asking me whether she is no longer a child?*"

Darleen laughed, and then clapped her hand over her mouth, not wanting to be laughing if her friend was still in pain. All of that loving kindness was a balm and a comfort, really, under the circumstances.

"I'll just have to wait to open that envelope until I myself am sure I'm ready, that's all," said Victorine.

"Well!" said Darleen. "You are much more patient than I could ever be! But I'm sure you must be right, since you know best of any of us what your grandmother would have wanted."

And then, a few quiet minutes later (after the last remaining cookie had been split into two sweet halves and thoughtfully consumed), Darleen said, "Vee, if you don't mind, I have had an idea about something else. Not about these letters of yours at all, you know, but about our future!"

When Darleen blossomed into one of her mile-wide grins, it was impossible not to smile back at her and nod in a way that meant, *Speak, Dar, speak!*

"Vee dear, it has come to me, and I'm absolutely *determined*!" said Darleen. "If any representatives of the Darlings of Matchless studios are going to California, and if the money possibly allows, two of those people should definitely be *you*—and *me*!"

## Chapter 7

# California

*A comedy is made up of complications . . .*
—How to Write for the "Movies"

"Absolutely not," said Aunt Shirley when Darleen first aired her plan about California. "We'll send Dan and Bill out West, and that's surely enough trouble for all of us, getting them organized and figuring out how to make do without them here."

But it turned out that Darleen could be very persuasive under the right circumstances. It was not just about herself and Victorine getting a chance to see the world! Her Papa's health was potentially in the balance, after all. She told Aunt Shirley that she (and "Bella Mae") had learned how to be sensible, practical people under the tutelage of Aunt Shirley (this was flattery, of course, but it was also at least partly true), that they could now cook a good supper as well as tell the difference between a solid, affordable, well-located house and a house that might misleadingly seem appealing to men who knew much more about machines and chemicals than they did about budgets and comfortable rooms. Aunt Shirley sniffed a little at that, but the Birdcage side of her had to admit that Darleen was making some good points.

Darleen was not yet finished with her role as Persuasive Niece, however: she hurried on to promise that she and "Bella Mae" could also be trusted to look up all sorts of useful practical information out in Hollywood about possibilities for a family troupe that consisted of a cameraman, a lab man and all-around technical expert, two girl actors (one with lots of experience and a moderate amount of fame), a director with an appropriately loud voice, and an accounting and organizational expert (that was another double dose of flattery and truth).

And then, the seed having been sown, as it were, Darleen kept watering it carefully by starting up conversations with Victorine whenever the adults were within earshot about useful, grown-up tasks they were doing or just had done.

And she also inquired of her Papa whether he really, truly had in mind leaving her behind. That, perhaps, worked best of all. Her Papa started asking Aunt Shirley whether perhaps it might be sensible to let the girls come along, seeing as they were such good, helpful young things, after all.

"Hmm," said Aunt Shirley.

But the next time the family was assembled (for coffee and pie), Aunt Shirley said, "I've been thinking about the girls, and how much they would like to go west. If I can just sort out the train fares and the money for food and housing, perhaps it might be possible." And then she looked quite pointedly at Victorine, which made both Victorine and Darleen blush, Darleen from the guilty conscience that started twinging every time Aunt Shirley implied the Darlings could benefit from the faint aura of money that still hovered around the person of "Bella Mae," and Vee from the trouble of finding herself in a rather sticky dilemma involving truth-telling and etiquette.

"Perhaps I *might* be able to help," said Victorine in a wobbly voice, since that was obviously the expected response, and since she still had a small reserve of money left from previous visits to the safety deposit box, even if the box was now (and seemed likely to remain) quite empty.

"Thank you, Bella Mae," said Aunt Shirley promptly. "That would be lovely of you, I'm sure. Now let's move on to the practical details. My old friend Mrs. Gish is out there in Hollywood now, of course. Maybe she can lend a helpful hand once you all arrive . . ."

It was amazing how when Aunt Shirley came

around to Darleen's view of the situation, she did so all at once and without blinking. She started talking about travel plans and budgets and the possibility of getting Pullman berths, at least for the second part of that long journey, from Chicago to Los Angeles.

In a flash it was all set up: the train tickets bought (for a five-day trip west!), the trunks packed, the local experts visited and asked for connections to helpful people already in Hollywood, the gears of the travel-preparation machine turning faster and faster.

Meanwhile Victorine found herself growing more and more worried about the awkward *Vanishing of Victorine* situation. Almost daily now she ran into someone who had come to Fort Lee to nose around. Once or twice, a stranger actually stopped her on the road and asked directions to the Phoenix studio, and whether she might have seen Victorine Berryman recently, and that felt like a close call each time.

The girls had explained some of these worries to Darleen's Papa, because he was the only other person in the family who knew who "Bella Mae" really was, and he had shaken his head with worry and affection.

"Sounds like it's about the right moment for us to shift ourselves west, then, girls!"

It felt like time to move on—it really did.

California! That would truly be turning over a new leaf. Starting a new chapter. It was such a long and melodious word, *California*, wasn't it?

And for Darleen, who had never been farther from New Jersey than New York City, one ferry ride away, California was a shining dream.

"You know what, Vee?" said Darleen sleepily one evening, as shadows of tree limbs played on the wall. "I've been thinking about trains. You know I've run on top of moving trains and stopped a train or two by bravely waving a flag in the tracks, and even pretended to land in a balloon in front of a train"—(all in the photoplays, of course!)—"but I've never ever been a *passenger* on a train. How about that?"

"You'll be an excellent passenger, I'm sure of it," said Victorine, smiling into the dark. "And it will be a comfort to know we have someone aboard who can fling villains off the top of a train into the water as we cross some trestle bridge, if it comes to that."

Dreams of California filled their heads like a bright and hopeful mist—and then the morning of the day they were all supposed to climb aboard that westward-rolling train, Darleen's Papa startled himself out of a fitful sleep with a bout of coughing so dreadful that Darleen wondered whether he might end up splitting himself right into pieces, like Rumpelstiltskin in the story.

"I'm fine," he said in gasps, but he was clearly not fine.

This was the cough that California was supposed to cure. But first he had to be well enough to get there safely, didn't he?

## Chapter 8

# Change of Plans

*Sympathy is the keynote of*
*the genuinely successful photoplay.*
—How to Write for the "Movies"

So there it was, very, very early on the day of their departure, and all the Darlings were standing around Darleen's Papa's bed while he coughed, and coughed some more, and tried to catch his breath to apologize for coughing.

"Must've breathed in some dust," he wheezed. "I'm sure I will be better soon."

"Well, the thing is, though, Bill, you sound pretty lousy now—I think you have to admit that, don't you, brother?—so I'm not sure what you think 'soon' means," said Aunt Shirley. (Her voice was kinder than her words, though, because like all of the Darlings, she had an enormous soft spot for Darleen's Papa, her oldest brother.) "You won't be traveling this week. That much is clear. So now what do we do?"

She heaved a huge sigh. Aunt Shirley really liked things to go according to plan.

They had their tickets. They had their trunks and bags packed. The girls and Uncle Dan were only hours away from being dressed in their traveling clothes.

If their travel plans had been a complicated but lovely Bach fugue of a plot, Darleen's Papa's cough could certainly be considered a very discordant note. Or even someone just stopping right in the middle of the piece and banging ruthlessly on the harpsichord keyboard—that's how awful it all was.

"I suppose we'll try again in a few days. Will you still be able to make your appointment, Dan?"

"What appointment?" said Darleen, whose eyes were ringed with worry shadows and sleeplessness.

"With Mrs. Smalley. About his very secret treasure," said Aunt Shirley. "When was that meeting, Dan?"

"September eighth," said Uncle Dan. "Next week. Well, never mind that, I guess."

"There's no help for it, we will have to hand in those train tickets and start over," said Aunt Shirley. "Can't have you out there coughing yourself into an early grave before the girls have found you a nice sunny cottage to move into, Bill, can we? It's too bad, but that's how it has to go. Trip is postponed. Now, girls—"

"No!" said Bill Darling, and heaved himself more upright against the head of his bed, although it meant another round of hacking and coughing.

"No?" said Aunt Shirley. "No, what?"

"No, can't keep 'em all here!" said Darleen's Papa, between dreadful coughs. "Shirley, think about it: we need the money, and we can't count on Miss Weber waiting forever. Dan can show the—secret off on his own; girls can—find a good house. Can't let a silly cough ruin everything for the Darlings, can we? No!"

And then he fell back against the pile of pillows Darleen had propped behind his back, which was as good as an exclamation point.

"You would let the girls go on their own?" said Aunt Shirley doubtfully.

"Not on their own," said Darleen's Papa, after another half minute of trying to catch his breath. "With *Dan*. Dan's there to help. And the girls are sensible and clever, both of them. I might be nervous about sending Darleen out West on her own, but Darleen and Bella Mae together? They will keep each other safe, I know. And Shirley, you'll nurse me through this cold in record time, I know you will. And then we'll all go out and join them, won't we? If it's really our destiny, you know, to go west—and there will already be a chair outside in the sun waiting for me . . ."

"But Papa!" said Darleen. "I should stay here and take care of you."

"Got to keep you both safe. Bella Mae can't go traveling west all on her own—"

"Now, now, Bill," said Aunt Shirley, patting him on his big paw of a hand. She clearly thought he was beginning to babble.

But Victorine heard the concern in his voice—concern for *her*!—and had to blink back tears.

Meanwhile Darleen's Papa pushed himself an inch more upright and said, "No, Darleeny, I'm thinking about what's best for the family here, and I will *not* be the one to hold you all back."

"Papa, how can you say that?"

But Bill Darling shook his head.

"No, Darleen, listen. You and Bella Mae and our Dan—you'll go out to that nice, warm California, keeping one another very safe all the while, and if that's the place we're meant to be, you'll find us a good home, and maybe some jobs in the photoplay business out there—and then I'll come and join you, sure as sure. I insist! This is about the Darlings—and you, too, Bella Mae! It's bigger than any one person. And I won't be the one keeping us from making our way forward, all of us and our work."

And then he coughed again, which just underscored how impossible it was to think even for a moment that he would be well enough to travel that afternoon.

Victorine looked over at Darleen and felt her heart twist a little in sympathetic pain. It was so clear that

Darleen was fighting off tears, while of course trying heroically not to let her Papa see. And the uncles were surrounding her and saying comforting things about how well they would take care of her father while she was away (that was Uncle Charlie) and about how much they were depending on Darleen and Bella Mae to help on this complicated trip (that was Uncle Dan).

And Victorine felt—oh, she felt such a number of things!

She felt the warmth you feel at watching a family come together, unite, and treat one another with tender compassion, yes. She felt the kindness of Darleen's Papa, whose love for his daughter spilled over into caring concern for Victorine, his daughter's orphaned friend. But if we are to be thoroughly truthful (and being truthful was something Victorine cared about very much), Victorine also felt the small, peculiar pang that comes from watching warmth and tenderness from just very slightly *outside*.

**Chapter 9**

# All Aboard!

*Register.—The expression by bodily and facial action of the emotions of love, sympathy, hatred, etc.*
—*Glossary,* How to Write for the "Movies"

A train station a few minutes before the departure of a major line is a very exciting and tangled place, a huge oxymoron, full to the brim with chaos and order both. The faces you see there express every conceivable emotion: sorrow, joy, excitement, anxiety about whether the trunk made it successfully into the baggage car—all of that. Victorine tried to study those faces as if she herself were a camera lens, and the passengers and porters and weeping family members were all *registering* their emotions, feelings, hopes, and fears on her inner band of celluloid.

That child over there, separated for a moment from its parents, turning around while its small face crumpled, only in the next second to reshape its whole expression into bursting relief and joy as it reached its small arms up to be swept into the arms of a rescuing parent—that was terror and then bliss, doled out in small, pure doses.

Darleen, enfolded at the moment in the arms of her Uncle Charlie (since she had had to say goodbye to her Papa back in Fort Lee), was in the grip of a most authentic and genuine flow of tears (remembering her Papa all over again), but when she glanced up over her uncle's shoulder at Victorine, she *registered* not just the sorrow of parting, but also (a little bit, around the edges) the thrill of setting out into the wide world beyond New York and New Jersey.

Uncle Dan, with his little black leather secret-containing satchel tucked securely under his arm, *registered* not only eagerness to get this trip underway, but also a hundred complicated thoughts about gears, currents, shutter speeds, and mechanisms, all buzzing away like bees in a hive.

Aunt Shirley's quite transparent face, meanwhile, plainly *registered* concern and determination that the schedule and program she had worked out be followed in every particular. She had already made quite sure that "Bella Mae" was in possession of the group's train documents and various letters of introduction. (Aunt Shirley still thought of Darleen as too young for such responsibility, although that was actually rather unfair, considering that the girls were born only a couple of months apart. She also sized up her brother Dan as being too caught up in the clicking gears of his own thoughts to be entirely trusted with practical matters—and that was probably also mostly unfair.) Aunt Shirley had had productive conversations with the train employee who was standing in the doorway of their car. She had examined the travelers' seats for this first long leg of the trip to California (two days from New York to Chicago on the Pennsylvania Railroad) and found them adequate. She had said, more than once, "And then from Chicago you will be traveling in the Pullman berths, so you'll get some rest eventually." And she had made several inquiries into the status of their luggage, just to be sure. Indeed, Victorine could see Aunt Shirley glancing up now at the big clock in the station and realizing there was nothing left to check, to double-check, or to check for the third time: it was time for the travelers to step aboard and the rest of them to get their handkerchiefs out for a hearty wave goodbye. And then Aunt Shirley and Uncle Charlie would go home to report every detail to Darleen's Papa, resting quietly in his bed in Fort Lee.

Tears! Smiles! Embraces!

Victorine, as the "camera" in this scene, could not see her own face, but she knew something was surely *registering* there, a mixture, probably, of her genuine affection for the Darlings, who had, a year ago or more, so kindly and wholeheartedly taken her in and allowed her to make herself a home with them in Fort Lee—and, with all that affection, again that slight sorrow ("Travel safely, Bella Mae," Aunt Shirley was saying now, "and I'm counting on your good sense keeping these Darlings of mine out of trouble . . .") of not actually being a Darling herself and perhaps, in fact, never again truly being able to be *herself*, whatever that might mean.

But Victorine was very impatient with self-pity. When it welled up in her, she firmly folded its rough edges over, as one folds a shirt, and stacked it off at one side to be ignored.

Victorine was stepping up into the train car at last when a man came bounding up to the car entrance, his hand protectively clamped to his coat pocket. He elbowed right past her, and as Victorine stepped to one side, she thought of how appalled her dear, beloved Grandmama would have been by such rudeness. But she noticed also that his red and sweaty face (under slicked-back black hair) *registered* annoyance and the heat of rushing so as not to be late, but also something Victorine had not seen on anyone else in that train station yet this afternoon: fear.

"Sir! Please be careful there!" said the man working the entrance of this car, and he got the rude man settled in a few feet farther down the carriage.

Victorine hurriedly took her seat next to Dar, with Uncle Dan facing them and next to the window. She and Darleen were incognito again today: this time as young people who were nevertheless old and mature enough to travel across the country almost—although, of course, not quite—on their own.

Acting in photoplays had alerted them to the fact that they were of a size and age to be able to dress like children when necessary, and then, on the very same day, and simply by putting on longer skirts and tying up their hair, to look just enough older to be able to run errands on their own without everyone thinking they must be lost and needed to be returned to some parent or guardian. That was very important for photoplay actresses, who must often be human chameleons when it came to appearance and age. Why, many of the best ones were *much* older than you would have guessed at first or even third glance. Take Miss Mary Pickford, for example: *she* played child roles all the time in the photoplays, and yet she was also a grown-up star and made business deals for herself and must be twenty-five if she was a day! She was surely what Aunt Shirley would call an inspiration.

To tell the truth, Darleen and Vee often found themselves needing to seem somewhat older (or, sometimes, younger) than they actually were. That is the nature of being twelve or thirteen.

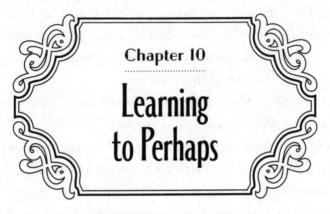

## Chapter 10

# Learning to Perhaps

*We will assume that a fertile imagination*
*has given you an original idea.*
—How to Write for the "Movies"

W hat is that you're reading, Vee?" said Darleen in a low voice, turning toward her friend again after a very quiet first half hour spent with her forehead pressed against the train window. (Victorine had tactfully absorbed herself in reading, as a way to give Dar some privacy with her emotions: the family in Fort Lee was being left behind more definitively with every clattering turn of the wheels.) Uncle Dan seemed to be napping in the seat facing them, his arm protectively circled around the satchel holding the mysterious treasure.

"It's this very helpful book I've been studying,"

said Victorine, showing Dar the cover. "Miss Louella Parsons's *How to Write for the 'Movies.'* I bought it a few weeks back, do you remember? If I'm going to enter that contest—if I'm going to write up a story about what should happen to the Vanished Victorine, you know—I will have to learn all the rules. And this book is good, I think, even if it does leave me feeling as if becoming a photoplaywright may be such a challenge as to be *practically* impossible."

"Why do you say that?" asked Darleen, perking up already. "You're so good with words, Vee. You know more of them than Aunt Shirley and Uncle Charlie combined. I'm pretty sure you should be in the running for becoming the best photoplaywright ever."

Victorine sighed.

"If it were only about knowing lots of words, I'd be more confident about the whole business," she said. "But it's not just the words, is it? Miss Parsons is so very strict on this point—her book practically brims with warnings. Look, Darleen, right here. She couldn't be clearer: 'We will assume that a fertile imagination has given you an original idea'!"

Victorine pointed to the dreadful line with one finger and raised both eyebrows at Darleen, but Darleen smiled and shook her head as if nothing at all were wrong.

"Vee, do you really think that's a *warning*?" she

said. "Sounds to me like encouragement, actually."

"Not if you're someone like me, with no imagination to speak of."

Now Darleen looked like someone trying not to laugh. (Victorine didn't mind; she was mostly just relieved that her friend was no longer spilling sad tears into her handkerchief.)

"That's just simply not true, Vee—how can that be true?" said Darleen. "Even tiny children have imaginations. And you are so intelligent and so artistic; think about how beautifully you play the piano. Of course you have an imagination!"

Victorine didn't think playing the piano was exactly the same thing as thinking up themes for a photoplay, but she was too touched by Darleen's faith in her to be openly contradictory, just at the moment.

"Well, be that as it may," she said diplomatically, "I've come to the conclusion I shall simply have to work extra hard to develop a real imagination. Miss Parsons also believes in training and practice, after all. There must be a way to learn how to imagine unreal things. Strengthening one's ability to say 'perhaps,' you know, as if it were some kind of muscle."

"All right," said Darleen. "Good. So—what are you going to imagine first?"

"The man who pushed by me when we got into the train," said Vee, very, very quietly, even though he was much farther up the aisle and couldn't possibly hear a word the girls said. "Right up there—you can see part of him if you lean past me, but don't let him see you trying. I've been attempting to imagine who he is, and why he was in such an anxious rush to get onto this carriage."

Darleen did a very skillful job of maneuvering herself to get a glimpse of this man, disguising it as tucking a loose bit of Victorine's hair back into place. Then she whispered to Vee, "He's not a very friendly-looking fellow. So what story did you come up with about him?"

"Not a story yet," said Victorine. "Just, you see, lists. Lists of things that might make someone red in the face and lead him to behave rudely when trying to board a train carriage . . ."

"Oh, do tell me!" said Darleen.

So Victorine read Dar her list:

—*running fast because late?*

—*ill health, such that running even less than fast might make him sweat?*

—*or* perhaps *he is prone to indigestion?*

—*bad mood leading to rudeness?*

—*worried about something?*

There was a brief pause after Victorine had finished reading these aloud (in a murmur) to Darleen—the *clackety-clack* of the train filled up the gaps with the comforting sound of distance being covered.

"Or, or, or!" said Darleen then, with a dancing

sort of smile. "Or *perhaps* when he was crossing the road to the station, he dropped something he cared about—*perhaps* a locket with some girl's pretty face in it?—only I don't think he can have won her heart, exactly, since he's such a scowler. So *perhaps* he is an unscrupulous type, and the girl was his ward, whom he was hoping to marry in order to get all her money. Anyway, she escaped him happily by sailing off in a yacht to—somewhere very pleasant and tropical, with palm trees—and he had to watch the boat sail off and then was stomping back to the station—because he probably manages a gold mine in the Rocky Mountains somewhere, don't you think?—and he dropped that locket and a motorcar came racing by—a black, shiny motorcar, of course—and smashed it, putting him into a horrible mood, but *perhaps* not nearly as horrible a mood as he actually deserves!"

They both laughed (very quietly) and stole another set of glimpses at the rude man, and then Victorine sighed, closed up her little book, and said, "And there it is, isn't it, though? How many practice lists will I have to work through, to be able to use a *perhaps* as well as you do, Darleen? What if an imagination actually *is* something you have to be born with, something that can't be acquired through hard work at this point in life, despite what Miss Parsons says?"

"Now you are being plain silly," said Darleen with such confidence in her voice that Victorine couldn't help but be a bit infected by it. "If anyone can work up an imagination from scratch, I'm quite sure you're the person to be able to do it, with your brilliant mind and your persistence and your notebooks. You'll be *perhaps*ing like the professionals in no time at all, Vee! I'm sure of it."

(And the train chattered along in its own private, ambiguous language: *Perhaps perhaps perhaps perhaps perhaps . . .*)

# Chapter 11

## Passing Dreams Along, Passing Dreams Along . . .

*Nearly everyone who goes to the picture shows night after night has
some plot stored in his mind that he feels would make a good photoplay,
if he only knew how properly to construct the story!
Ah, there's the rub!* —How to Write for the "Movies"

In Chicago they left the not-terribly-comfortable
seats of that ordinary railway carriage for the plush
accommodation of a Pullman car on the Union
Pacific, and they ate quite tasty meals at the tables in
the dining car too. Luxury! All of this fancy living—
the train tickets, the berths in the Pullman, the dinner
itself—was being paid for by Victorine's diminished
and diminishing stash of money, but still the girls
couldn't keep themselves from smiling in pleasure
when the plates of apple pie landed in front of them
while the train *clackety-clack*ed along. And when they
returned from the apple pie, they discovered that the
porter had pulled out the berth so cleverly folded into

the compartment above the seat and turned the seat into another bed. Then tactful curtains added privacy; Uncle Dan had his own berth across the aisle.

"How wonderful this all is!" said Darleen, clapping her hands. "Vee, have you ever seen anything so wonderful? No, don't answer, please."

That was because Victorine had traveled so very much in her younger years, and had been on all sorts of trains, some of them the sort that had elaborate inlaid wooden panels on their walls, as if they were an actual rolling palace. However (as she told Darleen in all honesty), none of those fancy trains had ever been quite so comfortable and cozy as this Pullman car.

Another curtain separated their part of the wagon from the other passengers. It was wonderful how cleverly all the details had been worked out.

They sat for a while in their compartment, Victorine reading comfortably and Darleen writing a letter home to Aunt Shirley, describing their journey thus far. The Pullman porter came by soon after they arrived back from dinner, just to check that everything was set up in a satisfactory way. When he saw Victorine's book, he smiled and said, "Are you planning to write for the movies, miss?"

Victorine tried not to sound even in the least bit discouraged. "I'm making a study of it, anyway," she said.

"Well, good for you, miss," said the porter, and he tapped his dark and regal nose like someone about to share a secret. "I was in a motion picture once, you know. Long ago!"

That was not what any of them had expected to hear!

"Really!" said Victorine, and Darleen put her pen right down and perked up her ears. (She was not a very eager writer of letters at the best of times.)

"What movie was it?"

"You probably won't believe this, girls," said the porter, "but it was in France, many years ago, when I was very young."

Now Uncle Dan was listening too. The porter brightened up another notch or two; he was clearly a person who liked to tell a good story.

"It was back in nineteen oh three, you see," said the porter. "Back when I was just a child, back when they called me Little Freddy, you know. But I was already world famous for the act I put on with my big sister, Ruthie. We were the Cakewalk Kiddies! You know what a cakewalk is?"

"It's a dance, isn't it?"

"It surely is," said the porter. "A dance that reflects some of those old African steps and traditions, you know, or so they say—and oh, back ten years ago or so, it was going around the world just like a wildfire spreading. Everybody wanted to see a good cakewalk on the stage! Quite a dance too. Not easy for anyone, you'd better believe, but my sister and I, we were nimble and clever and we worked hard, and they just loved us, all over Europe, if I do say so myself. Why, they sold little bronze statues of us as souvenirs, we were so famous! How about that?"

"Statues!" said Darleen. No one had ever made any statues of her, that was for sure.

"I would show you one, miss, if I still had any around, but none of those came back across the ocean with us. Anyway, it was moving pictures we were talking about, wasn't it?"

"Yes, that's right," said Victorine.

"Well, in Paris we were performing with a whole troupe of grown-up dancers, from just about everywhere you might imagine. And one day they had us do our act in front of a man cranking a handle on a little box. They had a funny name for that box—'cinématographe.' That was just the fancy French word for a motion picture camera, though. A big French movie company was making that film—company run by some big family, as I remember."

"The Lumière brothers!" said Victorine. "Did you meet the Lumières, then? They practically invented moving pictures!"

"Or Thomas Edison did," said Uncle Dan, being loyal to New Jersey.

"Well, I wasn't there when whoever invented the moving pictures invented them," said the porter, "so I can't really say who did it first. And I was just a kiddie in nineteen oh three, so I don't know who it was exactly who was cranking the camera that day, but I do know I was in the pictures, and that's my story."

"And now you've moved from stages to trains!" said Darleen.

"Yes, miss, I have," said the porter. "Plenty of ambitious people working for the Pullman company, you'd better believe. Why, one fellow came through some weeks ago on a different route—said he had been a Pullman porter himself, back in the old days. Gave him a leg up to buy some land out in South Dakota, and then he discovered telling the story was what he wanted to do, and he went and published a novel about it, *The Conquest*, he called it, *The Story of a Negro Pioneer*. He sold me a copy of that book, you better believe it. Look, here it is in my pocket, right now this very moment—"

He brought out a handsome book—dark blue cover with the title stamped on it in gold—and showed them some of the photographs in it serving as illustrations.

"And there he is, the man himself," said the porter, showing them the photograph at the start of the book. "He just calls himself 'a Negro Pioneer' on the cover, you know, but he told me his real name is Oscar Micheaux, and he could sell a book to a haystack, I do believe.

"Anyway, I said to him, 'Why not go to Hollywood and make your books into moving pictures, since it's a new century and all?' and he said, 'Think I might just try that one day, but it won't be Hollywood that makes *our* pictures—I'm thinking we have to do it for ourselves.' And I said, 'Now you sound just like my sister, Ruthie—she's been out in Hollywood a while, trying to make a go of it as an actress in the pictures. And she says the same as you—better find a way to build studios of our own, you know, if we want our stories told.'—Well, and now I'd better get moving, if you're all settled in nicely here."

"It's all lovely, thank you," said Victorine.

But Darleen said, "You have a sister out in Hollywood, Mr.—sorry, but what is your name, sir?"

"Waller," said the porter. "Fred Waller."

"Well, Mr. Waller, Hollywood happens to be where we're headed," said Darleen. (She left out the part about her being Daring Darleen, however.) "We're going to meet with Miss Lois Weber, the photoplay director—she's employed by Universal, you know."

The porter laughed. "How about that? My sister works in pictures for Universal. You keep an eye out for her, girls—Miss Ruth Waller's her name—and if you see her, go on and tell her her brother Freddy says hey."

The next day, when they were watching fields and prairies race by outside the window in endless waves and ripples of brown and gold—while they were thinking, in the spell of that landscape-induced daze that long train trips can cast on us, of how enormous a place this country was that their train was hurtling across—the porter came by with a little package in brown paper, which he handed over to Uncle Dan.

"That's just that book I was talking about," he said. "For you to pass on to my sister at Universal, out in California, if you see her. Miss Ruth Waller, that's her name. Figure she might know people who might know people who might want to make a moving picture out of it, you know."

At first Uncle Dan didn't want to accept that book and the errand it came wrapped up in, because, really, what were the chances of them finding any one particular person in a place as big as Hollywood? But the porter insisted.

"Way I see it, part of getting things to happen is passing things along, passing things along. Maybe you will run into my Ruthie, and she'll know who should see this story next. Or maybe you won't find Ruthie, but your Miss Lois Weber will hear about this book from you now. I'm just trying to do right by a man with big dreams, that's all . . ."

So Uncle Dan took the package and tucked it into the same little satchel where he was keeping that secret treasure of his, and the train clattered and raced toward the West as fast as it could possibly go.

Chapter 12

# Eggs! Happiness! Jewels! Shouting!

*Crisis.—A series of big situations leading to the climax.*
—*Glossary,* How to Write for the "Movies"

At breakfast in the dining car another day later, all three of them were in the extra sunshine-filled mood of people who have spent the past couple of nights sleeping better—much better—than they had been doing previously. Victorine tapped happily at the boiled egg brought to her in its own little egg cup, just like her Grandmama had always preferred. Darleen had her eggs scrambled, with amply buttered biscuits. Uncle Dan, meanwhile, with that black satchel (which had never been out of contact with some part of his body this whole trip) tucked safely behind his back, was concentrating on his ham and eggs, washed down with regular slurps of coffee.

"Tasty," he remarked. "Happy, girls?"

"I'm happy!" said Darleen. "How about you, Vee?"

"Of course," said Victorine. "This egg is perfect, and the toast most *beautifully* toasty!"

"Here's a question for you," said Uncle Dan.

The girls were surprised, because Uncle Dan was not the sort of person who usually asked a lot of questions over breakfast.

"What's that, Uncle Dan?" said Darleen.

"Bella Mae here—why do you call her Vee?" he said. "Been wondering that a while."

"Oh!" said Darleen, rushing in quickly to keep Victorine from filling up the silent spaces with one of those typical Victorine spillages of the truth. "Vee! It's just a nickname, you know. Like the letter V. Because V is for—"

What a terrible place in the sentence to get stuck!

"V," said Uncle Dan, sending the mysterious letter off to travel through the gears and cogs of his brain. "Let's see. V is for—*volcanic*? Naw. Not our Bella Mae!"

He chuckled, but the girls were still scrambling to find the best path out of this swamp.

"*Vivid*? *Violent*? No, no, none of those! *Violet*, then?"

"Um," said Darleen. "No."

"What's wrong with violets?" said Uncle Dan. "Pretty little flowers. Anyway. Thinking. V, V, V . . ."

"Oh, dear," said Darleen. "Uncle Dan, please don't!"

"It's a secret, you see," said Victorine finally. That

was telling the truth without spilling too much of the *actual* truth, so she was pleased with that. "Secret, like the treasure you've been carrying around in your satchel there."

"Oh!" said Darleen, grabbing this opportunity to change the subject. "That's it, Uncle Dan, yes! Do tell us, finally, what that is you have in there!"

"You'll find out soon enough," said Uncle Dan. "A treasure, as you rightly say. To make our fortune."

"That sounds good," said Darleen, lavishly buttering another biscuit. "A fortune would be very helpful."

"And you said it's something the director Miss Lois Weber might be interested in," said Victorine, thinking it over as hard as she could.

"Indeed so," said Uncle Dan. "I hope!"

"Give us a hint, Uncle Dan!" said Darleen.

"Absolutely not," said Uncle Dan.

"Oh, Uncle Dan, help us out with just one little word," said Darleen, and Victorine was impressed all over again by her friend's ability to produce a camera-worthy wheedle at the drop of a hat. "One word for a hint! And then we won't bother you about it anymore, will we, Vee—I mean, *Bella Mae*?"

"I'm sure we will try hard not to," said Victorine. It did seem unlikely that Darleen's curiosity could be satisfied by as little as one word, but perhaps?

"All right," said Uncle Dan, and he leaned forward: "—*aglyff*—," he said, but at the very moment he spoke, the dining car waiter collided with a railroad employee and dropped some spoons on a table, so the girls couldn't hear properly.

"What?" said Darleen. "What did you say?"

"Too late, sorry," said Uncle Dan with a chuckle. "That was your one word. Come and gone."

"Oh, Uncle Dan!" said Darleen. "How can you be like that? Was it *hieroglyph*, Vee? Is that what it was?"

"Hieroglyph!" echoed a very amused Uncle Dan, and the hubbub in that dining car had suddenly calmed down enough that the word rang out rather gloriously. A number of heads bent over other meals at other small tables turned to see who it was who was so amused by the thought of hieroglyphs that he thought it worth interrupting their breakfast with them.

"Did we guess it, Uncle Dan?" asked Darleen, but he merely shrugged and grinned.

Darleen frowned.

"But what can Uncle Dan or Papa possibly have to do with hieroglyphs?" she said. Victorine shook her head: she had no idea. And Uncle Dan, clearly delighted, took a last, deeply satisfied gulp of coffee.

The railroad man had started his announcement by then:

"Sorry to interrupt your good breakfast this morning, ladies and gentlemen, but we'll be coming into the Union Depot in scenic Ogden, Utah, shortly, and all are requested to return to their carriages and collect their things. Passengers to San Francisco and to Los Angeles will kindly transfer here to the respective Southern Pacific lines. And please know that whichever exposition you are headed to, the Union Pacific Railroad Company wishes you a safe journey and good weather . . ."

"Oh!" said Darleen. There were two major expositions going on in California at the moment to celebrate the opening of the Panama Canal, one in San Diego (smaller) and one in San Francisco (absolutely enormous), and Darleen had been cutting out newspaper pictures from the larger San Francisco one since its opening day. "The Jewel City, Vee! Imagine that! Wouldn't it be wonderful—?"

The Jewel City was another name for the Panama-Pacific International Exposition—apparently it featured a whole tower simply covered with jewels! No one could really blame Darleen for sighing a little about that.

"Let's just be absolutely sure we all get onto the right train, Darleen," said Victorine. "Southern Pacific to Los Angeles. No imagining anything until then."

The Union Depot, all red brick and pointed rooflines, must surely be by far the grandest building in Ogden, Utah. Darleen and Victorine stood on the platform there, guarding Uncle Dan's black satchel, which he had left in their care while he went off in search of a quick cup of coffee.

"You be careful, girls! I set it down at the ticket counter just now and nearly lost it!" Uncle Dan had said to them, in a bit of a dither. "Then saw this man was holding it, looking around—'Is that mine?' I ask—'You coming from New York?' the man says—'Yes, indeed!' I say, and I grab it. Can't let that happen again!" And that was a whole lot of story, practically a novel and a half, coming from the not-very-wordy Uncle Dan. Perhaps he was feeling the effects of this high-altitude Western air. Victorine was breathing deeply, very glad to be outside for a time. She had always liked wild air—the wilder, the better! Ogden is more than four thousand feet in elevation, which is not quite as high as Denver, Colorado, but still pretty impressive for girls who lived near the shore of the Atlantic.

"Goodness, the sun is so bright!" said Darleen. "Do you think the air smells different here?"

"Probably would if we were farther from the station," said Victorine. On this platform, however, the reigning smells were the usual coal plus railroad-station food. "I can see hills over that way, look!"

In between them and the distant outline of hills was a group of happy, chattering girls, some years older than Dar and Victorine, by the looks of them.

"Who are they, do you think?" said Darleen. "And golly, why are they waving at us?"

"No idea," said Victorine. "But look, now a few of them are coming our way—guess we're about to find out what they want."

Closer up, the girls looked even happier and better-dressed than they had from afar. Their hair had clearly been ironed into fashionable waves that morning, which is an impressive thing to see in the middle of a long train journey.

"Hello there, you two!" said the leader of that trio, a dark-haired, jolly-looking sort. "Are you more of us contest-winning girls, perhaps? Because if so—"

"I don't think so, miss," said Victorine very politely. "What contest would that be?"

"The Universal City contest, of course!" said the jolly young woman in a great rush of happy explanation. "A couple girls from each state—voted 'most beautiful,' ha ha, but really it was just 'who has the most friends and acquaintances willing to fill out the newspaper ballots'—but what a lark, right? Visiting the expositions, a tour of Universal City, movie town USA, the chance at a role in the movies! Such fun!"

"Oh, but see, Sally, they're just young things when you see them close up, aren't they?" said another girl, also jolly. "Sorry to bother you, girls. A bunch of us came from Chicago on the train, you know, but there was someone from San Francisco who was supposed to meet up with us here—to travel with the group, you know—and *that* train was delayed a bit because of all the excitement about the thieves, you know, so when we saw you—"

"Goodness, thieves?" said Victorine. "On a train?"

"Thieves everywhere these days!" said the second jolly young woman. "Don't you read the papers? Displays at the big exposition in San Francisco and that fancy museum in New York City—both robbed in a single week! 'Priceless Antiquities Nabbed in Brazen Theft,' said the paper today. And the same sort of stuff gone missing from both places—Egyptian, was it? Something like that! How's that for coincidence?"

"Or careful planning, Sally," said the third young woman darkly. "*That* would be more exciting, wouldn't it? And scarier."

"Anyway, it's all over the headlines everywhere today, I guess. Worth pots of money, too, all those ancient old things. Shocking what thieves will get up to, isn't it, girls? Guess there's still enough left to see at the exposition to make for a good visit, though."

She laughed merrily, just to underscore how vast the Panama-Pacific International Exposition really was, and how numerous its attractions.

"Oh, my, you all really get to see the exposition in San Francisco," sighed Darleen. "How wonderful."

"Yes, indeed! But didn't you hear the best part of it?" said one of the ones who wasn't named Sally.

"First, a chance to act in the movies! Might be seeing us on the screen, kiddies! How about that? Anyway, Sally here has already *been* to the exposition in San Francisco. Show them your jewel, Sally!"

And Sally fetched out a twinkling round gem she was wearing on a little chain around her neck. It was a lovely sea-green color and sparkled brightly in Ogden's high-altitude air.

"So pretty!" said Darleen. "Are there really so many of those jewels everywhere? All over the walls of the tower, like the papers say?"

"Simply thousands of 'em," said Sally. "All different colors too. They aren't real, of course—they're called Novagems—but you should see them at night when the electric lights shine on them. It's a marvel. And now I'll be able to see it all for a second time! But first: Universal City! And the movies! Oh, there's Mrs. Hanford waving at us now. She's our chaperone, you know. Guess we'd better scoot on back. Wish us luck, girls, won't you? Wouldn't you just *love* to be in a motion picture?"

"Sounds grand!" said Darleen, rushing in quickly, as usual, to head off Victorine from one of those little bouts of honesty she was prone to. Her caution was unnecessary this time, however; Victorine had already figured out how to navigate safely.

"I'm sure we wish you all the luck in the world!"

she said, and with enough sincerity that the older girls gave them the kindest smiles imaginable before turning to rejoin their happy band of contest winners.

"Well! A chance to be in the movies!" said Darleen, who had been acting in the motion pictures since she was a tiny tot jumping out of flour barrels. Just for fun, she added a twirl and a grin. "How about that, Vee? Now where's Uncle Dan gotten to?"

And that was the moment when all the shouting started.

## Chapter 13

# Catastrophe!

*Unless you have the punch and the action,*
*throw your efforts in the waste basket.*
—How to Write for the "Movies"

Such shouting and carrying on! All that hubbub had erupted a bit farther along the platform, closer to the concession and railroad offices and etcetera. Victorine and Darleen looked at each other in alarm: What was happening?

And then they both jumped a little, because one of those voices was very clearly the voice of Uncle Dan, and he was saying things like "CAREFUL THERE!" and "*DON'T!*"

A moment later Dar and Victorine were at the edges of a knot of agitated people, all drawn to the sounds of a fuss. From where they were standing they could see only occasional glimpses of Uncle Dan at the center of that knot, being pointed at and shouted at by various upset folks.

"Get the police!"

"Arrest him!"

"Thief!"

*What?* Accusing Uncle Dan of being a *thief?* How could that even possibly be?

Darleen and Victorine exchanged horrified glances.

"Oh, poor Uncle Dan!" whispered Darleen indignantly. "Vee, let me *go!*"

"Wait a moment," said Victorine, trying to corral her own rising sense of distress. But her instinct was telling her what Uncle Dan himself would surely have insisted—protect Darleen first, and only *then* worry about Uncle Dan—so she was holding on very tightly to Darleen's arm. "Just a moment, Dar. We have to figure out what's going on—"

A railroad official had just pushed his way to the center.

"What's happening here? *What . . . is . . . happening . . . here?*" he said. He had a reasonably fancy uniform, so his words all glittered some, like his shiny gilt braids and buttons.

The crowd reluctantly gave him an inch or two of space, while they shouted explanations at him.

"He was trying to pinch my case!" said a brown-haired man with twitchy hands and a mustache. "Just came off the San Francisco train, and this man misrepresented himself and grabbed it—"

"It is *my* case!" said Uncle Dan stubbornly, holding it to his chest. "You handed it to me yourself. And then I gave it to the girls to watch, but I guess they must have been careless, because here it is again—"

"You misled me—wasn't for you—was for *him*."

"Yep. That thing is mine!" said another voice, and the girls gasped when they saw him, because it was none other than the rude man who had traveled on the train from New York with them, the one who had been so very flustered that first day as he pushed past Victorine. And he was flustered again now.

He and the other man were plucking at the little satchel, which Uncle Dan was holding very close to his chest, while the expression on his face grew stubborner and stubborner.

"Oh, no," whispered Darleen. "This is awful!"

"Now, now," said the railroad official. "Has there been some sort of misunderstanding here, gentlemen? Should be easy enough to rectify, seems like. We'll see whose case it is, sure as sure. If you'll just be so good as to hand it over, we'll open it up, now, and take a look—"

Uncle Dan and the other two men all said "*No!*" at the very same time.

"Now that's no kind of attitude to take toward a station representative," said the railroad man.

Darleen was pulling Victorine forward now, through that broad-shouldered, mesmerized crowd.

"Thief!" said the twitchy-handed man.

"My treasure!" said Uncle Dan.

"Oh, please let my uncle go!" Darleen called out in alarm when they were still separated from him by a couple of tall fellows. "This is all an awful mistake! We've still got your satchel here, Uncle Dan!"

"What? Darleen? Is that you?" said Uncle Dan.

"Not yours? I'll take that, then," said the railroad official, plucking the case from Uncle Dan's arms. He turned toward the twitchy-handed man. "So this belongs to you, sir?"

"I was bringing it to *him*," said the man, pointing at the rude man from the New York train, and the latter fellow gave an unsavory grunt in agreement. "Yep. Mine," he said.

"And you fellows are heading—?" said the railroad official.

"Various directions," said the twitchy-handed man.

"Los Angeles, for me," said the rude man from New York. "That train right there. Soon as you hand me my bag that was nearly stolen, I'll be on my way."

The girls caught just enough glimpses through the crowd to confirm the railroad man went ahead and handed that satchel right off to the man from New York. Then the victors of this little tug-of-war slunk away and vanished from view entirely, leaving Uncle

Dan still standing there with his shoulders slumped, looking stunned and perplexed.

You would think that would have been the end of the whole scene: confusion over a satchel; confusion sorted out.

But the spectators were restless. Perhaps they had all been sitting too long on trains, letting the long hours of nothing-to-do make them peevish and fretful.

In any case the temperature of that crowd was beginning to rise again. New voices were contributing theories and suggestions, of which the girls could hear distressing little scraps:

". . . Newspapers!"

". . . Exposition!"

And then the showstopper, from a short, redheaded man:

"Why, I do believe I heard this very fellow talking about *hieroglyphs* this morning at breakfast! Hieroglyphs! Like the museum stuff that got stolen!"

More gasps from the crowd. Smaller, more horrified gasps from Dar and Victorine.

Dar actually said, "No, no, terrible!" right out loud, and Victorine caught a sliver's worth of a glimpse of Uncle Dan, hearing Dar's voice and turning to try to see where the voice had come from.

"This happened on the train from San Francisco?" asked the railroad official.

"No, Chicago," said the redheaded man. "But I seen

him before that, too, on the train from New York."

"Ah! Museum thief!" said someone in the crowd. "Metropolitan Museum! Read it in the newspaper this morning!"

"Or the exposition in San Francisco, you know—bandits simply everywhere," said someone else.

*"There's a reward!"* said another newspaper reader. "And here's the real police coming now!"

That woke up the crowd for real. Every single person there, it seemed, suddenly had the pleasant thought that maybe *they* could get a piece of that reward, if they just pushed and pulled enough to have a hand on the criminal when the police got to the scene.

So it was pandemonium for a while. It was chaos. The railroad official blew his official whistle, and that had no effect to speak of. The girls hardly knew whether to push forward or back away, so they stayed where they were, with Victorine's arms wrapped around both Darleen and Uncle Dan's little satchel as protectively as she could manage. Fortunately, nobody was paying two girls much attention just at that moment.

The policemen arriving could shout louder than the railroad official, it turned out, and almost as loud as a crowd of angry people trying to be the one to turn in a Wanted Criminal and claim any Possible Reward.

"Stolen? Stolen? Something's been stolen?" said a policeman's voice, once the shouting calmed down just a tad. "Satchel missing? And this is the only fellow left?"

A loud shout from a different railroad man: "ALL ABOOOOOOOOARD FOR LOS ANGELES! FIFTEEN MINUTES!"

The police: "We'll take this one into custody, then. This way, sir."

"Stay right here," said Victorine to Dar. *"Stay right here!"*

And then Victorine plunged forward until she could actually pluck Uncle Dan by the sleeve.

"Mr. Darling!" she gasped. "Uncle Dan! The train is going to leave. We have all your things. What should we do?"

The policeman leading Uncle Dan away looked down at Victorine in puzzlement.

"Who are you, young lady?" he said.

"That's just Bella Mae," said Uncle Dan.

"Is this young person all alone?" said the policeman. "Shall we take her in, too?"

"Oh, no! Not alone," said Victorine, meaning that, of course, she was with Darleen. "Not alone at all."

And Uncle Dan said, "The treasure, Bella Mae! Miss Weber's got to see that treasure!"

From the crowd: "The *treasure!* Listen to him, confessing!"

And from another, slightly nicer member of the crowd: "Oof, poor fellow! Don't care if he *is* a thief, awful to hear him ramble on that way. Listen to him—he's lost his mind for sure."

("ALLLL ABOOOOOOOARD!!")

"Go! Go!" said Uncle Dan to Victorine. "Get on that train! Can't risk missing Miss Weber, day after tomorrow. I'll be there soon, I'm sure. You'll call Shirley's Mrs. Gish from the station—she'll take care of you. I'll be along in a day or so. You'll take care of Darleen, right? *And don't you go worrying Shirley!*"

"Better get back to your people, little girl," said the policeman, and he pulled poor Uncle Dan away. Some part of the crowd flowed along with them, probably still hoping for a fight of some kind.

*Get back to your people,* the policeman had said.

Victorine's "people" was Darleen, who was pale with horror and shaking slightly.

"Vee!" Darleen said as soon as she reached her. "This is a nightmare! What do we do?"

"You heard him, Dar," whispered Victorine. "We have a *mission.* Stay with me now, one step at a time. We are going to get ourselves on that train. And then we are going to figure all of this out."

All the while she was angling the two of them away from the roughest part of the crowd and back into the friendlier company of the beauty contest girls, where Dar and Victorine would not stick out so much. Those older girls were also rather excited and distressed about what had just happened on that railroad platform:

"Did you all see that?" "Oh, so terrible!" "I think they caught the thief!" "One of them, anyway!" "Did you see his wild eyes?"

(That was unfair. Say what you wanted about him, but Darleen's Uncle Dan did not have wild eyes.)

"ALL ABOOOOARD FOR LOS ANGELES!" shouted the railroad man.

*All aboard!* thought Victorine grimly, using the older girls as a floating, chattering, eddying screen as she carefully maneuvered herself and Darleen—despite having lost Uncle Dan and nearly having lost his satchel—despite *everything*—right onto that Los Angeles–bound train.

## Chapter 14

# Onward!

*Each incident must be logical,*
*a consistent step to the next scene . . .*
—How to Write for the "Movies"

Somehow (the details of that awful quarter hour would forever be shrouded in clouds of horror and distress) Victorine managed to shepherd a very upset Darleen onto the Southern Pacific train and settle them both into their proper seats, with a gaping blank in the seat across from them, where Uncle Dan should have been. She also managed to make sure they had all their most important items close at hand (including her copy of *How to Write for the "Movies,"* which was surely as necessary as any toothbrush to a serious student of this new art), and she even remembered to check that their trunk had indeed made it into the baggage car and would arrive in Los Angeles when they did.

She managed all this while her own heart was boiling over with worry and alarm.

"What do we do now, Vee?" Darleen kept saying. To Dar's credit, she kept her voice low and tried to keep her tears out of public view, but there were, very naturally, some tears. "What are we going to do?"

"We are going to take this train to Los Angeles," said Victorine. "You heard your Uncle Dan! The *treasure*—" (This word she said in the lowest possible whisper, since after the awful display of mob misrule on the platform just now, she felt inclined to keep any bystanders well out of her private conversations.) "We have to be sure to get it to that appointment he made with Miss Lois Weber. But Darleen, that's not until the day after tomorrow. Uncle Dan will have caught up with us by then, surely. We will call that Mrs. Gish from the station, as your Aunt Shirley would expect us to do, and then we will just wait in safety for Uncle Dan to show up. Hopefully *soon*."

"But they were *arresting* him!" said Darleen (her whisper as small as Victorine's). "For no reason! What if he has to molder away his life in a dank cell? Why, oh, why didn't he want them looking in that case? It sounded so suspicious! And the case wasn't even his that he was protecting so foolishly!"

"He was so very intent on that treasure of his being a secret, you know," said Victorine.

"But now it's our secret," said Darleen. "Whatever it is."

"I suppose so," said Victorine.

"I guess we'll have to look and see what it is," said Darleen. "If we're going to be the ones taking it to Miss Weber. If he's going to be delayed more than—a few hours. More than a day."

The girls looked at each other and then looked down at the black case wedged securely between them.

"*Tonight*," said Victorine, meaning when the curtains were safely drawn around their berths. Then they could take a look at Uncle Dan's treasure.

And that thought added the tiniest little sparkle of interest and excitement to their general dark and gloomy spirits. Even a tiny sparkle was very welcome, to be honest. And despite everything, their spirits couldn't help but be amazed and inspired by the sheer beauty of the desert lands speeding by, the enormous spaces punctuated by bone-dry shrubs, bone-dry hills, and occasional displays of towering and strange-shaped rocks.

Victorine wrote a few lines for her contest entry—a scene in which the fictional Victorine tried to escape evildoers on a train through the Wild West—but her words couldn't possibly give justice to those immense and alien rock piles.

Hours later, the girls realized they were actually very hungry and went off to the dining car to find some dinner, carrying Uncle Dan's secret in its black case along with them out of respect for his wishes that it be kept, always, safe.

Darleen looked at the menu, which took the form of a typewritten sheet tucked into a pretty cover printed with a picture of a train whistling through a very scenic stretch of desert.

"You know what I like about eating in dining cars, Vee?" she said.

"The dear little saltshakers?" said Victorine. They were so small and handy!

"Not the saltshakers," said Darleen. "Although yes, they are very nice. What I like is that—unlike at Aunt Shirley's dinners, you know—you don't *have* to have the Boiled Ox Tongue with Tomato Sauce if you don't want to. And I don't want to."

She managed a wan smile, which, after all the stress and strain of that day, gladdened Victorine's heart.

"So what *will* you have?" said Victorine, who was happily constructing a menu for herself that included Cream of Celery Soup, Braised Beef Tenderloin in Bordelaise Sauce, and Fried Parsnips.

"Spaghetti and Hashed Brown Potatoes," said Darleen. "And then do you think we could have pie for dessert? 'Fresh Peach Pie Ala Mode'?"

"That's not how it's really spelled, you know," said Victorine. "'À *la*' is actually two *separate* words."

Then she looked up and found Darleen smiling a real—no longer wan—smile at her.

"Vee!" said Darleen. "Either way, it means ice cream, right?"

"In this country it certainly does," said Victorine.

"Then they can spell it any way they want, as far as I'm concerned—oh, but Vee, is this all too much money?"

Train food was expensive: sixty cents for the main dishes, twenty cents for the parsnips, fifteen cents for hashed brown potatoes, twenty-five cents for the soup. And Uncle Dan had most of their money (of which a good percentage was actually Victorine's) in his pocket.

Victorine had added everything up in her mind already, of course. Two dollars and thirty cents was a lot—a LOT—to pay for dinner, that was true. But whenever the question of expense had come up in the railroad dining cars of her childhood, her dear Grandmama had always smiled and said, "Travel, my dear, requires sustenance!"

The memory of a wise grandmother is a powerful force.

And Victorine still had a number of bills tucked away in her many secret pockets. And the girls were hungry.

"I think we shouldn't worry tonight, Darleen," she said. "We've been through the mill today, and we have to keep up our strength because tomorrow we will have to navigate Los Angeles, and I don't know

Los Angeles at all, so that will surely be a challenge. Anyway, peach pie it is!"

The jolly and well-coiffed young women who had won the beauty contest were just filtering into the dining car as Dar and Victorine left it, and they exchanged friendly pleasantries with them, including various divergent opinions on parsnips. Then Darleen and Victorine waved and went back to their carriage, where the berths had been set up already, as if by magic. The girls went to the washroom and brushed their teeth. They put on their sleeping attire, and then they huddled together on the lower berth and lay Uncle Dan's black case on their knees. The curtains were drawn. They had this small corner of the train to themselves.

"Here we go, right?" said Darleen, and, holding their breath, they unlatched the little case and looked inside.

They had been expecting some sort of *mechanism* to be in that satchel—a mysterious object that would have the definite look of an *invention*—but instead there were three small velvet bags.

"What's this?" whispered Darleen, putting an almost frightened hand on one of those bags.

It didn't seem right, did it?

Victorine picked up a bag, opened her left hand, and poured out the contents into her palm.

The contents, too, were terribly strange: a small

cylinder made of some stone—quartz or jasper, maybe?—quite rough to the touch, being absolutely covered with tiny, intricate carvings.

"How strange!" said Darleen in wonder.

Victorine turned the object about in her hand. The images were all carved quite deeply *into* the stone of the cylinder, quite the opposite way around from the usual way of carving things, in which whatever is being pictured—a face, for instance—will end up emerging *from* the surface. Here the picture bit into the stone: *concave*, thought Victorine, remembering geometry lessons of the past, rather than *convex*. It was rather hard to see what the images were supposed to be, but there seemed to be tall figures fighting with—was that a lion with wings?

"Does your uncle often make carvings?" said Victorine with a frown. "In stone?"

Darleen shook her head.

"Never," she said. "You know Uncle Dan! He's absolutely loyal to his cameras and machines. What *is* this thing, Vee? And what's in these other bags?"

In the other bags were more of the same: small cylinders with those hollowed-out figures carved into them. So peculiar!

For a moment the girls looked at those little cylinders and at each other, and could not think of a coherent thing to say.

And then an idea—actually, a memory *followed* by

an idea—rose to the surface of Victorine's mind, and she put a hand to her mouth in alarm.

"What, Vee?" said Darleen. "What is it?"

"I know what these are," said Victorine. "I've seen things like them before, in the Louvre—that's a museum, you know. In Paris."

"A museum?" said Darleen. "What are you saying? What are these funny things?"

"If we had some modeling clay, I could show you better," said Victorine.

"Clay!" said Darleen, and she almost smiled in disbelief. "Who goes on long train trips with *modeling clay*?"

"Well, actually," said Victorine, "my Grandmama, for one. She believed in travelers being ready to create art *whenever* the opportunity or necessity might arise: she always had some clay and some wax and her paints and good pencils, as well as a bit of charcoal for doing rubbings of interesting grave markers and suchlike. She would have brought out a nice lump of clay right now, and we could have rolled this cylinder over it, and you would have seen a whole little picture come into being. It's really too bad we don't have any clay."

"Oh, like a fancy rolling pin, for cookies! Aunt Shirley has one with snowflakes on it that she brings out for baking at Christmas," said Darleen. "But Vee, what is Uncle Dan doing with miniature old stone rolling pins?"

"Babylonian cylinder seals, I'm afraid," said Victorine, with the grim voice of someone sharing bad news. "I'm quite certain that's what these are. *Antiquities*, Dar."

That might not be such an awful word generally, but right here and right now it was terrible. Darleen clasped her hands and shook her head.

"Oh, no. No, no, no, Vee," she said. "You mean, like the things that were—stolen? From the museum in New York? But Uncle Dan couldn't have—he *couldn't* have—oh, but he said *hieroglyphs*, Vee, didn't he? And here are these dreadful *antiquities*, in his very own bag! But he couldn't have stolen anything. Not Uncle Dan. I *won't* believe it, Vee."

Victorine knew, based on past experience, that people can sometimes surprise us by being capable of good or terrible deeds beyond anything one could have expected from them. Nevertheless: Darleen's Uncle Dan! Even if the words he had used—*treasure, hiero-glyphs* . . . (Had he actually even said *hieroglyphs*? The dining car had been so noisy.) Even if those words were the kind of circumstantial evidence that might raise suspicions in certain people, like policemen, who didn't *know* Dan Darling, still—! Uncle Dan was the last person on earth likely to break into a museum and steal things. That seemed the sort of fact one could stand on with confidence. And anyway—

"Darleen!" said Victorine, sitting up a bit taller.

"I've just thought of something helpful. Hieroglyphs aren't Babylonian at all. Hieroglyphs are *Egyptian* things, you know, like the pyramids and the Sphinx. So I don't think he can have been talking about Babylonian cylinder seals—no, not possible. I don't know what he meant, but it wasn't all of *this*."

Darleen's little laugh was very hollow-sounding.

"I'm not sure anyone but you will care about the difference between something that's Egyptian and something that's *Babble-onion*, or whatever it was you called it. I'm sure the police wouldn't care. If they see what he's been carrying around in this case, they'll lock him up and throw away the key. And I guess that's why he wanted us not to show the case to the police. So this is awful."

"Wait, Darleen!" said Victorine. "I don't think that's the story here at all. I think there's been some kind of mistake. This is the wrong satchel, that's what it is."

The train rumbled along, *rattle rumble rattle rumble*.

"But it has to be Uncle Dan's," said Darleen. "It's black—it's the right shape. And it's been right with us, all the time."

"Remember, though: that other man had one just like it, back at the station. And there was some kind of confusion about the satchels, even before Uncle Dan told us to watch this one so very carefully. Remember that?"

Darleen was silent for a moment. Then she said, "Oh, my. Yes. Those men. Those suspicious, awful men! The one from San Francisco and the one from New York!"

"Yes!' said Victorine. "Them. I've been thinking all of this over, and I guess the New York fellow must have walked off with Uncle Dan's *actual* leather satchel."

"And he said he was taking this train!" said Darleen. "So if he's on this train, can we get Uncle Dan's own satchel back?"

"I don't know," said Victorine. "We can try."

The girls shared a look in which they tried to imagine themselves being brave enough to confront, somehow, that man who probably had Uncle Dan's black case, and thus also whatever Uncle Dan's "treasure" actually was.

"And whatever do we do with *these*?" Darleen said, running her hand over those velvet bags with their terrifying, perilous antiquities inside. "We can't take them to the police, Vee, because the police will misunderstand. They'll think these antiquities in a satchel we thought was Uncle Dan's are all the proof they need that Uncle Dan stole them. When he *didn't*."

It was a conundrum. That is to say, a puzzle.

"I suppose all we can do for the moment is try to keep them very safe," Victorine said. "I wish we could just hand them over to the museum without explaining anything to anyone. Anonymously, you know. But New York and San Francisco are both thousands of miles away by now, so that's no good."

"Or if we could prove somehow that this case *isn't* Uncle Dan's," said Darleen. "That would help, wouldn't it?"

They took another close look at that disappointingly generic black satchel. There were no initials stamped into the leather anywhere, nor was there any label. But then Darleen said, "Hey!" (Quietly.)

Because she had found an almost invisible pocket on the inside of the case, and in that pocket was a slip of paper with a Los Angeles address on it and a name: "Miss Withering."

"Stranger and stranger," said Victorine. "Who is this person with this peculiar name, and what does she have to do with antiquities? Well! Now we really need to go to sleep, Darleen. Tomorrow we arrive in Los Angeles!"

When they were tucked into their berths in their curtained-off section of that train carriage, and the lights were dimmed, and the rocking motion of the train was beginning to work its magic, and the black leather case filled with Dreadful Antiquities was tucked under Darleen's side so that it would stay perfectly, perfectly safe, Darleen spoke drowsily into the darkness.

"Vee, I just realized we still don't know what the treasure is. Uncle Dan's treasure."

"We know someone who might know, though," said Victorine.

"We do?" said Darleen. "You mean Papa?"

"Oh, your Papa knows, for sure, but he's completely far away. I mean someone in Los Angeles, Darleen."

"Who?"

"Miss Lois Weber, that's who," said Victorine. "With whom Uncle Dan has that appointment. When he wrote to her, he must have told her *something* that caught her interest. She may know what that 'treasure' of his was supposed to be. Maybe she can help us help him, if he hasn't been good about explaining himself to the authorities back in Ogden. Now let's go to sleep, though, Darleen. Good night, good night."

## Chapter 15

# Being Brave in the Dark

*Work out your plot with such delicacy of feeling
that it can only be likened to the music that comes
from a carefully tuned musical instrument.*
—How to Write for the "Movies"

Vee!" said Darleen, scrambling down from the upper berth the next morning. (Darleen always took the upper berth, because climbing, even the tiny amount of climbing necessary to get into an upper berth on a train, made her heart glad.) "I was thinking all night, and I woke up knowing what we have to do: we have to be brave!"

That made Victorine laugh, which brightened this brand-new day something considerable.

"That's certainly true," she said. "Courage will be a help today. Courage is always a help, I'm pretty sure."

Darleen huffed in impatience.

"I didn't mean being brave in a general sort of way:

I mean we have to be *very brave*, right *now*, and go see if we can find the man who has Uncle Dan's case, since we know he said he was taking this train—and then see if we can get it back from him."

Victorine remembered that man's angry, ruddy face, and her heart did quail a little.

"All right, Darleen," she said with a sigh. "We should try that, yes. But breakfast first. It's hard to be very brave before breakfast."

Here's what they did, trying to think ahead to all the morning's possible twists and turns. (Like reading ahead in an opera score, thought Victorine, inspired by Miss Parsons's helpful and musical thoughts on plotting. Only the problem here, of course, was that there *was* no score to read. They were going to have to be brave in the dark, which is true of all the bravest bravery—and true also, for that matter, of life.

They were going to have to improvise.)

First, they took the Dreadful Antiquities in their little velvet sacks and stowed them securely in three of Victorine's secret pockets. You couldn't risk handing goods that might likely have been burgled right back to the probable burglar, could you? So Victorine was determined to keep those Dreadful Antiquities out of sight and out of trouble.

Then they wrapped up the little black satchel itself, now empty, in a lacy shawl, so that they could take it along to breakfast without it advertising its own existence all over the place, should they run into that man from New York before they were ready to confront him.

Finally, they were careful to disguise themselves as people who were perhaps slightly older than you might think at first glance, because in the dining car they really needed not to look the least bit like abandoned children. They wore their longer skirts, for instance, and were a little more attentive to their hair. And quite a bit (they had learned from acting in the photoplays) could be achieved by modifying the way you stood and walked.

*"Mustn't act motherless!"* they reminded each other before setting out for the dining car, and of course they pressed each other's hands quite tenderly when they said it because, in sad fact, they *were* both motherless girls. That couldn't be denied. But they had learned to make their way forward in life nevertheless, hadn't they? Surely their mothers and grandmothers, if they could but see how their much-loved offspring had grown in resourcefulness and courage, would smile and approve and be glad.

To their secret relief, they did not run into the man in current possession of what they were now quite positive must be Uncle Dan's case as they made their way from their Pullman to the dining car. He must be in one of the other carriages. He was a challenge best faced after breakfast, anyway.

And—happy coincidence—the dining car was filled with the friendly faces of the contest-winning girls, who cheerfully found room for Dar and Victorine at one of their several four-person tables.

"We're two girls short, you know!" said one of them. "Families wouldn't let them go, in the end. So sad: Can you imagine? No California! No moving picture studios! Golly!"

Victorine sat down carefully so that the Babylonian cylinder seals in her deep and secret pockets would not clatter against the chairs.

The contest-winning girls might not even have noticed the telltale clattering of antiquities, however, because they were utterly bubbling over with the thrill of Hollywood approaching. They were staying in a very respectable rooming house, right in the center of Hollywood! Then tomorrow they would be heading off to Universal City! Had anyone ever been on such a lark in their lives?

Then the older girls looked again at Victorine and Dar and started asking the obvious questions, beginning with:

"Isn't your mother coming to breakfast?"

"Oh, dear, no," said Darleen. "I'm afraid we don't have any mother with us at all. We were traveling to Los Angeles with our uncle, but then he got—bad news. And had to step off the train."

Victorine winced a little, inwardly, at the way the

truth was being asked to tactfully bend itself around various hurdles and obstacles. Fortunately for the credibility of Darleen's truth-stretching explanation, none of the contest-winning girls seemed to have been close enough to the excitement in the Ogden station to notice that the "thief" arrested there had had any connection to their current breakfast companions.

"He will surely catch up with us tomorrow, though," she said, which she very much hoped was the simple truth.

"But where will you two go tonight?" said the girls, with real concern. They really were nice sorts.

"Oh, we're calling a friend of our aunt's from the station!" said Darleen.

"Well, then, that seems all right, doesn't it?" said the girl sitting across from Dar, whose name was Sally, and whose face was all long, soulful lashes and deep brown eyes. "Be a dear and pass the toast this way, won't you?"

After breakfast, though, they had to go on the hunt for the rude man. They really did have to: if they didn't do it then—if they didn't do their best to retrieve Uncle Dan's lost treasure—what kind of nieces (or almost-nieces) could they claim to be?

So now they paused in the women's restroom to make themselves just slightly younger (by braiding their hair) and then walked through the carriages, careful not to lose their balance when the train rattled extra hard, or to drop their own little black satchel, wrapped up inconspicuously (they hoped) in that lacy shawl.

The first two cars they went through were filled with people who were not the man they were looking for, and secretly they began to hope they wouldn't find him at all. But in the third car, there he was—and there was that familiar black leather satchel, right at his side! It was time for them to take deep breaths and leap.

Darleen, naturally, did the leaping.

"Excuse me, sir," she said.

"What? What?" he said, jumping a little in his seat and flushing red almost at once. He seemed still to be as nervous and jumpy a person as he had been days earlier, when he had pushed his way past Victorine onto the train in New York. "Who are you? What do you want?"

"We were wondering, sir, whether perhaps you might have acquired our uncle's carrying case, by accident, back in Ogden. The one you have next to you there. It does look just exactly like our uncle's case. Is it possible that—"

"Who *are* you?" asked the man, and the girls could tell he would have shouted those words if he hadn't at the same time been clearly wary of attracting attention. "Harassing a passenger, are you? There are laws against that."

"Oh, goodness, sir," said Victorine. "We certainly don't mean to be harassing anybody. We just thought, if there was a *mistake*, you know. Do you think there can have been a mistake of some kind? Perhaps the case is not the one you thought it was? Have you looked inside? Could there possibly be some kind of—mechanism you didn't expect in there? Because perhaps it wasn't your satchel at all?"

"Oho!" said the man, and Victorine could see (as they say in books) the light dawning in his eyes, only in this particular case, the light was full of angry and unpleasant sparks, like the approaching menace of a forest fire.

Then the man with the angrily sparking eyes actually grabbed at Victorine's sleeve, which she found very unpleasant indeed. "Are you two saying . . . ? Do you have that bag of mine? *Do you have my things?*"

"What do you mean?" said Victorine, shrugging his hand away from her arm. She was amazed by her own ability to speak without her teeth chattering or sweat popping out on her brow, because it really was looking more and more as if what this man was calling "his things" might be tucked away in her own pockets, far too close to the unpleasant man's grabbing hand.

"I think you know what I mean," he said, in a low whisper. "I am missing some very valuable—*very* valuable—objects, and it's beginning to look like *you* may know where they are. My case—do you know where it is?"

"Do you mean this?" said Victorine.

And she pulled the lacy shawl away from the little black leather satchel in her arm—the identical twin of the satchel resting beside the unpleasant man.

He gasped in surprise. For a moment, he could say nothing at all.

"Oh, wonderful—do let's trade!" said Darleen brightly, and she actually reached over and nabbed Uncle Dan's satchel, while simultaneously plucking the other case from Victorine's arms and thrusting it at the confused and ruddy man. "Thank you *so much!* Come on, now, Vee—let's go—"

The girls skedaddled. They had about five seconds to get out of that carriage, Victorine figured, before the man opened the latch of *his* bag—

"Hey!" they heard behind them (but they did not stop). That was him seeing the case was empty.

And then there was the strangest noise, a loud human gurgle that instantly swallowed itself up.

*Ha,* thought Victorine as they pushed through the doors to move into the next carriage. That sound— that swallowed gurgle—could mean only one thing, she was quite thoroughly sure.

"He's GUILTY! That man *knows* those things are stolen!" she said to Dar between the carriages, where the rushing noises from the outside were louder than whatever a girl might say. "That's the proof! He's not shouting! He can't very well be saying, 'Those girls have stolen my stolen antiquities,' now, can he?"

"Goodness, Vee!" said Darleen, and her smile was broader than anything she had managed since the dreadfulness in the Ogden station. "I don't think I've ever seen you quite so satisfied about anything. You're practically smug!"

"If I'm smug, I do hope it's because we got your uncle's satchel back, and not because I'm beginning to relish our new life of crime," said Victorine. It was thrilling, to have just been so practically fearless, so very, very bold!

"You know what?" said Darleen, skipping a little from one foot to the next as she reached for the next carriage's door. "Even if it's a little *tiny* bit you *relishing*, I think that's just fine. Robin Hood lived a life of crime, too, right? But not in a wicked way, I don't think. But let's get ourselves out of sight now, right? Next stop, Los Angeles!"

# Chapter 16

# How to Step into a New World

*Brevity, a few years past, was considered*
*the foundation of the scenario. Today the photoplaywright*
*is given a license to put in detail and business.*
—How to Write for the "Movies"

The "next stop" actually turned out to be a one-minute pause in the dining car so that Victorine could spend some pennies acquiring yesterday's *Los Angeles Times*. The expense was justified, she felt, because of the pressing need for research on several fronts.

Their berths had been tucked neatly away again, they saw when they arrived back in their own carriage. The girls took their seats and huddled together, Uncle Dan's case in their hands. The good news was that the people seated nearest to them were taking naps, and there was no sign of that awful man from the other car. The coast was, for the moment, clear.

They took the first five minutes to change their

disguises slightly: undoing the braids and switching to their slightly more mature-looking hats.

"Well?" said Victorine then.

Since Darleen was Uncle Dan's actual kin, it seemed right to let her decide what the next step was going to be.

"Here we go," she said quietly. "We're going to see what's in here, Vee."

They were, after all, about as curious as two girls could be!

So they opened the satchel and looked inside.

"Oh!" said Darleen, a bit disappointed. There was no machine or mechanism in there, after all, but instead merely that book from the Pullman porter, wrapped up in brown paper, a single small reel of film in its circular metal canister, and an eyeglasses case—"Oh, poor Uncle Dan! His glasses, must be!"

Victorine could read the rest of Dar's thought as clear as clear: *Is Uncle Dan moldering away in an Ogden jail cell without even reading glasses to help him pass the hours away?*

Remembering the other small black leather case—now in the hands of (shudder) that unpleasant man who had taken Uncle Dan's case, lied about taking it, and probably knew altogether too much about how Babylonian cylinder seals had gotten onto this train—Victorine ran her hands carefully over the interior of the bag, and yes! There was a small pocket sewn into the lining of this bag as well, and some sheets of paper there.

"Addresses and telephone numbers," said Victorine. "Those are always useful things to have. Here's an address for Miss Weber—for the appointment, goodness, *tomorrow!*"

"And there's a telephone number and address for Mrs. Gish, with a little note for her, too—I remember Aunt Shirley writing that out," said Darleen. "She gave a copy to you, too, didn't she, Vee?"

"Oh, yes. Our Helpful Contact in case of emergency," said Victorine. "Which this is, I suppose. She's a friend of your aunt's, I guess, this Mrs. Gish?"

Darleen laughed. "I should suppose she is! We were all bouncing around the New York theaters and studios around the same time, before the Gishes moved west a couple of years ago. But don't you recognize the name? Gish! Gish! Mrs. Gish is the mother of *Dorothy* and *Lillian*, of course! Whatever has happened to your supposedly clever mind?"

"Oh!" said Victorine, properly impressed. Lillian Gish was, after all, one of the most famous film actresses in the world, and Dorothy was her younger sister, also very famous. "Whoever could have thought that Mrs. Gish would actually be the mother of THOSE Gishes! Well, we'll try to telephone her from the station, then. That is to say, you'll do the speaking, Darleen. Since you've actually met her."

"What worries *me*," said Darleen, "is that strange man we got this satchel back from. What if he comes after us again?"

"We will keep ourselves well out of his sight," said Victorine. "As best we can, anyway."

"I'm not sure how we can do that, since we do have to get off the train," said Darleen. "And then we'll be on the platform, and I suppose he'll be able to find us pretty easily then."

"We will just have to be like the gazelles," said Victorine.

"Running very fast? With pretty horns?" said Darleen, who had only a vague idea of what a gazelle was like.

"No," said Victorine. "I mean: we will be excellent herd animals, so the hungry cheetah won't get us."

By the time the train pulled into the new Southern Pacific Depot in Los Angeles, Dar and Victorine were quite ready to implement their gazelle plan. The herd on this occasion was, naturally, the group of contest-winning girls. Darleen and Victorine stepped off the train and joined that happy, chattering group right away.

And it was good they had thought up this plan because they spotted the unpleasant man about three seconds later: he came off the train like someone in a very bad mood and was clearly looking for something— or somebody. The somebodies in question kept their heads down and stayed hidden in the crowd of contest-winning girls.

"The principles of Charles Darwin at work!" said Victorine to Dar as they moved with all the laughing girls along the platform—and then, when Darleen grinned and shrugged (which was her usual response when Victorine made references to things that Darleen, in her rather hit-or-miss education as a child raised in the movies, had never heard of), Victorine hurried to add: "Avoiding predators, you know, in this case by blending into the group and not sticking out."

It seemed to be working. The unpleasant man was left behind.

"Do you think it's this hot where real gazelles live?" said Darleen.

"Hotter," said Victorine, but really, it was remarkably warm here in Southern California in early September. The heat was lovely, though: it didn't leave you feeling soggy, like summer weather in Fort Lee, New Jersey. The air in Los Angeles was dry and comfortable and even a bit herbal around the edges. It felt like the air of a place where anything was possible.

"I guess we're off to make our telephone call," said Victorine to the contest-winning girls. "Have a lovely time in Hollywood!"

"We'll wait around until we're sure you're settled, won't we, girls?" said the kindhearted Sally, and the others clamored kindly that yes, of course, they would wait.

A railroad man pointed Victorine and Dar in the direction of the telephone pay station, a convenient cabinet with a telephone in it that could actually take coins! Victorine—more experienced with telephones than Darleen—had a little conversation with the operator, was told the price to call Mrs. Gish's number, and then carefully pushed the coins into their marked slots in the telephone device. Then she handed the telephone to Darleen, who at least had met Mrs. Gish before.

They stood there, waiting. And excited!

And then Darleen made a frowning face, said "Thank you—let me ask my friend," and turned to Victorine.

"Vee, the operator says nobody is picking up. What do we do?"

"Try again?"

But when they tried again, the call still did not go through.

"Oh, dear," said Victorine.

Darleen thanked the operator, who was able (thanks to the marvelous machine!) to make the telephone release the coins Victorine had fed it, and feeling rather glum and puzzled, the girls gathered their things and walked, somewhat in a daze, toward the front of the station.

Victorine knew about the ways of train stations from her years of travel with her grandmother, so she had already arranged for the girls' trunk to be brought from the baggage car to the place where the taxis were waiting to take people wherever they might want to go.

But where could they go from there?

To their surprise, however, there was a small crowd of young women waiting for them by the taxicabs out front. Those friendly contest-winning girls had been true to their word.

"All settled with your aunt's friend?" asked Sally.

"Oh, dear, no," said Darleen. "She didn't answer the telephone."

"You poor things!" said several of the girls.

And another added, "What will you do, then? Can you just go to her house?"

"But we can't be sure she's at home at all, just now," said Victorine. "If we go to her house, and no one is there, we're worse off than we are here, aren't we? At least there are taxicabs here, and telephones, and benches to sit on. What if they've left on vacation?"

"Oh, surely not!" said the older girls, and they started sending one another worry-filled glances. "Not if they knew you were coming!"

"But she may not have been expecting us just exactly today," said Darleen sadly. "We thought we were going to be finding rooms, you know, to stay in with our uncle."

"Well, now, don't you be too discouraged," said Sally. "There are the girls who didn't show up for the tour, remember, right at the last minute. The ones whose families changed their minds, you know—so sad. There has to be a room reserved for them, don't you think, that might be going unused? We'll just have to ask Mrs. Hanford."

Mrs. Hanford, the official chaperone of those cheerful gazelles, came over and shook hands with Darleen and Victorine, sized them up with slightly narrowed eyes, gauging whether they were "refined" sorts of girls, and then miraculously took pity and approved the plan after all.

Whew! Victorine realized suddenly that she had been holding her breath for hours, if not days. A place to stay that night in Hollywood, which meant also: not too far from Miss Weber's house, where they were supposed to go tomorrow! That was definitely a huge relief.

"Over here!" called one of the contest-winning girls, and she and Victorine and Darleen and five other girls squeezed into a taxi together: it was gazelles all over again, but now on wheels. The other five girls and Mrs. Hanford piled into the other taxi car, and off they went.

The pleasant warm air came rolling through the car, and all the girls in the taxi were leaning forward, soaking up all the details of this new world. This was not a vertical, towering city like New York, but a place where the streets were lined with little houses, like a simply enormous small town. And it was a town still very much in the middle of springing into being: the taxi car kept rolling by house after house that was still only a wooden frame and a pile of new boards.

"If the whole family is still going to come out to California to live, it will be up to us to find a house they all can live in when they get here," said Darleen, and Victorine smiled.

"But first, a room for us, while we wait for Uncle Dan to catch up with us," she said.

"You don't think he'll be here by tomorrow, do you, Vee?"

Victorine squeezed her hand. "I hope he will. Look at the hills! They're so close already."

"And they don't look like hills in New Jersey at all!" said Darleen.

That made the older girls laugh, but in a friendly way.

"They also don't look the hills in Michigan," said one of the girls.

"Or Wisconsin!" said another girl.

"Or the hills around Bangor, Maine," said a third girl. "For one thing, they're drier, aren't they?"

"Like the scenery in one of those films about the Wild West, I suppose."

"Universal City must be over there somewhere," said the tallest of the contest-winning girls, pointing toward a second row of hills ahead. "It's a whole city, you know! A city full of movie magic, how about that?"

It was all very friendly and pleasant in that taxi car, and when they got to the boardinghouse where they would spend that night, Victorine promptly brought out enough money to cover their stay that night, as well as the simple supper provided around the long table in the big main dining room downstairs.

"We'll be going off to that Universal City tomorrow!" the contest-winners said, while happily wolfing down chops and mashed potatoes. "Tomorrow and the day after! So exciting! Have you ever seen a moving picture being made, kiddies?"

"Yes," said Victorine.

And Darleen echoed her brightly: "Oh, well, yes, I guess we have!"

"We live in Fort Lee, New Jersey, you know," said Victorine. "There are a lot of photoplay studios there."

"Not as many as here!" sang out the older girls.

"I'm sure that's true by now," said Victorine. "And from what I have heard, the new studios here are sometimes simply enormous."

"For example: *Universal City!*" agreed one of the older girls. "Why don't you two young things come along with us? We're taking the trolley out there! It won't be too expensive, I shouldn't think. And they're feeding us all luncheon."

"Sally!" said Mrs. Hanford, setting down her fork.

"Let's not get ahead of ourselves, please. Your visit to Universal City is *expressly* limited to contest winners and chaperones."

"You are all so kind to us," said Victorine. "We appreciate it very, very much. But in any case tomorrow we have an appointment we can't miss, isn't that so, Darleen?"

"That's true," said Darleen.

"'Darleen,'" said another one of the girls thoughtfully. "Come to think of it, that's sort of an unusual name, isn't it? Where have I heard it before?"

Darleen and Victorine exchanged glances.

"I suppose it might be a little unusual," said Darleen. "I'm used to it, though."

"Now 'Bella Mae' is more of a Betsy-Sally-Mary sort of name, seems to me," said the girl. "You might have to change that name, Bella Mae, if you get yourself a role in the movies!"

"Oh," said Victorine, suddenly a bit tongue-tied. Fortunately the other girls were too busy laughing to notice she had gotten stuck, and then Darleen came to the rescue with a pretend yawn, and the two girls got themselves safely extracted from the dinner table and up to their neat little room, a pleasant haven for tonight—even if unaffordable over the long haul.

"How much money do we have left, Vee?" said Darleen as they got ready for bed.

"Sixteen dollars and thirty cents," said Victorine.

That was a large amount for everyday life in Fort Lee, New Jersey, but very little for two girls trying to find their way in a place they didn't know at all. "We'll need to be careful with it, I'm afraid."

She had been studying the prices of rooms and houses in the newspaper, and she didn't think sixteen dollars would cover the costs of life in Los Angeles for very long at all.

"We'll have to stretch it pretty carefully," she said.

"With any luck, Uncle Dan will catch up with us tomorrow," said Darleen. "That will help! But of course if we want to make a life out here in the West, we will have to get ourselves some paying jobs."

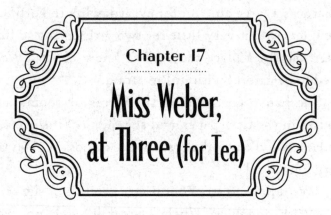

## Chapter 17

# Miss Weber, at Three (for Tea)

*Don't under any circumstance
use a real name or a correct address.*
—How to Write for the "Movies"

The nice thing about having the trunk with them again was that the next day they could change out of their traveling clothes into something a little fresher for their meeting with Miss Weber. They couldn't do a real washing, of course, but they did sneak down to the laundry sink near the kitchen after breakfast to repair the damage done by the train as best they could. Then they hung those dresses up to dry. (The air was so toasty warm here in Hollywood that it seemed likely the dresses might be wearable again by the time they had to pack them back into the trunk for the next move.)

"Ready?" said Victorine. She had studied a map and

the address and discovered that Miss Weber's bunga-low, which was on a street with the sweet-sounding name of Sierra Bonita, was within walking distance of the boardinghouse—fortunate news if you were girls who had counted their money and now were trying not to let more pennies melt away than strictly necessary.

Darleen nodded. She had Uncle Dan's satchel firmly in hand. They had their clean clothes on (longer skirts, since they still were worried about looking too *motherless*), and they were wearing summer hats too. People didn't dress as formally out here in California as they did in New York City, but the sun was strong overhead, and they wanted to look neat enough that Aunt Shirley, if she were suddenly to bound across the country to see how Darleen and Victorine were doing, would approve.

A half an hour later, they were standing in front of the door—solid wood, decorated with eight square panes of glass—of a very pretty house with vines climbing up a trellis that framed the front entrance.

"It's not as grand as I was expecting," said Darleen. "Not a palace, many stories high."

"Not that at all," agreed Victorine. "But it looks like an awfully pleasant place to live, doesn't it? Well, here we go—"

It was Darleen who bravely rang the doorbell. (They could faintly hear the chime of it inside.)

A woman opened the door.

"Yes?" she said, and then took another look. "Goodness! Two girls, just like that horrid man predicted! How odd!"

"Miss Weber?" said Darleen doubtfully, while Victorine tried to understand what the woman had just said.

"A man *predicted* us?" she said, half to herself.

The woman laughed.

"Yes, miss," she said, and then, turning to Darleen, added, "And also, my dear, no. That is to say, a man paid us a visit earlier, looking for two girls he insisted would be coming here, but no, I am not Miss Weber. I am Mrs. Hatch, and I keep house here. And who might you be? I understood Miss Weber was to have some scientific fellow join her for tea today—not a pair of little girls."

*Little girls!* And here they had their longer skirts on and everything! Both of them tried to straighten up an extra half inch, and Darleen said, "Oh, Mrs. Hatch, that would be our uncle you're speaking of: Mr. Daniel Darling. But he has been detained and couldn't come, and so he sent us instead."

"Oh, really?" said the woman. "What a perfect muddle! I suppose you'd better come in, girls, and we'll try to make some sense of all of this."

They filed into the house, which was a lovely warm gray on the inside, a perfect place to retreat from the sun and heat outdoors. The floors were polished wood.

Everything was tidy—neat as the proverbial pin. And a pleasant-looking woman with dark curling hair tied neatly up on her head and the most expressive eyebrows was coming toward them now, using her eyebrows to say to the woman who had opened the door, *Are these really people who need to be inside this house right now?*

"Who have we here?" she said out loud. You could see that she was a very busy woman, and used to having things run smoothly under her direction.

Victorine and Darleen curtsied a little, which was probably the least Californian thing they could possibly have done.

The woman's lips twitched a bit, in the direction of a smile.

"Miss Weber?" said Victorine, "We are—of necessity—representing Mr. Dan Darling. This is Darleen Darling, his niece. And I am 'Bella Mae Goodwin.'"

(She always added the quotation marks in her mind because that made the statement more completely truthful.)

"*Are* you?" said Miss Weber. "This *is* a surprise. Fancy two girls showing up here, after all, when until this morning we had been expecting at most one man! And here you show up only hours after that other nasty fellow surprised us by knocking on the door. Not a scientific type, certainly! Full of threats and nastiness, and I'm afraid he was looking for you—at least,

I suppose it must have been you he was looking for. Two girls, he said. And we sent him packing, but here you are. I trust *that* person wasn't your Uncle Dan."

"Oh, *no!*" said Darleen in horror. "Oh, Miss Weber! Uncle Dan wouldn't ever threaten a soul!"

"He most certainly wouldn't," added Victorine, and all the while her brain was jumping up and down and waving its hands at her. (That was the image that came to her in this moment of stress, even though of course she knew perfectly well that *brains* don't technically have *hands*. Nor were they likely to do much jumping, come to that.)

But really: someone was looking for them! That had to mean the rude man from the train, right? And that wasn't good news, not at all.

"All highly peculiar, I'd say," said the housekeeper. "Shall I set another place for tea?"

"Yes, Mrs. Hatch," said Miss Weber. "Certainly. Please do. These young people don't look too frightening, after all, despite what that fellow earlier gave us to understand. Come sit down over here, girls, and we will figure this all out."

A pleasant little table had just acquired another plate, fork, and teacup, and there was a homey little loaf cake there, waiting to be served out.

"It's persimmon," said Miss Weber, nodding at the cake. "Do you know about persimmons?"

"Yes, ma'am," said Victorine, at the same instant

as Darleen said, "No. Is that a fruit? I thought pos-
sums were furry little things. Oh, now I'm all rattled!
Please, Miss Weber, do tell us more: Was there really
a man looking for us?"

"Yes, I'm afraid there was," said the woman,
and she gave them each a slice. "An unpleasant one,
but Mrs. Hatch and I sent him away. And persimmon—not possum, my dear—is a fruit, but a rather
mild-mannered one, so I prefer it in a cake, with plenty
of sugar, you know, to bring out the flavor. Tea?"

She poured out tea and handed around a small but
elegant creamer.

"Now, about that unpleasant man," said Miss
Weber. "It was rather early this morning, wasn't it,
Mrs. Hatch? And he came pounding on this door and
startled good Mrs. Hatch with questions like 'Where
are the girls?' When of course we knew nothing about
any girls."

"Had a nasty way of asking it, too, if I may inter-
ject," said Mrs. Hatch from where she was fetching a
couple little pots of jam. "I said, 'What girls, sir?' And
he said, 'Two girls that have something of mine I want
back. If this Lois Weber person is hiding them, I'll do
everything horrible.' (He didn't say exactly that, you
know—he listed some of the specific horrible things in
all their horrible particulars.) And so I took alarm, as
you'll understand, and I said right away, 'This, sir, is
the residence of Mr. and Mrs. Smalley. There are no

girls here. And I'll beg you to remove yourself from the premises before I call the police.' And then, finally, off he went, but all the while saying very upsetting things, I will not deny it."

"By the way, girls, I am truly Mrs. Smalley," said Miss Weber. "Even if I use 'Lois Weber' for my professional work."

"Oh, we know!" exhaled Victorine and Darleen together in perfect unison, since they were close readers of Aunt Shirley's movie magazines.

Miss Weber's eyes crinkled at them.

"And that man was a thief!" said Darleen with some fervor. "IS a thief, I mean! He's a *thief*!"

"A thief?" said Miss Weber. "You'd better explain."

So they did explain, as best they could, pausing only for sips of tea, and leaving out only the minor footnote that the stolen goods themselves—the mysterious Babylonian cylinder seals—were indeed in this very room at this very minute, tucked into Victorine's very practical hidden pockets. The main thing was that that man had mixed up Uncle Dan's black case with his own—or rather, with the one that other man had brought from San Francisco and handed off to him—and then Uncle Dan had been unfairly and inaccurately accused of being a thief and was now in custody in Ogden, Utah. Which was why it was the two of them who had had to come to Miss Weber today, and not the inventor himself, Mr. Daniel Darling.

There was a brief, contemplative pause at the end of their account.

Miss Weber took a bite of cake, and then said, "Well! Now that's quite a story. Seems to me we need to find some way to keep you girls safe, in a world harboring so many thieves and ruffians—and yes, of course, we must help your poor uncle too. But I warn you, I don't have much extra time today because I'm hosting *quite* a fancy party for Miss Anna Pavlova at the Alexandria Hotel tonight—"

"Anna Pavlova!" said Victorine. She could not help it—*Anna Pavlova.* "Oh, my!"

"Who is she?" asked Darleen.

"A wonderful Russian ballerina," said Victorine, feeling very peculiar all of a sudden. "Oh! I saw her with my grandmother once—a real gala, Darleen, at the Metropolitan Opera House—all the fanciest people in New York—with dancing and the daintiest food in the lobby after—I think it was the czar's birthday that day—girls dressed up as Russian peasants with hothouse flowers for the guests—so elegant—I practiced my fanciest curtsy all day so that when I met her—oh, never mind!"

She stopped short, not only because both Darleen and Miss Weber were now staring at her with identical expressions of surprise, but also because the name of Anna Pavlova was tied up with many feelings for Victorine: that evening in 1913 had been the last lovely outing with her beloved grandmother. Then there had been sickness, sadness, all the trouble in the world. And now that whole elegant chapter of her early life was a part of the book that must not be opened in public, wasn't it?

"Never mind, never mind," said Victorine again, more faintly this time. "You were saying—"

Miss Weber gave a forthright, businesslike nod.

"Yes, well, indeed: Miss Pavlova," she said. "She has just finished shooting a wonderful film with me at Universal, and so I thought I had better give her a bit of a banquet to celebrate. I still have my toast to write for tonight, you know, and I won't be easy in my skin if I'm not there well ahead of time, making sure everything is organized just exactly right. So that is all to say, I don't have much time. But don't look so disheartened, goodness!"

And a smiling Miss Weber actually clapped her hands together quickly twice, as a signal that it was time to buck up and be encouraged.

"I did have a few minutes scheduled in my calendar for a conversation with Mr. Darling. And you two are here as representatives of your uncle, yes? So let's talk—but efficiently, girls! Is this the black satchel in question? Your uncle's, I mean? He did write to me about his invention, so now I'm quite curious now to see it."

"Oh, yes!" said Darleen. "He would say that's the

most important thing of all, I'm sure. He did keep calling it his treasure, you know—I think that's partly what made people so suspicious and got him into trouble. But then we looked, and we didn't see anything that looked so special at all. See, Miss Weber? What is this?"

Darleen had opened the satchel and was already pulling out the round metal tin.

"Well, now, that looks like a reel of film, my dear," said Miss Weber with a laugh. "I would think you would know all about film reels, having been raised up in a studio, as I believe you have been."

"But what's special about it? He thought it was special. He thought it might bring in a lot of money, even," said Darleen. "And he thought of you, Miss Weber, as someone interested in all sorts of technical experiments—he said there was a place in one of your photoplays where you managed to have three parts of the story showing at once, 'just like a chord on the piano,' he said. I don't remember the movie's name, though— the one about a poor mother at home alone with her baby, and the bad man comes looking for them—"

"*Suspense,*" said Victorine and Miss Weber at the very same moment. Even though Victorine had not been raised in a movie studio, she had had an adventurous grandmother who liked the modern art of the motion picture as much as the older arts of ballet, opera, and chamber music.

Miss Weber was already opening the little canister,

and now she carefully drew out a few frames' worth of that roll to hold up to the light.

"Ah, yes, look what's here," she said. "I think I know what this must be. He wrote to me about some of his experiments, you know. I think there must have been something else in the case? Eyeglasses, perhaps?"

The girls were amazed.

"Eyeglasses? Well, yes," said Darleen, reaching back into the satchel. "But we thought they must be his reading glasses."

"Reading glasses?" said Miss Weber as she opened the case. "No, I don't think so."

There were, it turned out, several pairs of spectacles in that case, not just one. And they were very odd. Miss Weber held them up to the light, so that the girls could see.

One lens was green, and the other was red.

"Aha! Shall we take a look at this bit of film, girls?" she said, already standing up, with the film in her hand. "I have a projector set up in the back room, you know. For situations like this one, when a projector is just what's needed."

She had the film laced through the projector in a matter of seconds—which, to be fair, was only a few seconds less than it probably would have taken Darleen. Even Victorine could now handle a projector quite well.

"Turn off the lights, Miss Goodwin—is that the right name?—if you would be so kind."

The projector clattered into life, saving Victorine from having to answer the question, and a strangely fuzzy picture appeared on the screen—it looked a bit as if someone had been experimenting with color and things had gone terribly wrong. A fuzzy Darleen was twirling around on the fuzzy grass under fuzzy trees near the fuzzy building of Matchless studios.

"Glasses for you and you," said Miss Weber, handing them around. "Quick now, put them on, and I think you'll see—"

Victorine tucked the glasses around her ears and looked back at the screen—and gasped. There was Darleen, but now she was no longer a fuzzy flat image, but a girl with depth and solidity, now reaching right out *toward* the people watching—now blowing a kiss and dancing away.

Darleen giggled next to her.

"Oh, I remember him making this!" she said. "I had no idea—I thought he was just testing film stock, but this—"

"This is a bit like a stereoscope," said Victorine. Stereoscopes allowed you to see photographs in three dimensions. "Isn't it, Miss Weber? A stereoscope, but moving?"

"It's called *anaglyph*, the technique he is using here," said Miss Weber, switching off the projector and going over to the light switch to bring light back into the room.

*Anaglyph!* The girls looked at each other through their red-and-green glasses and felt the light coming on not merely in the room, but in their brains: not hieroglyphs at all, but *ANAglyphs!*

Miss Weber collected the strange spectacles and tucked them carefully back into their carrying case.

"Your uncle is very clever, Miss Darling. And I'm sure, yes, that one day films will be stereoscopic as a matter of course—stereoscopic, three-dimensional, and in all the colors of the rainbow, and even with people talking! I worked on talking pictures with Monsieur and Madame Blaché, you know, some years ago."

"So why aren't moving pictures all those things already?" said Darleen.

"Money, my dear," said Miss Weber. "Think of all the hundreds and hundreds of theaters in this country—think of what it would take to put complicated machines in all of those places so that movies can speak out loud or look as real as anything. How much money would that be? Who would want to take the plunge?"

"Oh, dear," said Victorine. Her heart was sinking.

And it took Darleen only a few seconds longer to arrive at the same depressing point.

"Oh, Miss Weber! I see what you're saying. You're saying that no one is going to pay Uncle Dan thousands for his treasure, after all. Oh, but that's awful, awful news!"

## Chapter 18

# Disappointments, Hopes, and Dangers

*But, if your means will permit, I would most earnestly recommend that you rent a typewriter. Then, later, if you have any success marketing your scenarios, you can easily buy your own machine.* —How to Write for the "Movies"

Good gracious," said Miss Weber. "I've never seen such discouraged faces. Would more cake be helpful?"

"No, thank you, Miss Weber," said Victorine, and then she glanced to her left and became a little worried that Darleen might be about to lose the battle not to cry. "Although it's very delicious cake, of course."

Victorine was trying to be cheerful, but of course it all came out sounding like the most doleful words ever spoken, because her mind was full of worries such as these:

If there was no money to be hoped for from Uncle Dan's treasure, what was the point of any of this? What was the point of their coming all the way to Hollywood?

And Victorine could just tell that Darleen was thinking about her Papa, who needed a house in the sunshine if he was going to get rid, finally, of that awful cough.

They had all been counting on the "treasure" to see them through.

"Let's pull ourselves together a bit, shall we!" said Miss Weber brightly. "I do think the most important question at the moment has to be: What do we do with you girls?"

"Do with *us*?" said Darleen. "Oh, we're all right. It's Uncle Dan I'm worried about. And everyone else in the family. And Papa! We're supposing to be: What do we do with you girls?"

"'Establishing an outpost for the future efforts of the Darlings,'" said Victorine, quoting Aunt Shirley. "I'm afraid, Miss Weber, that everyone has been very much hoping Mr. Darling's invention might save the day."

"By raising money, you know," added Darleen. "To be honest, we're awfully short of money at Matchless."

"Of course you are," said Miss Weber. "Moviemaking is a very expensive and uncertain proposition. But it is my firmly held belief that young women these days—if they have an entrepreneurial spirit, you know, and are willing to work very hard—will find they have all sorts of practical opportunities opening up for them in this world. Let's consider your situation, Miss Darling—"

"But first, oh, please, Uncle Dan!" said Darleen,

which was almost interrupting. "You said there might be a way to help him. Can you help him?"

"Good point," said Miss Weber. "I shall write to the police in Ogden, giving them all the necessary information about the anaglyph experiment he intended to share with me. A telegram today, and an explanatory letter to follow. That should clear any lingering suspicions."

"Oh, thank you so much!" said Darleen. "Thank you! We've been so worried!"

"That won't make you late for your banquet?" said Victorine.

"I don't think so," said Miss Weber. "I still have some time before I have to fly away to that. And luckily for me, I happen to be a very speedy typist."

"Oh!" said Victorine, startling upright once more. "You know, Miss Weber, I've been thinking about typewriters!"

"You have?" said Darleen.

"Miss Parsons, you know, in *How to Write for the 'Movies,'* says that nearly all authors of note are self-taught typists, so I was thinking—perhaps I should learn."

"Excellent idea," said Miss Weber. "Are you in the process of becoming a photoplaywright, Miss—was it 'Goodwin'?"

Victorine winced at the name; the trick, she found, was to focus *very hard* on all the other words in the question.

"I hope so," she said. "Eventually. I am currently working very hard on developing an imagination. There's a contest, you know, for writing an ending for this serial, *The Vanishing of*—"

"Oh, yes, yes, so many contests!" interrupted Miss Weber. "Well, if your imagination shows up and you find you have something to show off, bring it to me, and perhaps I'll take a look. We have a busy troupe of scenario writers at Universal, you know, and could always use more. But you, Miss Darling—"

Darleen looked up. "Oh, please don't suggest typewriters to *me*, Miss Weber!" she said. "Because *I'm* not writing any scenarios. I just need to find a film to act in, I guess. And Bella Mae can act, too—she's had little parts in many of our movies at Matchless this past year."

Funny how these small gifts of loyalty and faith from a friend can make our hearts feel a degree or two warmer, just like that. Victorine brushed her hand against Darleen's arm, which meant *thank you* in the language of good friends and near-sisters.

"I'm sure Miss—*was* it Goodwin?—has done perfectly well," said Miss Weber. "But *you* are Darleen Darling and have been acting in front of movie cameras since you were a wee tyke. And had that whole adventure serial to star in last year—*The Dangers of Darleen*. No, don't look surprised. I saw some of it. I'm of the opinion, you know, that the era of the adventure serial is ending, and just as well, for the most part. All that action, action, action! Absurd villains! Cliffhanger endings every week, just to get the audience back in for the next episode!"

(None of this sounded so terrible at all to Victorine or Darleen. Wasn't that how it was all supposed to work? But Miss Weber's face conveyed distaste, and she dismissed the whole idea of *adventure serials* with a crisp flick of her hand.)

"My point, girls, is that the movies have more important roles to play in our world," she continued. "They can be such powerful forces, photoplays—why, they can affect the way people think about things. They can change minds. So I prefer to make films that teach you something. That make you *think*, like the best newspaper editorials, about the issues of the day. Not just entertain by showing people jumping off bridges and trains. But never mind: I have to admit, Miss Darling, you acted very well in some of those more touching episodes, when you weren't too busy running and jumping. How old are you now?"

"Perhaps just a little older than you think?" said Darleen, after a pause. Victorine was probably the only person in the room who could tell—from a slight straightening of the back and a tiny, tiny amount of ice in the words—how much Darleen must still be smarting from the "jumping off bridges and trains" comment. But Darleen was an actress, through and through, and the script here called for her not to let Miss Weber see even a hint of hurt feelings, *so she did not.*

Miss Weber smiled.

"I see," she said. "All right. Twelve? Thirteen? Definitely not too old to play a child, and that's the main thing. Come out to Universal City tomorrow, and we'll see if we can get some small parts for you girls. A bit of income to tide you over until you're reunited with your uncle. But first—"

And now she became very stern. Anyone who works as a photoplay director can sort of expand in size when necessary, to capture the full attention of whomever they are speaking to.

"Even if you are older than I think you are, you are still far too young to be fending entirely for yourselves," she said. "Where are you staying now?"

They explained about the telephone call to Mrs. Gish that hadn't gone through the day before, and how they had then thrown themselves on the mercy of the contest-winning girls (Miss Weber was delighted— "Very resourceful," she said approvingly) and about the boardinghouse they couldn't quite afford.

"Very nicely done, girls," said Miss Weber. "But we can't have you floating around this way any longer than necessary, can we? Especially not with that unsavory fellow on the prowl. If you have that number for Mrs. Gish with you, I'll put a call through for you right away."

These fancy Californians with telephones in their private houses!

A minute later Miss Weber was chatting in quite a friendly way with someone on the other end of the telephone line—presumably Mrs. Gish herself.

The adults conversed for a minute or two. It was rather amusing to have only one side of a conversation within earshot—Victorine had had more telephones in her childhood than Darleen had had, but even for her it always felt a little odd, to see and hear someone speaking with such natural animation into a tube made of wood and metal. Then Darleen was summoned to the telephone and had to answer what must have been a cavalcade of friendly questions. Her answers seemed to be satisfactory, though; Victorine could see relief spread gradually over Darleen's face, despite all the newfangled strangeness of speaking into a machine and having voices come leaping right out into your ear.

"Thank you so very much, Mrs. Gish!" she was saying in quite a normal voice by the end of the call. "So grateful to you. Thank you!"

She turned around after carefully hanging up the mouthpiece of the telephone and grinned at Miss Weber and at Victorine.

"She'll do it! She'll have us stay with them there for a little while—she said not to worry about a thing, and they'll be expecting us tomorrow evening," said

Darleen. "We can manage one more night at the boardinghouse without any trouble, and we're all set up there, you know."

"How lovely! That certainly eases my mind," said Miss Weber. "And now my banquet does call, girls! No, no, don't worry—before I get into my fancy gown, I'll get that telegram off to Ogden, Utah, about Mr. Darling's importance to the motion picture industry. We can't have your uncle languishing a moment longer than necessary, can we? And you'll come up to Universal City tomorrow—tell them I sent you. Who knows? Perhaps I'll see you there at some point during the day—I'll be looking tired, I suppose. You know how banquets are. In any case, stay well away from mysterious criminals. Good luck and goodbye!"

A moment later they were out on the front walk. Victorine felt just a little bit dazed. They had been in such dire straits, and now suddenly they were more or less rescued! And the sun was very bright.

She did remember to scan the street for any sign of thieves from New York, but there was no trace of anything but sunshine, pretty flowers, and hope. The girls—and the little cylinders tucked into Victorine's pockets—seemed safe enough for now.

Darleen took a couple of dancing steps.

"Universal City, here we come!" she said. "Too bad about Uncle Dan's treasure, but at least Miss Weber will help him get back to us, won't she? And perhaps he'll find somebody else more willing to spend money on his hieroglyphs!"

"*Anaglyphs*," said Victorine.

"Right, those," said Darleen. "Anyway, he's a cameraman and an inventor, and there's simply got to be work for a cameraman out here in California! That's 'establishing an outpost for the future efforts of the Darlings' right there, wouldn't you say?"

"I'm just relieved our sixteen dollars—minus tonight's boarding, of course—will stretch a few more days," said Victorine, but she grinned when she said it, because of course it wasn't just the rescued finances that were making her heart tingle at that moment: it was the many talents of Miss Lois Weber, and the thrill of having spoken some part of her private dreams aloud. Perhaps she really could, with hard work, someday become a photoplaywright. (If only she could figure out how to develop an imagination, of course.) Even the simpler dream of typewriters and learning to use them properly was a fizzy, lovely thought. Oh, in California, dreams really did seem so much closer to hand than they ever had back in New Jersey!

# Chapter 19

# Universal City

*You must cultivate patience . . .*
—How to Write for the "Movies"

W hat are you up to today, kiddies?" said Sally (of the contest-winning girls) at breakfast the next morning.

"Universal City! We've been invited!" said Darleen, and the older girls clapped their hands in approval. They were really a remarkably good-hearted and cheerful bunch. Victorine couldn't help liking them all quite a bit.

"Lovely! Wonderful!" they said. "We're headed back for our second day there! Come along in the bus with us, why don't you? Mrs. Hanford's taking the day off to go visit her cousins."

So Dar and Victorine had lots of friendly company on the ride out to Lankershim, where the new

Universal City was spread across the grassy hills. The contest-winning girls were in the best of moods and even belted out a rousing rendition of "Kitty, the Telephone Girl" (*"Kitty! Kitty! Isn't it a pity in the city you work so hard . . . !"*) while the bus bounced along the road north.

"Our Betty Ann here really *is* a telephone girl!" said Sally to the younger girls, and one of the singers (evidently Betty Ann, all blond curls and dimples) gave them a friendly wave.

"Not today!" said Betty Ann. "Today, I'm busy being an extra in the motion pictures!"

The contest-winning girls cheered.

It wasn't a very long ride. They all got off the bus in front of a very long two-story building, bright white against the tawny hills behind.

"We'll just all go in here and register," said Sally, shepherding Darleen and Victorine into the office at the entrance. "Go ahead now—give your names to the nice lady at the desk there and tell them you want to see the sights."

Darleen and Victorine exchanged slightly embarrassed glances. Some of the other girls had already given their names and been sent with a brisk, no-nonsense wave on through the door that led (presumably) out into the wilds of Universal City.

"Go ahead," said Dar to Victorine.

Fine! Sometimes Victorine did have to be the one

being brave. That was only fair. She took a deep breath and stepped up to the counter, where the woman at work hardly lifted her head to glance at her.

"Excuse me, miss," Victorine said to the secretary. "We were told to tell you Miss Weber was sending us—"

The bored secretary woke up all at once, raised her eyes to look over the counter at Victorine and Dar, and then actually jumped to her feet.

"Oh, yes! You must be the girls! She gave us a ring on the telephone about you. Over this way—"

And she gestured toward a different door, down the hall a bit.

Sally was staring at them in surprise.

"Where are you headed, then, you two?" she said.

When Darleen paused to try to explain ("Miss Weber called about us, you see, and then—"), the bored secretary actually clapped her hands together loud enough to make anyone in that room jump an inch and then added "Don't let's dawdle now!" in a voice that was about three notches bossier than necessary (in Victorine's opinion).

But Sally, good-natured as ever, simply laughed and waved.

"Never mind, girls! You have a nice day, wherever you're off to!"

Dar and Victorine ended up in an office in the back, where their feet dangled a little awkwardly from chairs that seemed to have been designed for tall cowboys.

"Hello, girls!" said the woman there, looking right square at Darleen. "So, you're Darleen Darling, aren't you, dear? I recognize you from the pictures."

"Oh!" said Darleen, and she straightened up a bit. Victorine, of course, was already sitting with quite a straight back, having been taught since toddlerhood the importance of good posture by her Grandmama and a series of dance teachers. She had never been able to relax as fluidly into the steps of a dance as those teachers might have hoped, but at least she had triumphed over her childhood slouch.

"Yes, ma'am, that's right—I'm Darleen Darling," said Darleen. "Miss Weber mentioned us?"

"In between yawns," laughed the woman. "Not because you're dull in any way, I assure you! Because she stayed up late banqueting at the Alexandria, you know, with Miss Anna Pavlova and all."

Victorine sighed, and the woman's head turned very fast to take her in too.

"Excuse me for not knowing," she said. "But are you perhaps Miss Darling's maid, my dear?"

That came so out of the blue! Before Victorine could even figure out what feeling was bubbling up inside of her, Darleen was already saying, with some fire in her voice, "No, ma'am! That's—Miss Bella Mae Goodwin! She is going to be a photoplaywright one day, but at the moment she is still taking small roles in the motion pictures. She's very good at dancing and playing the piano and can ride a horse, too—"

And that was when Victorine found herself doing something quite un-Victorine-like: she *giggled*. Of course she clamped her hand over her mouth right away, but the giggle had moved faster than her hand and was already out.

Dar turned to stare; the woman across the desk was staring too.

"Vee?" said Dar.

Victorine swallowed hard.

"So sorry," she murmured. "Caught by surprise—"

Which was the truth of it. Not that long ago she had been *Victorine Berryman*—practically a princess, living in that old castle of a home in New York City. And now (surprise!) she was no princess at all. Now a person might look right at her and think, *Oh, this must be the maid.*

It wasn't that she was offended—nothing like that. It was more the dizzying sensation of being on a merry-go-round (the carousel of life!) that was spinning very fast. Every now and then, we glance away from our wooden horse (as it were) and realize just how quickly that merry-go-round is now turning. That's enough to make anyone giggle. Or cry. Or giggle and then feel suddenly about to cry—

"Ah, well, then," said the woman, turning back to Darleen, thank goodness, so that Victorine had a chance to settle her mind and her facial expression. "If I may say so, Miss Darling, it's such good luck for all of us you've shown up here this morning. Little Annie McDonald has come down with the chicken pox, just when we were supposed to start filming *The Orphan by the Sea*—but Miss Weber says you should be able to jump in and swim right away."

"Do you mean *actual* swimming?" asked Darleen. Victorine knew what the quaver in her voice was saying: swimming was one of the rare things involving muscles and movement and strength that Darleen Darling was not very good at.

"No!" said the woman, with a laugh. "Metaphorical! Tell me, Miss Darling: you can play a girl of eight or nine, can't you? Stand up and let me take a look."

Darleen stood up—in child mode. The angles of her knees and ankles were slightly askew; her hands suddenly looked smaller and more pleading.

The woman nodded, evidently satisfied.

"Excellent," she said. "Off you trot to wardrobe, then. I'll get a runner to take you and a copy of the scenario, just to give you an idea."

She pressed a button, and a little bell rang somewhere far away.

Darleen hesitated.

"Excuse me," she said. "But what about . . . Bella Mae? What can she be doing? I'm sure she'd be glad to help—she had a lot of experience this year at Matchless."

"Oh, goodness," said the woman. "We can't be experimenting with just anyone, can we? We're a very professional enterprise, here at Universal. I'm sure your friend will find a lot to amuse her. And then she can watch your picture being filmed from the bleachers! Won't that be fun, my dear?"

"Don't worry, I'm sure I'll be perfectly fine," Victorine said as a boy came through the door. He must be the "runner" who would take Darleen off to the important, secret places of Universal City. "I brought my book with me, of course."

She held up How to Write for the "Movies," but nobody else in that room even pretended to look at the book. The boy was looking at the woman (his employer) who had summoned him; the woman was looking at Darleen; Darleen was looking at Victorine, and there was a certain amount of puzzlement and worry in Dar's eyes.

"Really, Dar," said Victorine. "Just larking about all day—I'll be fine!"

And that—she realized as soon as the runner had ushered Darleen out in one direction, and the woman had sent Victorine off to the main entrance again—was perilously close to being a lie.

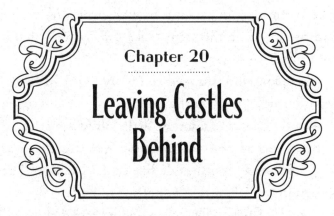

*Never overlook the commonplace things in life in your
efforts to find the unusual plot. It is these same unpretentious
things that unfold for you the possibilities for a story.*
—How to Write for the "Movies"

Victorine was stubborn about a number of things,
but especially and particularly about the truth. So that
meant, in this case, that she was bound and determined to transform what she had said so confidently
to Darleen in that office ("Just larking about all day—
I'll be fine!") from possible falsehood to actual fact.

She might not be someone who was very good at
"larking about," but she could still make the most of
this day, couldn't she? She could still "be fine." She
could!

In a daze that was part sudden sunlight and part
lingering emotion, she stepped out from the office
building into the studio lot, where at first she hardly

noticed the people rushing by her, everyone so busy with the hundred different tasks that go into making motion pictures.

Then someone stopped suddenly, right in front of her, and said, "Are you the maid?"

Again! That was another little jolt of surprise.

But even as she was opening her mouth to say, "No," someone right beside her said, "I believe I am. Do you know where I'm supposed to be?"

—And it turned out the person who had stopped in front of Victorine hadn't been speaking to Victorine at all, but to a young woman next to her. A young woman with posture even better than Victorine's, by the way, and with the loveliest warm brown skin. She had a maid's uniform folded neatly over her arm: that must be the costume she was supposed to wear.

"Right, then," said the studio employee, checking a list on her clipboard. "Ruthie, is it? We're headed this way."

"It's Miss Waller," said the young woman.

"What?" said the employee.

"That's my *name*," said the young woman. "*Miss Waller*. That direction, you said?"

And off they went.

Victorine thought she had perhaps never seen so much dignity radiate off a single ordinary person ever before. A person does have to carry her own dignity around with her everywhere, doesn't she?

(*Miss Waller*—did that name ring a tiny bell? But a pigeon flew in front of Vee's feet and distracted her, and the bell was silenced.)

Victorine dodged the pigeon and took a steadying breath.

She was intending to have a very sober conversation with herself as she walked, but she kept getting distracted, not just by pigeons but also by the ridiculous marvel that was the administration building—the four sides of which were each built in a different style, with German angles dominating one wall, and interesting curves (Egyptian perhaps?) taking over the decor as you turned the corner. Did they really make films with those walls in the background, each part of a different "set"? Or was it just another—aha!—*metaphor*, this time saying something about the way the photoplay business depends on a mix of varied scenery and illusion?

And when she turned her eyes to the hills, she saw a "castle" set up there for some fancy medieval picture (she assumed), and that was charming too. It had been built less than half normal size as a way to make it look bigger and farther away than it actually was—the perfect background for impressive shots of knights-in-armor riding along the foot of the hill.

It was fake, of course, that little castle—it was pretending to be something it wasn't—but Victorine felt only affection for it. She certainly couldn't be too scornful of that make-believe castle for not being real, not when she herself had lived all those years in the sort of pretend castle that exists on Fifth Avenue in New York City.

She remembered the tall ceilings, the winding elegance of the main staircase, the lovely blue walls of her own childhood room, the kind voice of her Grandmama suggesting they play a game of cribbage after Victorine finished practicing her piano . . .

That castle was gone now. Her Grandmama had faded away out of this life, and the building itself had burned down in a fire, along with almost every remnant of her childhood as a girl who wanted for nothing and could simply bask in the sunlight of a grandparent's love.

Victorine shook the sad cobwebs out of her head and started walking back toward the long series of stages where interior scenes were filmed.

She was thinking quite hard about that strange moment back in the Universal office, when Darleen had so evidently been worried that she might have been offended by the secretary mistaking her for a maid—for *Darleen's* maid.

Was it strange—was it awfully peculiar—that she had not been offended?

Surprised, yes! Knocked out of her old names and roles all over again. Reminded that she was no longer the same person she used to be.

But, oddly, what made her feel bad was mostly the thought that *Darleen* might think that she, Victorine, minded.

Could it be—could it be—that she, Victorine—despite being someone who felt strongly that all people should be valued equally, no matter what kind of work they might do—somehow gave off the impression that she felt she still belonged in a *castle*? Or should be treated like a *princess*?

Ugh!

"Not a princess!" she said out loud, and then jumped back to avoid a line of horses pounding by, with men dressed as cowboys on their backs. They were heading toward a camera set up far over there to the left.

Victorine smiled. They knew what they were doing on horseback, those "cowboys." Back in Fort Lee, New Jersey, Victorine had seen plenty of people riding for the camera who plainly didn't belong on any horse.

Well. She had her book, *How to Write for the "Movies."* She just needed a quiet place to sit and read it, in order to practice being the new sort of person she hoped to become: not a princess of any kind, but a *photoplaywright*.

She would work to find the stories hidden in commonplace things.

There was a long, shaded stand with benches set up right across from the studio stages for tourists who had come to see the movies being made. That would be the perfect place. She could read her book, and every now and then she could look up from Miss Parsons's excellent advice and watch Darleen at work, and that would be about as close as Victorine could come to "larking about"—that would be Victorine really and truly being fine.

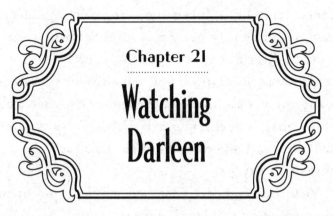

**Chapter 21**

# Watching Darleen

*"Punch" is the motor that makes the painter, the writer, the genius, and gives them their talent. No two people ever agreed upon its meaning, but all must agree that it is the heart interest, the main idea, and the suspense of a story.* —How to Write for the "Movies"

Here was something that struck Victorine very deeply as she wandered around the grounds of Universal City: everything—*everything*—here at Universal was on a simply enormous scale compared to any of the studios back in Fort Lee. Why, there must be at least nine pictures being filmed at once on the long stage there! *Nine* pictures! It boggled the mind.

Victorine climbed the stairs to get up to the benches the Universal people had thoughtfully set up for their guests—there was a nice awning above, protecting spectating tourists from the sun, all very comfortable. She chose a spot on the bench across from the set most likely to be depicting a sea captain's humble home, opened her book, and began reading about the deeper mysteries of being a photoplaywright. There was, for instance, this thing called "punch." Miss Parsons kept saying it was necessary if you wanted your scenario to be any good at all. And yet the author couldn't really define what "punch" might be. Miss Parsons said it was "the heart interest, the main idea, and the suspense of a story."

Victorine sighed. That seemed like too many things for one small word to mean at once.

"What's wrong, honey?" asked a friendly and oddly familiar voice. "Something worrying you? And where's the other one of you?"

Sure enough, it was Sally, who had just arrived in the stands with a whole little bevy of the contest-winning girls.

"Don't mind us. We're just the ones who are done for the day," said that friendly Sally as she slipped onto the bench in the stands right next to Victorine. "I guess we're not meant to be movie stars, after all. Oh, well. Isn't it interesting, though, to watch them all cranking the cameras and shouting for people to get into position? And don't tell me that's a *book*! Are you really sitting in the middle of all of this glorious Universal City hubbub reading a *book*?"

"It's by Miss Louella Parsons," said Victorine, showing them the cover. "It's about learning to write scenarios."

"Oh, well, thank goodness!" said Sally with a laugh. "I was afraid you were reading some weighty French novel or something—at least this book is about the movies!"

"I don't mind telling you I'm writing something of a photoplay scenario right now," said another girl (Marge?). "For the contest, you know."

"I thought you all had already won the contest," said Victorine, and the older girls laughed.

"For *another* contest," said Marge. "The one about thinking up a good ending for *The Vanishing of Victorine*—have you seen that serial, Bella Mae? It's wild, honestly!"

Oh! Victorine froze for a moment, unable to say a word.

Fortunately, Marge was patting Victorine on one of her frozen hands.

"I think you'll find many of us enter contests all over the place!" said Marge. "Gives a person something to dream about, doesn't it?"

"And every now and then," said Sally, "once in a blue moon—am I right?—an ordinary telegraph dispatcher or secretary or—remind me what you do, Marge dear—"

"I keep accounts for my father," said Marge. "He runs a dry goods business in Sioux City."

"Or *accountant*, then, *wins* one of those contests, and finds herself all the way in Universal City, watching motion pictures get made!" Sally finished triumphantly.

"Yes, even if we're not quite lucky enough to be picked to be *in* those pictures," said Marge with only the hint of a sigh. "But I'm happy for Betty Ann. She's going to be in some party scene over that way, just standing in the background, but still! She'll do beautifully, I'm sure, with her sweet looks and her dimples."

They all settled comfortably onto the benches. The older girls were focused on the part of the stage that was across from where they were sitting and slightly to the left: it featured an interior of some sort of ballroom, all light walls and fanciness. There was a group of extras standing around in the back of the set, and one of those extras was evidently Betty Ann, because all the older girls waved in her direction, and Betty Ann (presumably) waved back, although then somebody said something stern to her, it seemed, because she pulled her waving hand very suddenly out of the air and went back to trying to look inconspicuous.

Meanwhile, most of Victorine's attention was focused on the set to their right, at the end of the long stage. That set had been built up to suggest the interior of a lonely, rugged house, presumably perched on rocky ocean cliffs (not visible here, of course). The scenery was painted to look like everything was made out of slabs of rough wood, and there was an old-fashioned iron light hanging over a wooden table.

Victorine watched the cameraman check his camera position and chat with the director a moment, and then the director waved and called out something, and a couple of actors filed into the set to consult with him: a burly old fellow in what Victorine thought of as classic lighthouse-keeper apparel, all woolen sweaters, bristly beard, and long boots. That poor man must be awfully hot in all that wool! And with him, a child. That is to say, of course: Darleen. She was listening very intently to everything the director had to say. This would not be the first or even the fiftieth time Darleen Darling had had to act in a photoplay without much (or any) time to read scripts or prepare.

"It's not Shakespeare!" Aunt Shirley liked to say, back in Fort Lee. And unlike some of the older actors who remembered their time on the "legitimate stage" with nostalgia, Aunt Shirley meant that as a compliment. No need to worry over the fine details of your lines—just get to work and get the job done: that was Aunt Shirley's way of seeing things.

That had always made Victorine nervous, though, and not just because she liked Shakespeare, but because she really, really liked being prepared for any sort of performance, whether it was playing a Chopin waltz on the piano or acting some role in front of a motion picture camera. Which is all to say, she watched Darleen now with affection and awe both.

On the set Darleen listened to the director, made

some practice motions with her arm to see what the director thought of them, and then was evidently told to tuck herself into the cot set up by the "fire" (not real).

The director said something. The cameraman started cranking film through that machine of his. The burly fellow in his lighthouse-keeper garb came in through the door and walked over to the bed where Darleen was lying. She turned around, opened her eyes, raised her arms toward him, asked some sort of question—"Where am I?" it seemed to be—and then fell back against the pillow. So well done, all of it! And then they stopped the camera, had the set people come in and shift the cot away and set bowls on the table. In this next scene, Darleen was apparently supposed to be healing from whatever had put her into that cot: while the technical crew got everything set up, she sat at the table, chatting cheerfully with the man playing the sailor or lighthouse keeper or whatever he was supposed to be.

The cameraman shifted the position of his camera forward a little so that Darleen would look larger in the frame. Not exactly a "close-up," but closer!

And then the director said "Go!" and the camera started cranking, and Darleen was now suddenly shy and weak, trying spoonfuls of whatever it was in the bowl (Victorine hoped on Darleen's behalf that whatever it was wasn't too nasty to eat) while the old lighthouse keeper (or sailor?) looked on anxiously. At first—her hand even wobbled a little, as it lifted the spoon, and then, bite by bite, she seemed to regain her strength, until, several spoonfuls later, she looked up at the old sailor, with a smile that brightened her face like (oldest possible simile) the sun coming out from behind a cloud.

"That's it!" said the director. "Stop film! Well done!"

And some of the people watching actually applauded, which made Victorine's heart swell.

And *that* drew the attention of the contest-winning girls, who turned their heads from the stage where Betty Ann was lost in a crowd of extras over to the set on the right, where Darleen was sitting at that rough-hewn table.

"Wait a moment," said Marge. "That little girl—is that—"

"It is!" said Sally. "Goodness gracious, Bella Mae, that's your friend Darleen! What's she doing there?"

"Wait, wait, wait, *wait!*" said Marge again. "*Darleen!* Now I'm realizing where I've seen her before!"

Not only Marge was realizing this. The whole group of contest-winning girls had turned toward Victorine and were absolutely abuzz with excitement.

"Why, you sneaky little kid!" said Sally to Victorine with a wink. "You never *once* told us that your friend named Darleen is actually *Daring Darleen!*"

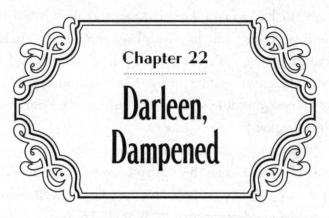

# Chapter 22

# Darleen, Dampened

*Often the introduction of a child will help your scenario.*
—How to Write for the "Movies"

The cat, as it were, was out of the bag.

Victorine looked around at all of those incredulous, flabbergasted faces, which were themselves toggling between looking at Victorine and looking at Darleen there on the set, acting in front of a motion picture camera as if she were a professional photoplay actress—because, of course, Darleen *was* a professional photoplay actress!—and Victorine couldn't help feeling a little delighted and proud on Darleen's behalf.

"I think perhaps we did mention that we lived in Fort Lee, New Jersey? Where the studios are?" she said to all those faces surrounding her now. The older girls exchanged glances and shook their heads vigorously.

"That's hardly telling us one of you is *Daring Darleen!*"

"You didn't drop us a crumb!" said Sally.

"It's just—" said Victorine, but the girls were already two steps ahead of her explanations.

"You were trying to keep things quiet! You didn't want to create a big fuss!" they said, and Marge added, "So we forgive you."

The other girls nodded, and then Sally bumped her elbow gently against Victorine's side.

"So, are you another hidden star of the moving pictures, Bella Mae?" she said. "Better confess to us right away if you're actually Mary Pickford in disguise or something—well, not Mary Pickford, of course, because I'm *sure* we would have recognized you if you were Mary Pickford!"

(Mary Pickford was probably the most famous personage in all of Movieland, even more famous than Lillian Gish.)

"So not Mary Pickford. But some other star, you know. Are you?"

Victorine sat up very straight.

"I'm afraid I'm not any kind of star," she said. "I've been in some movies, but just in the background, you know. I'm more interested in—"

She held up the book again for them, as a reminder: Miss Parsons's *How to Write for the "Movies."*

"So you have been in the movies! Goodness! And which famous people have you met?"

That last question came from one of the short-
est of the contest-winning girls, whose name was, if
Victorine remembered correctly, Velma. Poor girl!

"Oh, I don't know," said Victorine. What she did
*not* say was that most of the "famous people" she had
met in her life hadn't anything in particular to do with
the motion picture industry. They had been princes and
princesses and archdukes and suchlike back in the days
when she traveled the world with her Grandmama.

But that was all from the world and the life she had
left behind.

"Oh, come on, Bella Mae! You must have met
*somebody* we'd know!"

"Well, there's Madame Blaché," said Victorine,
with some hesitation. "Alice Guy Blaché. We know
her in Fort Lee. She has made a lot of photoplays. And
then we met Miss Lois Weber just yesterday—"

"Aha!" said Sally, who of course must have heard
that name this morning in the excitement in the office.

But the other girls were simply awed and amazed.

"LOIS WEBER!" said Marge. "You met LOIS
WEBER yesterday? But she's one of the most important people here! She makes all sorts of really serious
films. You know she used to be 'Mayor' of Universal
City, don't you?"

Victorine had not known that, but it seemed to her
to explain quite a bit.

"I suppose that's why they trusted Miss Weber's

word on Darleen," said Victorine. "They just popped her right into that lighthouse story."

"If Lois Weber says you're in, you're in!" said Sally.

"Anyway, Daring Darleen is wonderful—I loved all of her pictures," said Marge, and several of the other girls nodded and made agreeing sounds.

"And now there she is, acting right there in front of us," said the one whose name was actually Velma (poor girl). "And to think they're making a half dozen different pictures, all at the same time! How do they keep all their sceneries straight?" She swept her hand across the long line of the stage on which all of those moving pictures were being filmed at once. The pale walls and gilt decoration of the ballroom scene contrasted almost comically with the rough wood of the sea captain's cottage. And farther along to the left were other rooms of very different houses, and what looked like a store, and . . .

"Well, if it's like Matchless studios—only this place is about a hundred times larger than Matchless!—I imagine they have a whole crew of carpenters on the staff," said Victorine. "And a warehouse where they store the flats to bring out when needed. I mean: bits of walls and rooms that they can reuse whenever they need a rustic cottage or a palace or whatever."

"Like a library of walls," said Velma.

Victorine smiled at her. The thought of libraries always made her happy.

"Yes, exactly!" she said.

"All right, thank you," said Velma. "But why don't the rooms have ceilings? Just those large swatches of pale cloth draped above—"

The girls asked questions and more questions, and Victorine was quite tickled to discover she knew the answers to a fair number of them. She felt herself relaxing. The practical side of moviemaking was, after all, perhaps the most interesting thing in the world: everyone always having to come up with clever solutions to every kind of little creative challenge. She could talk about sets and cameras and editing until the end of the day and not be tired of it. And then Marge put a gentle hand on her arm and said, "It must be rather strange being an ordinary person living with a motion picture star. Is it strange? Do you get jealous inside? Don't you ever wish you were famous, too—"

Ah! The funny thing, of course, was that the person named Victorine Berryman *was*, in fact, famous enough to have a whole serial made about her (fictionalized) life. But what did Vee have to do with that make-believe version of herself? Or, for that matter, with the long-ago Victorine who had been in the newspapers as the "RICHEST GIRL IN THE WORLD"?

She hardly knew what to say, to be honest. But at that moment Sally gasped and pointed at the stage.

"Oh, now. They've gone and dunked Darleen right into a water barrel, poor kid!"

The last scene of the day for Darleen, it turned out, was going to a slightly earlier part of the story, when the old sailor or lighthouse keeper or whatever he was supposed to be brought the half-drowned child into his cottage or lighthouse or whatever *that* was supposed to be. They were filming that episode last, Victorine knew, to save them the trouble of drying off Darleen for the other scenes. (Then eventually, of course, the editor would snip and paste to put all the scenes together in the proper order.)

So now poor Darleen, in a damp frock and with dripping hair, sagged in the arms of the old sailor as he carried her in through the door and draped her on the cot in front of the (fake) fire.

That was the first try. The director wasn't too happy with something. He gave new instructions (inaudible from the bleachers where all the girls were watching the filming), and Darleen, still dripping, got up from the cot and headed back through the door with the older actor to try again.

In they came, Darleen looking very damp, her hair even wetter than the first try. Were they really dunking her in that water barrel again every single time? She was so convincingly limp in the old sailor's arms that Victorine felt a twinge of distress—and then, when the director came back with more comments, something directed toward the older actor, something about how he had stepped through the door with his left foot when his right foot might have looked better, Victorine rose up from her seat.

"Are they making her do that a third time?" she said.

"I do believe they are," said Marge, and the older girls made disapproving sounds. Wet hair and wet clothing! Even in warm California, that didn't seem wise. And a little breeze had come up, now that the sun was lower in the sky.

When Darleen got up from the cot to go back through that door for yet another attempt, she was— Victorine was quite sure—shivering. That did it.

"No," said Victorine to herself, and quick as could be, she sidled by the older girls and down the steps of the viewing stand—and then ran right over to the front of the stage, where the director and the cameraman were positioned.

"Excuse me, mister!" she said to the director, and she stretched herself to be as tall as possible (which wasn't actually very tall, but she had noticed that *firm intention* is at least seventy-five percent of *the impression of height*). "Darleen Darling there! She needs to go indoors somewhere and get warm and dry!"

"What?" said the director, obviously irritated. "What's this?" Various assistants started coming toward Victorine as if she were a fly that really needed to be swatted or shooed. But Victorine stood her ground.

"That last take looked quite good enough to me,"

said Victorine. "Look at her: Darleen is shivering. She needs to get inside somewhere right now. I hope you have some good warm towels around here!"

The director gaped at Victorine. He was probably not used to being interrupted by young people of slightly indeterminate age.

"Who in the name of everything are you?" he said.

"I'm—" said Victorine, and then in the stress of the moment, she got stuck. "I'm—"

But who was she really, anyway? Suddenly she couldn't finish that simplest of sentences: the "Bella Mae" seemed to have gotten stuck in her throat.

"Enough of this nonsense!" said the director. "We can't have nobody in particular interrupting filming this way! You girl, get out of here!"

"She's *cold*," said Victorine. "It's not safe. You have to—"

And by now Darleen had popped her head through the door—she was shivering hard enough that when she spoke her teeth chattered together.

"Th-that's my sister!" she said.

The director was swiveling his head from the still dripping and shivering Darleen to the stubborn and standing-as-tall-as-possible Victorine, and his irritated face froze in place.

"Her sister? You saying you're . . . the one responsible?"

Victorine knew what he meant by this—he was

not asking about Victorine's general character traits (though, yes, Victorine was very *responsible* as a general sort of thing); he was asking whether Victorine was the person who negotiated with the studio on Miss Darling's behalf—and thus had the right to demand towels for a shivering child actress. Usually that responsible person would be the child's mother, but Victorine had had a lot of practice sidestepping this question on her own behalf, hadn't she? Both she and Darleen were motherless girls, even if they were absolutely determined to transcend the limits implied by that category.

Victorine made her eyebrows stern and her voice as close to flinty as she could manage.

"I'm responsible for Darleen, yes," she said, and she meant it not in the legal sense (of course), but on a deeper and truer level than that. "And so I trust someone will find a good towel right away?"

"Very well," said the director with a sigh, and to the crew he said, "Action will stop for today, all! Everyone back on set tomorrow morning, crack of nine! Good work, Miss Darling."

(That was presumably his olive branch for having done his best to give Darleen a bad case of pneumonia.)

And then there was a lot of hustle and bustle.

In the dressing room Victorine made sure Darleen put on entirely dry everything, while Darleen smiled at her.

"That went fine!" she said. "And they're going to pay me fifty whole dollars! Imagine that!"

"Wonderful," said Victorine, and she meant it. "But I thought they promised you that you wouldn't have to swim."

That made Darleen laugh outright, and her teeth no longer chattered when she laughed, which was a relief to hear.

After restorative cups of cocoa provided by the canteen, Darleen and Victorine made their way back to the bus stop out in front—where the contest-winning girls had very kindly been waiting.

"Darleen, you were simply crackerjack up there!" they said, but they also said, "Well done, Bella Mae!"

"That was so very brave of you," said the one named Eleanor. "Speaking up like that. I don't think I would have dared."

"Vee's the best and bravest," said Darleen, and then she caught herself almost immediately. "Bella Mae, I mean. Did you all have a nice day?"

They had all had excellent days, especially Betty Ann, who was in raptures about her ballroom adventure.

"Tomorrow we're heading up north, you know," said Sally. "Off to beautiful San Francisco."

"The Panama-Pacific Exposition!" said other girls. Even five or six days into their adventure, they were all evidently having the time of their lives.

"Oh!" said Darleen. "I wish we could come along."

"No, you don't," said Sally. "You're busy being the star of that photoplay. That's better than any exposition."

The girls nodded vigorously, but Victorine could tell that Darleen wasn't entirely sure that was true.

"And when were you going to tell us who you are, *Daring Darleen*?" said Velma. "Will you sign my album?"

Suddenly there were little books and pencils being pressed in Darleen's direction. Albums filled with signatures of anyone who might be a little bit famous.

"Why not do that at the boardinghouse, where you can use a pen?" said practical Victorine. "We'll have a few minutes before we have to go."

"Go where?"

"We found a place to stay for a while," said Victorine. "Thank goodness!"

"Mrs. Gish said she'd take us in," added Darleen. "Since she knows my aunt and everything."

"Mrs. Gish, as in *Lillian Gish*?" said someone. "You didn't say you knew Lillian Gish, Bella Mae!"

"Oh, I don't!" said Victorine a bit feebly, but her protest was lost in the general happy hubbub.

"Not to mention *Dorothy Gish*!" said another someone. "Dorothy's always been my favorite. She's a sweet little thing. The two of them together in *The Sisters* last year—oh, my. What a pair!"

"But Lillian!" said Marge. "No one ever looked like a candle just blown out by the winds of cruel fate as well as Miss Lillian Gish. And she's so young too."

"And *so* famous," said Velma. "I mean, especially since February—why, *Birth of a Nation* must be one of the most successful motion pictures ever . . ."

Here Victorine found herself in an even more awkward position, since she was someone who had not liked *Birth of a Nation*. She preferred her history to be at least somewhat accurate—and she did not like hatefulness dressed up in fancy clothing. Mr. D. W. Griffith's *Birth of a Nation* told the story of the rise of the Ku Klux Klan after the Civil War, and it made the history of the South look like it was all about noble white people being put in danger by those who had previously been enslaved and now wanted to do things like *vote*. It had very fancy camera tricks in it, and the scenes were edited together in a way that made your heart race—but what good are camera tricks if they're used to tell lies? That was something Victorine felt all the way down to the marrow of her truth-telling bones.

"I didn't care for that picture, honestly," she said now, but everyone else was too busy with their own opinions to hear a word from Victorine.

"Anyway, it's Mrs. Gish we'll be staying with," said Darleen to the girls clustered so eagerly around her. "Not *Lillian*!"

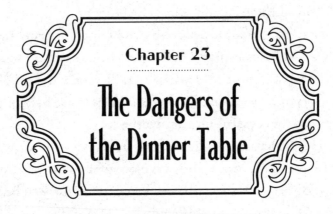

## Chapter 23

## The Dangers of the Dinner Table

*Be honest, photoplaywrights. Honesty is*
*always the best policy and pays best in the long run.*
—How to Write for the "Movies"

It was some hours before they arrived at the home of Mrs. Gish, of course. First they had to return to the boardinghouse to pick up their things, to bid fond farewell to all the contest-winning girls, and to sign quite a large number of autograph albums. (That was mostly Darleen doing the signing, of course, but Sally warmed Victorine's heart by coming over with a pen and a grin and asking for the signature of the "future famous photoplaywright Bella Mae . . .")

Then there was the awkwardness of lugging all of their possessions across Hollywood to the house Mrs. Gish was renting. That hour was uncomfortable and a chore and to be forgotten as soon as possible.

But at the end of that miserable slog, Dar and Victorine found themselves at the front door of a large house. Through that door came the slightly jangly sound of somebody playing etudes rather badly on the piano. (Victorine felt a pang, since it had been a long, long time since she herself had last practiced the piano properly.)

They bravely rang the bell, and a moment later the door swung open to reveal a kind-looking woman in an old-fashioned lace cap. Staring at them curiously from behind the woman's shoulder was a rather tall girl, who was, Victorine noticed, holding a book in one hand. (Vee felt another pang, since she loved books even more than the piano.)

"Hello, my dears," said the woman. "You must be little Darleen Darling and her friend! Goodness, Darleen, look at you now! You were just a bitty little thing when I last saw you!"

"Mrs. Gish?" said Darleen.

"Yes, indeed," said the woman. "Come in, come in. I can't believe you poor little things have been all on your own here! How old *are* you?"

But before Dar and Victorine could so much as exchange glances or say "Umm," the tall girl standing right behind Mrs. Gish laughed and said, "Now, Mother, you know we don't ask questions like that of people who act in pictures!"

There was no doubt about it: only a few feet from

them and in the flesh was *Lillian Gish*. Even without the makeup required for a face to be properly visible for the camera, her eyes were large and soulful in a delicate, narrow face, her eyebrows expressive, her blond hair piled in curls, and her mouth ever on the verge of looking quizzical.

The piano etude stopped in the middle of an arpeggio, and a moment later another girl, not nearly as tall as Lillian, had bounded over and joined the knot at the door. And that must be the younger Gish sister, Dorothy. She was about seventeen, if Victorine remembered those articles in *Photoplay* correctly. Lillian's age was more of a mystery—the gossip columns said one thing and then said another. But surely she couldn't be that much older than her sister?

"What questions don't we ask?" said Dorothy. "You know I'll ask anything!"

"Dorothy!" said the older sister in a distinctly older-sister way.

Meanwhile, Mrs. Gish was shepherding the girls into the house, leading them upstairs and showing them the little room they would share, all the while asking friendly questions about how the day had gone at Universal—and once she heard about Darleen's damp experience on set, she clucked her tongue and said it was a good thing, then, that they were having some nice, old-fashioned soup for supper.

"That should go a good distance toward warming up your bones, my dear."

And it certainly did. There was also a hearty slice of meatloaf with gravy and some buttery mashed potatoes.

"I'm famous for my plain cooking," said Mrs. Gish with a laugh. "No one suffers here when it's Cook's night off. Glad to see you girls agree."

"And your dressmaking, Mother dear," said Lillian. "You've always been a genius with a needle."

"I trust your aunt has made sure you know all the essential skills of life," said Mrs. Gish to Darleen.

"We can do enough cooking to get by, can't we, Bella Mae?" said Darleen. "But I'm afraid I'm not very good on the sewing side of things. You're better at that, Vee—"

"Only when it comes to embroidering silk roses on lacy handkerchiefs," said Victorine. "Not the useful sort of sewing."

Mrs. Gish eyed her guests with tolerance.

"Well," she said, "I do always say that if you can thread a needle properly, the dress is already half made, so I'm sure you're well on your way, both of you. And now, Lillian darling, tell me how your day went? I know you weren't filming anything."

"Playing secretary for Mr. Griffith," said Lillian. "He had some correspondence that has been vexing him for a while, so I said I would take a look. Some ailing old Miss Withering who seems to have become quite obsessed with him and all of his work. She keeps sending helpful advice along, you know, about the new picture."

"What's the new picture about, Miss Gish?" asked Darleen.

"About *everything*!" said Lillian. "And do call me Lillian—we can't be all formal when we're eating meatloaf together, I don't think. Unless you don't want to be Darleen—no, of course you don't mind, I see that—and I'm afraid I've forgotten *your* name already, young friend of Darleen's—"

"She's Bella Mae Goodwin," said Darleen very fast. "What does 'everything' mean, though?"

Victorine was curious about that, too; it seemed so unlikely that any one photoplay could be about *everything*.

"It's the most brilliant design for a photoplay!" said Lillian, with the deep enthusiasm other people might have for a painting by Rembrandt or the Gothic arches of the Cathedral of Notre Dame in Paris, France. "Mr. Griffith is braiding four stories together with the help of editing, you know, all about one particular theme, and each set in such different times and places: France during a time of religious wars; and the life of Christ; and a story set in today, with love and tragedy and a thrilling chase to save an innocent man from the gallows; and even the most spectacular views of the fall of

Babylon to Cyrus of Persia, thousands of years ago—that's the part that has got old Miss Withering going!"

"Really!" said Dar and Victorine, almost at exactly the same time. Darleen was impressed by how complicated this picture seemed to be, and Victorine was reacting to the word *Babylon*. Babylonian things seemed to be popping up in their lives so frequently these days!

"So what is the theme you mentioned, that ties all the parts together, though?" asked Darleen.

"Intolerance!" said Lillian. "It's a great work, and all about *intolerance*, and how bad and harmful it is. Mr. Griffith thinks it is motion pictures and the stories they tell that will eventually bring us all together, you know. He sees making photoplays as a higher calling—something that can make our world a happier, better place."

"How well you put things, dear," said the contented and motherly Mrs. Gish. "Do have just a bit more meatloaf. The rainy season will arrive eventually, even here in the land of endless sunshine, and then we'll all need a little more flesh on our bones."

Victorine was thinking very hard. She opened her mouth as the thoughts went in one direction, and then closed it again as the thoughts wheeled around and came back. *Making the world a better place*, she was thinking. Could a photoplay really do such a thing? And what did that actually mean if it *could*?

"You could write a column for the papers, like our Gladys does!" laughed Dorothy. "You'd like that, wouldn't you, Lillian? Being a bookworm all day long?"

"Mary Pickford's Daily Talks," said Lillian. "Well, now, Dorothy. If you think Gladys is writing every word of those things, you have surely had the wool pulled right over your eyes. She's got one of her writing friends doing the work, trust me—you see, we knew Gladys Smith *years* before she became *Mary Pickford*, girls."

"You did?" said Darleen in awe.

"Why, dear child, Mary Pickford (that is to say, Gladys Smith) has probably had more slices of my good, plain meatloaf than anyone in the world other than my own darling girls," said Mrs. Gish. "They lived with us for a time, the Smiths."

"Long, long ago," said Lillian.

"Very long ago," agreed Mrs. Gish.

There was a nostalgic pause. Dorothy finished the mashed potatoes.

"Do you really think," said Victorine suddenly, "that the motion pictures can make the world a better place?"

That took everyone at the table by surprise.

"Yes, of course!" said Lillian. "That's Mr. Griffith's foremost conviction. That's why he's making *Intolerance* right now."

"But *Birth of a Nation*," said Victorine. "That seems

a different sort of photoplay, doesn't it? Not really about making the world happier and better."

Victorine was the sort of person who read newspapers and paid attention, and so she remembered that although many people had indeed rushed to see Mr. Griffith's film about the Ku Klux Klan when it came out in February, others had protested, picketed, and pleaded with city and state officials not to let false history poison the screens of the movie houses.

"Actually it's a very elevating picture," said Lillian, and a bit of that older-sister tone was coming back into her voice now. "About overcoming differences between the North and South. Why, even President Wilson saw it and praised it!"

"But the people doing terrible things in that picture are all mostly people who had, you know, been stolen away from Africa and held in bondage here— aren't they? So then anyone watching that photoplay might think everyone who had once been so cruelly enslaved—or whose ancestors had been—couldn't now be trusted, right? And then, if it's the sort of picture powerful enough to *change the world*, as you were saying, don't we have to be extra careful, you know, not to do *harm*—"

Victorine was trying to work this thought out for herself as she went, which meant she wasn't paying much attention to the expressions of the people around the table.

Dorothy said, quite merrily, "Careful there, Miss—what was your name? You should know my sister isn't going to tolerate a *word* of criticism leveled against Mr. Griffith!"

"I was just wondering about the effects motion pictures can have on people," said Victorine. "Since that's something Miss Weber also said to us, you know, yesterday: she wants to make photoplays that are—what did she say?—like the editorial pages of the newspaper! Motion pictures that can change people's minds about things, you know . . ."

Victorine must have sounded earnest enough to soften the general effect on everyone around that table, because Lillian laughed a little and said, "Newspaper editorials! Oh, now, that's dry fare, isn't it? Who is ever *inspired* by a newspaper?"

And that gave Darleen, who was not much inspired by newspapers ever, the cue to indulge herself in the loudest, largest possible yawn—and then beg everyone's pardon.

"I'm *so* sorry! It's been such a long day, and tomorrow's going to be another one, I guess! Thank you so much for supper, Mrs. Gish. For supper, and for a place to stay, and for *everything*."

Fifteen minutes later they were upstairs, with their nightgowns on and their teeth freshly cleaned.

"You know, Vee dear," said Darleen as they settled into their beds in that pleasant guest room on the second floor, "you won't be cross with me, will you, if I say that at supper tonight, you were *almost*—well—not polite."

"I know it," said Victorine. "But Darleen, if I had been polite, it would have been—a lie. Right? Oh, it's a mess."

She did feel quite twitchy and dissatisfied with how that dinner conversation had gone.

"Well," said Darleen, "Aunt Shirley says, 'Least said, soonest mended.' Not that she follows that advice herself, of course!"

Darleen laughed at that idea, but Victorine was still trying to sort out all of those tangled thoughts that seemed so important and so difficult, both at once.

"Honestly, Dar, I'm thinking now it's worse than lying to say *nothing*, if there's something that really has to be said," said Victorine. "Not that I've got it figured out at all yet, obviously. How to say what I think is the truth, without seeming so rude that the other person just gets angry and closes their ears. How to change the way people see things. As Miss Weber was saying about her films, you know—wanting them to be effective. Oh, but what if only the hateful things are effective? Now that would be terrible!"

Darleen's face was wearing the sort of tolerant smile that comes from simply being too warm and contented and happy to argue.

"You do know, don't you, Vee," she said, "that if what you think is true makes other people unhappy or uncomfortable, you *will* seem rude. I don't think there's any way around that. Is there?"

"Then we're stuck, I suppose? Because we can't lie, can we? Or not say what we know *is* true—can we?" said Victorine. For some reason this puzzle made her feel desperate in some small, deep corner of her soul. "Oh, Dar, I have to feel more hopeful about the truth than that! There simply has to be a way to be truthful that will help people hear what you're saying and, you know, maybe even be convinced, if you've put things logically enough—without being made angry. I mean, I suppose I don't mind much them being angry, if it can't be helped, but the thing is that if they are angry, they won't listen, will they? What an awful puzzle it is! Because it has to be possible, changing people's minds! I simply have to figure it out, seems to me. The right words to use, and so on."

She could tell from Darleen's expression (affectionate, but also slightly amused) that she might have gone on a bit long—but it *mattered*. She couldn't help thinking that all of this mattered a great deal.

"Vee!" said Darleen. "You always have such a peculiar way of seeing the world! It's part of your goodness, actually, I guess. And I suppose if anyone can ever figure out how to tell unpleasant truths while somehow miraculously—magically—keeping everyone from becoming furious and shouting at each other, maybe that person will be you." And then, after that burst of loyalty, Darleen seemed to think she had to be extra truthful too. "But of course it *might* be impossible, telling everyone the truth without making them mad, that's the only thing. Anyway"—the smile crept back—"don't be sad! Things are looking up so beautifully, don't you think? Mrs. Gish is being so kind, and Miss Weber sent that telegram off to the Ogden police, and surely Uncle Dan will be able to come find us. And I have a job! At least for this week and next—a foothold for the Darlings!"

"Well, we do still have to figure out what to do with *those*," said Victorine, and she waved her hand toward the three little velvet bags, which sat on the bedside table near her head, along with the book given to Uncle Dan by Mr. Waller, the Pullman porter.

In each one of those sacks was a Babylonian cylinder seal. Unfortunately, there was no anonymous collection point in Los Angeles where people who had accidentally come into possession of stolen antiquities could turn them in without having to answer difficult questions that might make the police suspicious of Uncle Dan all over again (the girls' chief concern), while at the same time being quite sure the little cylinder seals would be perfectly safe and would be safely returned to the museums they had come from (Victorine's secret secondary concern). "Without involving the Gishes, of course," said Victorine.

"Something will come to mind," said Darleen.

"And if nothing does, Uncle Dan will get here, and everything will be clearer then, I'm sure."

"Oh!" said Victorine then, having looked twice or three times at the objects piled on the bedside table. "That book! Darleen!"

"What is it now, Vee?" said Darleen. "You look as though you just saw a ghost."

"Not a ghost!" said Victorine. "Miss Waller!"

Darleen stared.

"Miss who?"

"Miss Waller! Miss Ruth Waller! The sister—the Pullman porter's sister—the one we were supposed to deliver this book to! I think I saw her today, up at Universal."

"You did?" said Darleen. "Are you sure?"

"Almost positive," said Victorine. "I was just so caught up in my thoughts, you know, that the name didn't register."

"Well, how about that?" said Darleen, reaching over to turn off the lamp. "We'll carry the book along with us, then, won't we. Just in case. Imagine running into the one person we were asked to find! That has to be a good omen, don't you think?"

Victorine wasn't confident that "good omens" were properly scientific sorts of things, but did she feel a little warm glow of hope and encouragement at the moment? She did!

# Chapter 24

# Shots Fired in the Night!

*Punch may be nerve-racking suspense. . . .*
—How to Write for the "Movies"

But then in the darkest, deepest hour of the night, Victorine found herself suddenly sitting up in her bed, wide awake, and not knowing why.

"Darleen?" she whispered.

Despite the gloom, she could tell that Darleen was awake too—also bolt upright.

"Someone's in the house," whispered Darleen. "I hear footsteps, Vee. Sneaking around, rattling the knobs of things."

And now Victorine could also hear those sneaking steps. And the squeaks of floorboards too. The footsteps seemed to be coming closer and closer.

Victorine slipped over to Darleen's bed and took her hand, which was cold with fear.

"We'll just sit here quietly," she whispered. "It'll be all right. It'll be all right. We're going to be all right."

And then—oh, horror—the door of their room opened, and a man came sneaking in, holding up a lantern so bright that they could not see his face.

But apparently he could see *their* faces.

"You!" he whispered furiously. "The little thieves! The thieving girls! You *are* here! And where are—oh, there! I see them there!"

That voice! Even in the form of an angry whisper, it was clearly the voice of the unpleasant man from the train!

The burglar swept his large hand across the nightstand, and that hand swallowed the little velvet sacks there, while Darleen and Victorine shrank as far away from him as they could possibly shrink, all the while hanging on to each other so tightly their fingers hurt.

Fortunately, the man was in a terrible hurry (as thieves so often are). A second later he was heading back out through their door, into the big, dark hall. But wait! Another light came into the hall—and Mrs. Gish's voice, ordinarily so motherly, and now full of steel and determination.

"Who are you? What are you doing? OUT OF HERE!"

And then the loud, deafening pop of a pistol!

"Oh!" gasped Darleen, and Victorine could say nothing, nothing at all. All she could do was hold on more tightly to Darleen's cold hand.

The man shouted and his heavy feet scurried away down the hall.

"I said OUT! OUT OUT OUT!" said Mrs. Gish's voice. Mrs. Gish's *stentorian* voice, thought Victorine. (Sometimes terror will send a person's mind scurrying in surprising directions: Victorine, for instance—in spite of being thoroughly overwhelmed by shock and fear—found herself pausing to appreciate the word *stentorian*, which is simply a fancier way of saying "resonant—and loud!")

There was another gunshot! The man's feet were now not sneaking but thundering away down the stairs, fast, fast, fast.

And then, after another terrible moment, the front door slammed shut. Victorine was quite sure he must be gone. But she and Darleen clung to each other without moving or speaking until Mrs. Gish—and right after Mrs. Gish, Dorothy—came bursting into their room and turned on the lights, which made everyone blink.

"Girls, girls!" Mrs. Gish was saying. "Are you all right? That horrible man—that burglar—he came into your room!"

"We're—we're all right," said Victorine, for the first time feeling that yes, they were. All right. Basically fine. But she couldn't take her eyes off the pistol in Mrs. Gish's hand.

That was what Dorothy Gish was looking at, too, with her hand to her mouth.

"Mother! You *shot* him!"

"I'm pretty sure I missed," said Mrs. Gish calmly. "We can look around for bloodstains in the morning, just to see for sure. Is Lillian telephoning the police?"

"Yes," said Dorothy Gish. "What did he want? What did he take?"

Darleen pointed a shaky, cold hand at the floor at Dorothy's feet, where there was a little velvet sack.

"Oh, my. Look what he dropped," said Victorine.

You would think that a burglar ruthless enough to invade someone's home in the middle of the night would hold on very tightly to all the objects he had burgled! But apparently burglars can be clumsy too.

Dorothy had immediately swooped down to pick up that little sack, and now she emptied it right into Mrs. Gish's hand (the hand that was not holding the pistol): even from as far away as the little bed, Victorine could tell it was the tiny little rolling pin with the winged lions on it. The Gishes looked at it in wonder.

"Whatever can it be?" said Mrs. Gish.

"The girls just said the burglar dropped it, Mother," said Dorothy. "Maybe he was burgling many houses tonight, not just ours. What *is* this funny little thing?"

Darleen and Victorine looked at each other, dazed by all of these turns of events.

"I've seen things like it in museums before," said Victorine. Still the truth.

"In the Louvre, that museum in Paris," said Darleen, her voice still a little dreamy from shock and lack of sleep.

"That's right," said Victorine. "What this is, Mrs. Gish, is a Babylonian cylinder seal. I'm quite sure of it. It must be very old and very valuable."

"Does mostly look like a dollhouse rolling pin, though," added Darleen, and a giggle welled up in her.

"Oh, dear," said Mrs. Gish. "You two are practically in hysterics! And no wonder. I'll make you some warm milk to settle you down, and then I want you to get back to sleep. No need for you poor girls to fuss with the police."

As the Gishes walked back down the house's long second-floor hall, Victorine could hear Dorothy saying to her mother, "Are you sure you didn't hurt him? Are you sure?"

"Hush, hush, darling Dorothy. Don't you become hysterical too! I can see now it will have to be restorative warm milk for everyone," said Mrs. Gish's voice. "What a night!"

## Chapter 25

# An Errand and a Mission!

*You can very quickly learn to manipulate the keys.*
*Nearly all newspaper writers and authors*
*of note are self-taught typists.*
—How to Write for the "Movies"

As the girls were rather droopily brushing their hair the next morning, Darleen stopped suddenly and said, "But how did that awful man know we were *here*?"

And Victorine, who had been thinking about this problem hard at approximately four in the morning and was still thinking about it now, at seven, said to Darleen, "Mrs. Gish's address was in the pocket of Uncle Dan's satchel, remember? With Miss Weber's address too. The burglar must have found those addresses there when he took the bag in Ogden. So he has been searching for us everywhere ever since— well, not really for us, but for the pilfered antiquities, you know."

"Golly. I think you may be right about that," said Darleen.

"And that makes me worry quite a bit because, Darleen—remember how Miss Gish—Lillian, that is—was talking about a woman who keeps writing to Mr. Griffith? Wasn't her name—"

"Oh, no!" said Darleen, catching on right away. "*Miss Withering!* Like the note we found in the *burglar's* satchel. It's not a very common name, is it, Withering? Perhaps they are one and the same? Do you think he's planning to steal from that poor lady?"

"He may be," said Victorine, feeling rather grim. "Maybe she has something valuable in her house that he has his eye on. And what if she comes to harm? I think—I think perhaps it may be our solemn duty to warn her, Darleen."

"Oh, dear," said Darleen. They looked at each other.

But the clock was striking the breakfast hour, and as it happened, they were ravenous. Midnight struggles with burglars can leave a person feeling rather drawn and undernourished.

There were only three tired people around the breakfast table that morning, however. Mrs. Gish had decided that Lillian and Dorothy (who had stayed up through the police's visit in the middle of the night) should sleep late and restore themselves.

"And I'll take an old woman's cat nap later today,"

she said with a laugh. Victorine figured that the laugh was just by way of acknowledging how ridiculous it was for Mrs. Gish to call herself an "old woman," even in jest. As far as Victorine could figure, Mrs. Gish must have become a mother at a very young age.

"All that fuss with the police—and more telephoning this morning—do you know they think that funny little stone the man dropped was stolen from the great San Francisco exposition? Apparently thieves are hard at work these days, all over the country. Antiquities have gone missing from the big New York museum too. Well! What I say is, what can that thief possibly have hoped to find *here*? And what I also say is, let's have some nice breakfast."

Exhausted as she must have been, Mrs. Gish had gotten up to make oatmeal for Darleen and Victorine before they went racing back to Universal City for another day's work. Mrs. Gish was a stage-and-photoplay mother, so she understood that even a burglar in the night could not be allowed to keep an actress from her second day on the set.

"I do hope they don't drown you again, though, my dear," she said to Darleen.

"They had better not try," said Victorine with determination. And while washing up the dishes after breakfast, Victorine had a private conversation with Mrs. Gish about some little errands she and Darleen needed to run after filming had ended for the day.

"Vee," said Darleen once they were en route for Universal City, "I'm sure you didn't tell her we were going to go looking for that Miss Withering. So were you perhaps actually *lying* just now to Mrs. Gish? About the 'errands'?"

"No, not at all—you'll see!" said Victorine.

Victorine's errand was perfectly real. After a long, enjoyable, and blessedly uneventful day filming a courtroom scene for the little drama about the orphan and her kindly sea captain or lighthouse keeper or whatever he was supposed to be (but a day when Victorine, despite having Mr. Freddy Waller's book close at hand in its brown paper wrapping, did not again run into Miss Ruth Waller to pass it along), Darleen and Victorine went off to a very ordinary storefront, inside of which were . . .

Typewriters!

"I've decided to take Miss Parsons's advice and rent one of these!" said Victorine. "Now that you're earning money, we can afford the investment, and Mrs. Gish says she doesn't mind a typewriter in the house as long as I *resolutely promise* not to bang away on it in the middle of the night."

Victorine, who had been studying the advertisements in the newspaper, chose a lovely Underwood, at $2.50 a month.

"They're supposed to be very reliable," she said to

Darleen, by way of excuse. There were cheaper type-writers available, but they didn't have the charm and razzle-dazzle of the Underwood. They arranged for the typewriter to be delivered to Mrs. Gish's house and then stood a moment outside the storefront, looking at each other and gauging how brave they wanted to be.

"I think we have to do it," said Victorine. "We have to warn this Miss Withering. That burglar fellow seems quite ruthless and determined."

"Yes," said Darleen. "And I suppose you memorized Miss Withering's address just by glancing at it that one time?"

"I didn't mean to, but yes," said Victorine. "The address just got itself lodged in my head."

Darleen laughed. That did sometimes happen with Victorine.

"Lead on, Vee! We'll give the nice lady a quick warning and then come running back home as quick as we can. I'm hungry and tired, and I bet you are too."

They consulted their map and discovered that Miss Withering seemed to live at the foot of a hill. What the map neglected to mention, however, was that Miss Withering's house was a mansion of the spooky-old-house variety, like something you might find in a really creepy photoplay. And above her house, up on top of the hill, was another mansion, even more enor-mous and built to resemble some kind of temple in a faraway land.

"I think I've seen that other one in a film before," said Victorine, squinting up the hill. "Is that possible?"

"*Anything* is possible here," said Darleen.

That really seemed to be the case. Anything has to be possible in a place where the air smells slightly of orange groves.

# Chapter 26

# Warning Miss Withering

*Suspense is an essential sensation
to the dramatic photoplay when not overdone.*
—How to Write for the "Movies"

It ended up taking a little more courage than they had expected to need to walk up to the door of such a palace (even if not the largest palace in that neighborhood). It helped that they were hungry and tired and wanted to get this necessary duty over with as briskly as possible.

"Onward!" said Victorine, only it accidentally came out with a question mark instead of an exclamation point tacked onto its end: "Onward?"

"We'll talk very quickly, give her the bad news, and scoot right home to Mrs. Gish's," said Darleen as she pulled Victorine up the walk to the mansion's very imposing door. "Because honestly, after last night's excitement and today's work on the set, I'm ready for a bit of a rest."

When they pressed the doorbell, it started an appropriately spooky deep chime somewhere far away inside that building.

"Goodness," said Darleen.

And then the door creaked open, and an elderly servant—the butler?—asked in a rusty old voice what they wanted.

"We're here to see Miss Withering," said Victorine. "We have some information for her that may be important."

"Please to wait here," said the butler (if that's what he was), and he disappeared down the long hall.

The girls, still on the threshold, looked around. Everything was shadowy. Everything looked very old and as if at some point in the previous century it had been worth a lot of money. And there was even a set of old armor standing in that hallway, which really did seem like something taken from a *very* bad photoplay.

A minute later the butler was back.

"Miss Withering will see you. Come this way, please."

They were committed, then, to entering that spooky house. Victorine reluctantly pulled the front door shut behind her, and the girls followed the old butler down the hall and into an elaborate old parlor on the left. The proportions in here were large. The ceiling was so far above their heads! The walls were so very tall! And almost every inch of the walls was covered with old-fashioned paintings, darkened with age, mostly of people in long-ago clothes standing in front of large houses and trees. There were cabinets and drawers built into the walls all around, and a simply enormous white dress folded into an armchair next to a rather anemic fire. That extravagant dress was, of course, not merely a dress, but a person wrapped up in that dress, and the person in question—the only object in the entire room whose size was smaller than normal, not larger—was staring quite sharply at the girls now as they approached.

"Miss Withering?" said Victorine.

"That's my name," said the wizened old person, who seemed (Victorine couldn't help thinking) to have taken her name much too seriously and indeed become by now the very essence of *withering*. "Who are you? And what have you come here for? I don't make a habit of having visitors here in my inner sanctum. I don't make a habit of it at all."

"I'm Darleen Darling," said Darleen. "And this is Miss Bella Mae Goodwin. We've come here because—"

She took a deep breath, and that gave Victorine time to jump in and carry on with the necessary recounting of bad news: "We have come here to warn you, Miss Withering. You see, we're a little worried you may be in some danger."

"Me, in danger!" said Miss Withering. "Well,

now, that would be an interesting change of pace, wouldn't it?"

For some reason that amused her enough that for a moment she actually laughed. The laugh was rather ghastly. (*Like dry branches scraping together*, thought Victorine, practicing her similes.)

"What kind of danger am I in, then?" the old woman asked, after her dry, autumnal laugh had faded away.

"There's a burglar," said Victorine. "Who seems to be rather ruthless, I'm afraid. He has stolen treasures from museums—"

"What museums?" said the old woman, leaning forward.

"The Metropolitan Museum in New York," said Victorine. "And also—from the Panama-Pacific International Exposition in San Francisco. Which isn't exactly a museum, of course, but apparently has cases full of valuable things on display."

"I see," said the woman. "And what did he take from these museums that aren't exactly museums?"

"The Metropolitan Museum in New York *is* a museum, though, Miss Withering—one of the most famous museums in the world, in fact," said Victorine, feeling a little wounded on the Met's behalf.

"What he took was *old things*! Very old things!"

That was Darleen, helpfully jumping in to get Victorine unstuck. It worked.

"A set of Babylonian cylinder seals, yes," said Victorine. "But Miss Withering, that doesn't matter. What matters is that he has your name and knows where you live. We are worried that he—that he might come this way."

"And so we wanted to warn you," said Darleen. "Which is what we are doing now before we have to go home for supper, which we really have to do very, very soon."

Victorine understood the little tremor in Darleen's voice: this room, this old lady burrowed into that huge dress in the huger armchair, the shadows—all of it was as creepy as one of those old-fashioned fairy tales.

Just as they were looking at each other, asking the silent question (*Do we stay? Or do we skedaddle?*), there was a sudden upsurgence of voices in the hall, the door flew open, the butler's head appeared, and then he was rudely shoved to one side by a male figure pressing urgently into the room.

A familiar, awful figure!

Next to Victorine, Darleen gasped out an accurate and horrible summary of their situation: "Oh, *too late!*"

# Chapter 27

# And Then the Plot Twisted!

*[A]nd for a moment it looks bad . . .*
—How to Write for the "Movies"

Yes, it was indeed the man from the train, the burglar, the very person whom they had come here to warn old Miss Withering against and about.

"Miss Withering! It's him!" said Victorine, feeling grammar and logic evaporating under the pressure of the current shock. "I mean, I mean—it is *he!* Miss Withering! What should we do?"

There was a pause in which the horrible man turned his gaze in their direction (which was awful in itself) and then widened his own eyes in surprise and growled, "*Those* girls again!"

In short, everyone in that room was in a state of shock and surprise—everyone, that is, except one.

Miss Withering, Victorine noticed, had *not* leaped to her feet in horror *nor* screamed in terror and distress *nor* indeed reacted to the sudden entrance of a dangerous burglar as one would expect a frail and vulnerable old person to react. She had become, instead, a small island of chiffon and serenity in the middle of all that frantic turmoil.

Her wrinkled face was calm, amused, even shining.

This expression was so *wrong*, in the context of the current awful situation, that the temperature of Victorine's heart plummeted about fifty degrees, as if her soul had just opened a door and found itself in an entirely unexpected landscape, all ice and snow and peril. (And that, some obsessive corner of her mind still managed to notice, was *metaphor*, shifting to *simile*, shifting to *metaphor* again!)

The unfrightened, even radiant Miss Withering straightened up in her armchair and pointed commandingly at one of the cupboards built into the walls of that room—the cupboard closest to her chair, as it happened.

"Open that drawer there!" she said to the girls. "Open that now!"

Victorine looked at Dar, who widened her eyes and shrugged unhappily.

So Victorine walked over to the drawer and pulled it toward herself.

"Oh," she said (still half frozen).

It was—*of course*—filled with Babylonian cylinder seals, each displayed against a background of cotton wool.

"Miss Withering—" said Victorine, but Miss Withering interrupted her with a wave of her hand.

"Mr. Smith," she said. "The new additions for my father's collection, if you please!"

The burglar—"Mr. Smith"—lunged toward that drawer, and Dar and Victorine shrank to the side. And out of his pockets Mr. Smith drew two familiar little sacks, which he emptied, one by one, into the waiting palm of Miss Withering. Both times, she examined the little rolling pin of the cylinder seal, made admiring and satisfied sounds, and then passed it to Victorine with the command "Into the archive, my girl!"

Victorine did not know what else to do, so her hands went ahead and obeyed. She found herself placing each of those Babylonian cylinder seals—the very seals that had been swept off Victorine's bedside table at Mrs. Gish's house the night before—into its little waiting display case, while Victorine's eyes and mind looked on in growing alarm.

"But Miss Withering," she said finally (and she was rather amazed to find herself talking, given the imposing, unpleasant, and far-too-nearby presence of Mr. Smith). "Perhaps you do not know—surely you cannot know—these cylinder seals—I'm afraid these are the ones that have been stolen—from the

Metropolitan Museum, you know, and from the exposition in San Francisco—"

"Nonsense!" said Miss Withering.

"Nonsense?" said Victorine.

"Utter nonsense," said Miss Withering, and then she declaimed a few lines that accelerated quite as if rolling downhill—and then veered to one side at the bottom of the figurative slope: "They have been *collected*! And at great expense, I might add. But no matter. They have been *collected* so that they may join my great father's *collection*—you will have heard of my father, children, surely: Dr. Pritchard Withering, whom the *New York Times* once called 'the Greatest of Armchair Archaeologists,' you know, in a review of his book? *That* Pritchard Withering?"

Victorine could only shake her head. She had never heard of any Pritchard Withering at all, much less a Pritchard Withering who was "the greatest of armchair archaeologists." And Darleen (cheeks a little puffy and red) looked like someone trying very hard not to ask a saucy question about whether an "armchair archaeologist" was an *archaeologist* who collected *armchairs*.

"Then you girls are uneducated fools," said Miss Withering. "What a disappointment. I can tell from your faces, you know. You are wondering, why is she bothering with such old, old things today, in the twentieth century?"

That was not exactly the question uppermost in Victorine's mind, but Miss Withering shook a finger at her and went rolling right into her next sentence.

"Because I am modern! That's why! Do you know what those actually are, those little scrolls?"

"Babylonian cylinder seals?" murmured Victorine.

"Oh, posh! Listen, you girls! These are the very first *motion pictures*—yes, now you're surprised. They are the very *seeds* of the movies. That's what they are. Story machines, that's what my father used to call them. Pictures that unfurl from a turning reel! *They* printed them by rolling them out on clay, and *we* use celluloid film, but what tiny difference is that?"

"Oh," said Darleen. "Miss Withering, you really think the little rolling pins are like moving pictures?"

But surely there was more than a "tiny difference" between these ancient cylinder seals and a modern reel of film!

"My father understood how important these things were, didn't he? The movies had not been invented yet, but he somehow *knew*. He collected these seeds of the moving pictures! Oh, my girlhood was very happy, in our home under the great magnolia trees of Mississippi, surrounded by my father's treasures . . ."

Victorine saw Darleen give a little start; it was the word *treasures* that had done it, probably reminding her of Uncle Dan and all his woes.

"So it is right and fitting for me to honor him by

continuing his great project," said Miss Withering, spreading her tiny arms very wide, as if to emphasize how strongly she felt all these things. And then she bent forward and said, with great earnestness, "Tell me, girls, do you know what it is to have a family? To have a *family—tradition—*and a *past*?"

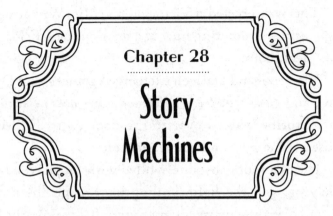

# Chapter 28

# Story Machines

*In simple language, there must be a reason why.*
—How to Write for the "Movies"

*A family! Tradition! And a past!*

Miss Withering's words went through Victorine like swords. She felt herself swaying for a moment, but steadied herself by putting a hand on the cool wood of the shelf.

"Well, I hope we do," said Darleen, pulling herself together. "We have those things, I suppose."

"Or have had them once," said Victorine very quietly.

"My father called them 'story machines,' didn't he?" said Miss Withering, ignoring anything the girls tried to say. "Yes, roll the things out in clay, and their story appears! And now the world has new kinds of story machines! Go open that door, girl—"

That was directed at Victorine, and Miss Withering's right arm was pointing now at a door on the far side of this great room.

Victorine and Darleen exchanged glances, and Dar gave an *I guess that doesn't seem too scary, does it?* shrug, so Victorine walked over to the door (with Darleen close behind her) and opened it wide.

It was a room absolutely filled with rough wooden shelving, and the light spilling in through the door glittered against many, many round, flat, shiny tins.

"Oh!" said Victorine. She had seen tins like these—many of them—back in Fort Lee, New Jersey.

And Darleen said, "Film reels!"

Then she spun around very fast to Miss Withering.

"You're keeping *films* here, Miss Withering? Just piled up on shelves like that?"

"They are the story machines of the new century, are they not?" said Miss Withering, evidently quite pleased with herself. "I am, you see, expanding my father's collection! In his honor!"

"But it's not *safe!*" said Darleen, with the urgency of someone who has grown up in a photoplay studio. "Miss Withering, look at you! You have a fire burning right this minute in the fireplace! And then right here in the next room—a hundred reels of film, just sitting there! Miss Withering, the films are made of celluloid—do you know what celluloid is?—it is so dangerous—"

"Pish posh," said Miss Withering. "I find that you

are both very tiresome children. And entirely uncourageous, unlike myself. I grew up in one world, you know—the lovely soft world of the South, long ago, where life was so easy and comfortable, and all I had to do was be beautiful all day long, while my father wrote about his Babylonians—and then that world ended, and eventually I moved out here and embraced the New—"

*Embraced the New?* thought Victorine doubtfully. Miss Withering was so old, and so withered, and so surrounded by things from centuries gone by. She seemed so very distant from anything *new*.

"My own dear story machines!" said Miss Withering. "And they, in turn, bring life again to the glorious old past. Have you seen Mr. Griffith's *Birth of a Nation*, girls? There is a story machine at work! That beautiful, true history—"

"Oh, dear," said Darleen, looking over at Victorine, who carefully closed the door behind which all those terribly flammable movie reels were sitting on their shelves, like bombs in an armory (flatter than most bombs, of course, but quite full of the potential for explosion).

"Yes, Miss Withering, we have seen it," said Victorine, once the door was closed and she could face the eccentric Miss Withering with what she hoped was determination and strength. "But you can't possibly call what that picture shows us 'true history' or the 'glorious old past.' It's all actors, you know. All made up. And a lot of those actors are people in blackface, pretending to be what they aren't so that they can make us think awful things about the past! How can that be glorious?"

"Rude girl," said the old woman, tipping her head away from Victorine. "Slandering the work of Mr. Griffith—and of the beautiful Lillian Gish! I was beautiful, too, you know, when I was young! Mr. Griffith understands. I'm sure he understands. He is from the South. And he is working right now on a picture about *Babylon*, do you understand? It is a sign! *It is a sign!*"

"A sign?" asked Darleen. "A sign of what?"

"A sign that *he* must be the one to make a picture about my magical girlhood, about my beloved father and his beloved story machines of the past—"

"Are you saying you want Mr. Griffith to make a photoplay about Babylonian cylinder seals?" asked Victorine.

"Not just about my father's story machine collection! Mr. Griffith is the one to bring my girlhood to life again! How lovely it was, when a person could just relax in the shade and feel comfortable, knowing a good dinner would be waiting at the end of the day, knowing her dresses would be sewn up overnight if need be. Comfort and luxury. Magical! That is the film Mr. Griffith must make! I have told him so many times. He must use his story machines to bring that magic back to life—"

"Oh, my," said Darleen. "You're hoping Mr.

Griffith will make a whole film about your magical childhood? I mean, about your father who collected very old things *and* about your magical childhood? Oh, my goodness. Vee, what would your Miss Parsons have to say about that?"

But Victorine found that it didn't even so much matter what Miss Parsons, author of *How to Write for the "Movies,"* might think of any of this—whether she would think such a story had "punch" or could be the useful basis for a photoplay.

In fact, Victorine felt a galvanizing chill run through her.

"Miss Withering, excuse me, but the thing is, that wasn't *magic* at all, what you are describing," she said. "*That* was never magic! That was living in a castle! That was someone else doing all the work, cooking all the dinners, mending all the dresses. There is nothing glorious about being used to other people doing all the work. Nothing glorious about thinking that perhaps you are special because other people are doing all the work. I know this very well, Miss Withering, because I—because I—"

—*used to live in a kind of castle, too*, was what she meant to say, but Darleen had already taken alarm and jumped in: "Oh, goodness, how late it must be! Mrs. Gish won't be pleased if we're out too late."

And Miss Withering, of course, leaped right on that little syllable and said, "*Mrs. Gish?*"

**Chapter 29**

# Perfect Little Messengers

*If we do not get these crises under control they may
make our story end differently . . . than we at first planned.*
—How to Write for the "Movies"

That was when the thief, who was still standing
there like the hulking menace he was, said, "Oh, yes,
ma'am, that's where they're staying, the little thieves.
Mrs. Gish shot her pistol right at me!"

(That was bold, thought Victorine. For the thief to
call *them* thieves!)

"How convenient this is, then," said Miss
Withering. "The perfect little messengers, to carry
my demands to Mr. Griffith."

"Carry your demands!" said Victorine, taken aback.

And Darleen said, "You mean, take him some
kind of a note? But we've never met him, you know.

And goodness, it's really, really time for us to go, isn't it, Vee?"

"Oh, yes, I think so," said Victorine, and she took Dar by the hand and let the impulse to escape from this place, to *run*, take over her feet. But only two quick steps later, the burglar—that awful man—had inserted himself in between the girls and the door of that room.

His face was ruddy and sweating again, as it had been days ago when he had first pushed past Victorine so rudely to get onto the train. And his voice was very rough: "But don't you understand me? These are *those* girls!" he said to the old woman in her armchair. "The thieves on the train! Them! You're not letting them get away?"

"Of course not," said the old woman. "Kindly bar the door, Mr. Smith."

Victorine glanced at Darleen and saw that her friend's eyes were busy, darting around the room, seeking, seeking, seeking some kind of escape. Victorine thought: *I am not here alone. We will find our way out. We will.*

"Now we both have something we want," said the old woman. "*You* want to leave through that door. And *I* want Mr. David Wark Griffith to use his story machine to honor my father and bring my lovely girlhood back to life. And that's not all I want. I want one of my father's story machines embedded into

Mr. Griffith's story machine! He has been building Babylon in Hollywood—I know, I know, my spies have told me. You must take one of these Babylonian cylinders I've collected in honor of my father and plant it in Mr. Griffith's new Babylon. The seed of moving pictures *planted* in a moving picture! Isn't that perfect? And from that seed, truth and beauty will grow, and *that* will be a proper tribute to my father, will it not? Take one! Take one from that drawer! Go!"

Darleen and Victorine looked at each other, and then Darleen shrugged and walked back to the drawer, where she picked out one of those cylinder seals that had already traveled so very far in its lifetime, from Babylon to New York to this strange house in Hollywood—and from the very far distant past to this confusing, chaotic Now.

The man at the door made some disgruntled sound.

Miss Withering laughed at him.

"Don't be discontented, Mr. Smith!" she said. "You will still be handsomely paid! You know I pay very handsomely! Open the third drawer from the bottom in the cabinet to the left of the door—do it now!"

He opened that drawer—and pulled out a paper envelope stuffed with money.

"That is yours," said Miss Withering. "And more to come, because you, Mr. Smith, are part of my insurance plan. These girls are deceitful—all young people these days are deceitful. And flighty and forgetful, I'm sure.

Children of the modern, careless era! Not as we were when I was young: thoughtful, careful, obedient. No! So how can I be sure they will do these tasks I have assigned them? Ah, the tasks. Let us put the children to the test: stand straight, girls! What are your tasks?"

"To plant this little rolling pin in Mr. Griffith's Babylon?" said Darleen, with wide and innocent eyes. Victorine was impressed by the skill with which Darleen was acting the part of a Very Good Child: polite, obedient, and oh-so-trustworthy.

"Yes," said the old woman. "Yes, in honor of my father. In the Babylon that Mr. Griffith is building at Hollywood and Sunset! That is your first task."

Darleen looked at Victorine and almost imperceptibly shrugged again—she obviously could not have dared to roll her eyes, but there was, nevertheless, a flicker of irrepressible light in them.

"Yes, Miss Withering," said Darleen. "Of course, Miss Withering. And now we are going."

Miss Withering waved a hand in the air impatiently.

"We are not done yet! What, then, is your other task?"

Here both girls were stumped, however.

"Foolish girls! Not listening! The young people, they never listen! You must tell Mr. Griffith to use his story machine to re-create my own girlhood—to create beautiful pictures of those happy years—my family— my father—my lovely young self—I was lovely, you know. I have preserved myself well! I can still wear my old gowns!"

She patted the chiffon all around her.

"Yes, Miss Withering!" said Darleen. "We understand you perfectly. Hiding a story machine in Mr. Griffith's Babylon and telling him you think he should make a moving picture about when you were young and your father was studying history and collecting rolling pins. We will get to work on all of it, right away. Come along, Bella Mae."

"Yes!" said Miss Withering. "But you haven't heard my threats yet."

She laughed, and that laugh was like a gust of cold wind through dead leaves. Victorine found herself shaking a little, in sympathy with those leaves.

"My *insurance* plan, that is," said Miss Withering. "To make sure you do these things. Number One: Our Mr. Smith! He will be watching you always! He is a rough sort, have you noticed? Do not go wandering near policemen, you girls, or *he will see*! Number Two: You are thieves and children! I can telephone the authorities quietly and have you put somewhere safe, can I not? And by the way, if you haven't noticed, I am remarkably single-minded and persistent. Have you noticed that?"

The girls looked around at that strange room, at the drawers holding the enormous quantity of Babylonian cylinder seals (gathered over the course of how many years?) and the door behind which were stored a possibly lethal number of moving picture reels, and what could they do but nod? Whatever else she might be, Miss Withering was also, clearly, *single-minded and persistent*.

"So what that means for you, young ladies—and this is Threat Number Three—is that you had better accomplish what I've asked of you, and promptly, or I will turn all my single-mindedness and persistence onto the sole task of *destroying your lives and careers*. And the careers of your family, whoever they may be. Have I made myself quite clear?"

Darleen squeaked slightly in horror, and at that point Victorine had had *enough*.

She pulled Darleen right out of that room, past the looming Mr. Smith (who was counting his money), down the hall, past the butler (if that was what he was) standing like a statue in the shadows, and out through the front door. At which point the girls began to sprint at full speed, eager to get as far away from that awful mansion as possible.

When they finally stopped running, and had finished gasping for air, Darleen turned to Victorine in some wonder. "Vee, you say you never leap boldly forth, but you sure did leap a moment ago!"

Victorine, trying very hard, managed a wobbly smile. "I guess maybe your courage, Darleen, has been gradually rubbing off on me all this time!"

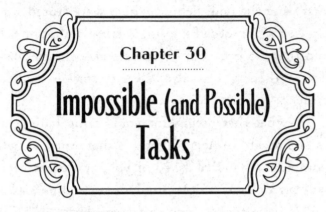

## Chapter 30

# Impossible (and Possible) Tasks

*This is just a way of showing you how one idea
suggests another, and thus you can take a simple incident and
build it up until you have both a plot and a climax.*
—How to Write for the "Movies"

W e simply can't seem to be rid of it, can we?" said
Victorine sadly. She was looking at the Babylonian
cylinder seal, once again lying on their little bedside
table at the Gishes' house.

"What do we do now?" said Darleen.

"I think we go to the police tomorrow morning, bright and early," said Victorine. "I think we go
quickly, before that really quite terrible Mr. Smith can
come after us again. I'm afraid we will have to confess
the truth and simply hope for the best."

That plan, desperate as it was, brought a certain
feeling of comfort to Victorine. She had been suffer-
ing from the feeling that they were getting themselves

ever more trapped in a kind of spiral of unintentional deceit. That weighed on her very much. Indeed, it was as if those little cylinders in her pockets were growing heavier and heavier with every passing day. She imagined what it would feel like to be suddenly free of all of these little guilty weights, and for a moment she almost floated.

But then the next morning, as they came out of the door bright and early, off to Universal City for a third day of filming, that dreadful burglar was waiting for them on the street, just lolling against a tree and looking mighty dissatisfied with his lot, too, it must be said.

"Oh, no," said Darleen. "I guess he's really watching us, then. We can't go to the police, Vee. He'll know."

Victorine's heart sank. Her pockets grew terribly heavy again. She had to struggle a little, not to shrink down under that awful weight.

*Be strong!*

(Sometimes a person has to speak very sternly to herself.)

"Don't let him see we've noticed him," said Victorine, straightening herself back up. "We'll go off to Universal, just as if everything were absolutely peachy, and then, while you're working, I'll do my best to come up with some sort of a plan, that's what I'll do."

At Universal the girls noticed (using peripheral vision so as not to alert the burglar to the fact they had spotted him) that Mr. Smith parked himself near the gates, but did not seem eager to come into Universal City through the official entrance. Which was a relief: it is unsettling to feel oneself being watched all the time.

Darleen went off to the dressing rooms, and Victorine wandered slowly, her mind full, toward the stands by the stages and toward all the incredible racket that went along with creating silent movies. Seven different pictures were being filmed at the same time on this particular day—so mixed into the general noise were the sounds of seven directors shouting different sorts of instructions on the seven stages in use for the day, while seven cameramen positioned their cameras in the best place for whatever the next image was they wanted to imprint on their long rolls of celluloid film. A couple of the scenes even had musicians playing along, to give the actors in that photoplay whatever the feeling was they most needed to be having at that particular moment. A photoplay actor had to have admirable powers of focus, that was sure, to be able to do a convincing job amid all that din and hubbub.

It was quiet and a bit lonely in the spectators' bleachers, however, without the cheerful presence of the contest-winning girls, who had so happily set off to San Francisco. But perhaps that was just as well.

Victorine was able to put her mind to the problem at hand, while reserving about fifteen percent of her attention to watch Darleen at work and make sure the director wasn't taking the picture in some perilous direction, involving water or other risky elements.

Today's scene seemed safe enough, however. It was a courtroom scene, with a judge (you could tell from the robe) sitting high above the rest of the set. Extras were brought in to sit in the jury, and there were even a few token "audience members" in chairs in front of the camera, to give the impression that the set was really a true courtroom, with all sorts of people there, eager to hear the outcome.

Darleen came in, dressed in her own short white frock (for those days when she wanted to look as young as possible). Apparently Universal, despite being so much more enormous than the studios in good old Fort Lee, also liked its actors to provide their own costumes when possible, to save a dollar or two. Today they were filming a later moment in the story, when the little orphan rescued by the old sailor or lighthouse keeper had been taken away and given to rich city people to raise, but had been languishing in all that luxury, without her beloved Cap'n there to love her. So this was the scene where the little girl was going to plead with the stern old judge—plead to be sent back to her lighthouse keeper—and move that judge to tears and compassion.

In short: no floods, no fires, nothing unreasonably risky for a young actress. Victorine was free to mull over the problem of Mr. Smith and Miss Withering's unreasonable demands. Her first instinct, as usual, was to open her helpful little book; after all, Miss Louella Parsons insisted that "one idea suggests another," which was exactly the sort of advice one longed for when facing the plot twists of life. But then she glanced again at the photoplay unfolding farther down that long stage, and saw a scene in some rich living room—in the corner of which stood a maid. And not just any maid, but a maid who radiated dignity and gave the distinct impression that if she had been given a better role to play, she would have acted everyone else on that stage right out of the (so to speak) water.

*Miss Waller!* said Victorine to herself. It was surely, certainly Miss Ruth Waller. Victorine patted the other book she had been carrying so carefully, the one wrapped up in brown paper, and jumped up from her spot on that bench with purpose and conviction. All the other problems that Victorine had to solve seemed so overwhelmingly difficult. But this, this was just something simple. Gloriously straightforward. This was delivering a package, and delivering a package— unlike evading hired ruffians, sidestepping the plans of a dangerous old lady, rescuing Uncle Dan, choosing a path in life, finding a new home for the beloved people of Matchless Photoplay, or, goodness, figuring out when a person has grown old enough to read secret letters from her Grandmama—is wonderfully, beautifully possible!

So she made her way to the alley running behind the photoplay stage, and there she *lurked*, trying to seem as unimportant and shadowlike as possible until, some minutes later, the actress, still in her maid's costume, came walking right by.

"Miss Waller?" said Victorine.

The woman was turning around, puzzled.

"Yes?" she said.

"Miss Ruth Waller, I mean? Whose brother is Mr. Freddy Waller?"

"Yes, that's right!" said the woman in surprise. "Why do you ask?"

"I have something for you!" said Victorine. "We met him on the train, you know, and he was talking about this book, and when he heard we were headed here, he wanted us to pass it along to you."

The woman hesitated a moment, and then she took the package from Victorine, turned it over a couple of times, and then unwrapped it.

"It's called *The Conquest: The Story of a Negro Pioneer*," said Victorine, a bit shyly. "Mr. Waller thought it would make a good motion picture."

"Ah, Freddy is always such an optimist. Maybe it would, but who would make a picture like that? Not the people here."

That was surely true. They stood there for a moment in silence. Then Miss Waller said, "I know some people who want to make pictures—not for white audiences, you know, but for ourselves. Pictures where *we* are the actors and the directors. Where I would not always have to be a maid, standing in the background."

Victorine nodded. How galling it must be always to be given the small, unimportant roles, no matter how much of a true actor one actually was.

"Well, thank you for the book, I'm sure," said Miss Waller briskly. "Maybe Noble Johnson will find it interesting. Who knows?"

"He's one of the people who wants to make films?"

"Yes, he's been talking about it. But at the moment he is busy being a Babylonian soldier for Mr. Griffith's big new picture."

"Really?" said Victorine, and she was rather awestruck by how those Babylonians kept coming into everything and popping up everywhere. "On that big set he's been building? Old Babylon?"

"Mmm-hmm," said Miss Waller. "I'm thinking I should just *pass this along* to him, as Freddy likes to say. And see what he thinks. Well, goodbye—what was your name?"

"Oh, I'm . . . 'Bella Mae Goodwin,'" said Victorine, and sighed. Sometimes she just felt so tired of wearing this particular mask. "I mean, that's what I'm called. Here. At the moment, anyway."

Miss Waller didn't follow up with any prying questions, however; she evidently had things to do and places to be. She simply nodded and walked off like someone determined to find a way forward, no matter what. So that was that!

*But there I've done one thing that needed doing,* Victorine said to herself as she turned back to the viewing stands. One very tiny thing, true. But as her Grandmama liked to say on hard days, *we take our small comforts where we can.*

Chapter 31

# New Ideas Baking

*The climax, we have decided,*
*is in a way the solution of your play.*
—How to Write for the "Movies"

Back on her bench in the viewing stands, Victorine returned to wrestling with the more impossible problem of how to do enough of what Miss Withering wanted done to keep that strange and ruthless old lady from destroying the lives and careers (and hopes) of all the Darlings, while not committing even more accidental crimes—like, for instance, actually leaving a priceless antiquity somewhere on the set of a photoplay in honor of Miss Withering's father.

By the end of that day, Victorine thought she might be close to an idea—an odd idea—but then, every part of this situation was odd, was it not?

"Darleen," she said as they headed back to the gates

of Universal City, "I have had a thought. Listen—if he is still out there, that Mr. Smith, then on the way back to Mrs. Gish's house, we have to go to the—don't laugh now, Darleen—the grocer's."

Darleen did laugh. Victorine couldn't really blame her. In fact, she laughed with her, but secretly inside she had a tiny little bubble of a thought: perhaps this strange plan of hers might actually work!

Of course, the girls were both hoping that the unpleasant Mr. Smith would have evaporated, like a bad dream, at the end of the day. But no. There he lolled, waiting for them outside the gates.

The worst moment was when he growled at them as they went by. One single word of warning: "Babylon!" That was enough to let them know that he knew they had not come any closer to fulfilling Miss Withering's bizarre demands. He knew where "Babylon" was located in Los Angeles, and Universal City was not that place.

They did not reward him with so much as a look; they simply ignored him. But of course *inside* they were not ignoring him at all!

At the grocer's, Victorine carefully bought a small quantity of flour and salt and powdered alum (often used in pickling and baking). Nothing that would raise the hovering Mr. Smith's suspicions in the slightest.

"I don't want to be borrowing everything from the Gishes," she explained to Darleen, after she had given her just the very briefest description of what she had in mind. "And we'll have to do our best to be very tidy too."

Although Mrs. Gish did pride herself on her "plain cooking," in fact on most nights of the week a Mrs. McNulty did the cooking, so when they arrived back home, Victorine and Darleen headed to the kitchen to mollify that good woman and gain access to a corner of her workspace.

"What sort of little cake do you want to be baking then, girls?" asked the cook.

"Not a very tasty cake, I'm afraid," said Victorine. "We have to make ourselves something out of modeling clay—well, the sort of dough that's so *very* much like modeling clay, you know! Anyway, it's a sort of prop that's needed, you see, for a photoplay."

"Oh, for a photoplay!" said the quite kindhearted Mrs. McNulty. "One of Mr. Griffith's, perhaps?"

"Well, yes, actually," said Darleen.

"Well, then, that's fine, isn't it?" Mrs. McNulty was used to photoplays governing the ins and outs of that household. "Go ahead, go ahead. But you won't be making a mess of my clean floors, now, will you?"

"Oh, no indeed, Mrs. McNulty," said Darleen. "We'll be so very careful, you'll see."

They borrowed a bowl and a mixing spoon, and they were indeed very, very careful as they huddled around their little table in the corner.

Victorine had remembered a trick her resourceful Grandmama had had, of making a substitute for fine modeling clay out of a very simple dough: flour, salt, alum powder, and some water. It was a good enough substitute to make a child very happy, and sometimes her Grandmama had hardened the little creatures Victorine had made from that day by baking them in a not-very-warm oven.

And now Victorine could pass on that little sample of her Grandmama's life lessons.

"If the oven's too hot, the clay risks cracking, you see," she said to Darleen. "But first we need to do our modeling!"

"With our little rolling pin!" said Darleen. She was clearly delighted to see what that "rolling pin" could do—for that matter, so was Victorine.

"And here it is," said Victorine, drawing the Babylonian cylinder seal, wrapped in a handkerchief so it wouldn't acquire any bumps or scratches, out of one of her very practical secret pockets. She was careful to speak very low so that Mrs. McNulty wouldn't be tempted to turn their way or bustle over to them.

Victorine patted together a little cake of the modeling dough and sprinkled some flour on the engraved and ancient stone so that it wouldn't dare stick.

"Oh, let me roll it out, won't you?" whispered Darleen happily.

Victorine handed it over, and Darleen rolled out a

neat strip of the cylinder's strange images: little people in skirts with many folds, some of them fighting those winged lions—or being eaten by them, perhaps. The figures stood out, solid and convex now, from the "clay" of that dough, the exact opposite of those hollowed-out images of the cylinder.

"It *is* a bit like a strip of celluloid film, isn't it?" said Darleen. "You roll it along, and the pictures repeat."

The movies were really—as Darleen and Victorine knew very, very well—an illusion produced by many, many little pictures printed on a very long strip of a special celluloid film, translucent to bright light, so they could be projected onto a screen or a light-colored wall. The eye and brain are mechanisms with certain very interesting habits: for instance, if they see many images very quickly in succession, and if each of those images changes only very slightly from the one previous, the eye simply cannot see those images as separate things—and the brain, to make sense of what it is perceiving, interprets all those many different images as one single image, *moving*.

The Babylonian cylinder seal's images did not repeat quite like the frames of a modern-day moving picture, but still they repeated, they rolled, the cylinder turned—quite a bit like a reel of film, if Victorine thought about it. She could almost see why that batty, dotty Miss Withering had decided that those ancient cylinder seals were the "seeds of the movies"!

While Darleen was busy rolling out her little "film" in the modeling dough, Victorine had formed two small cylinders of dough, roughly the same size and thickness of the Babylonian cylinder seal itself. And into each of those cylinders she carved the semblance of the "people" and "winged lions" that decorated the original.

She was not as fine an artist as whoever had carved those cylinders thousands of years ago. That was certainly true. And modeling clay made from flour and water was not at all the same substance as stone. But she made her little forgeries, and then she and Darleen put them into the coolest baking drawer of Mrs. McNulty's oven. And the other piece of dough, too, the one Darleen had rolled the actual cylinder seal across. They did want to keep a souvenir of that.

Ten minutes—that's all the little "clay" objects needed.

Then the girls brought them out carefully, using the thick towels so as not to burn their fingers.

One of the little cylinders had cracked, but the other looked just fine. It wasn't the same color as the original, but with a little paint or beet juice—why not?

And both girls were delighted with the way Darleen's "movie" had turned out: like the fanciest of Christmas cookies, but perhaps (they hoped) less fragile. They thanked Mrs. McNulty and then got out of her way while she finished fixing supper.

"Very neat, you've been," said Mrs. McNulty approvingly. "You should feel free to come down to do a little baking whenever you want, girls—you're not at all like that careless, harum-scarum Dorothy in the kitchen, thank all goodness."

(But she said that with fondness and affection.)

Then the girls scampered upstairs and hid their creations in their room.

"Now what?" said Darleen.

"Now we merely have to take this to Babylon, of course" said Victorine.

"Oh, yes!" said Darleen, brightening up. "Babylon! I wouldn't mind paying a visit to that fancy old town, would you?"

# Chapter 32

# Old Babylon

*No one need draw upon antiquity, or lure visions*
*from the clouds. Write something that tells the simple truth . . .*
—How to Write for the "Movies"

Supper that night was plain cooking: boiled mutton and potatoes, but very tasty for all that. And Mrs. McNulty had baked an apple pie, in some other, hotter compartment of that oven, and it was quite delicious.

"Miss Lillian," said Victorine over that pie, "we are really so curious about the Babylon section of that photoplay of Mr. Griffith's. Could you tell us more about it? I've always been interested in ancient history."

This was quite true, of course, so even though Victorine was trying something sneaky with her questions, she was also, at the same time, being perfectly sincere. And as it happened, her honestly interested tone of voice seemed to win over Lillian Gish's good feeling, despite Victorine's comments about Mr. Griffith the first evening.

"I don't mind telling you," said Lillian Gish, "that this part of the great photoplay Mr. Griffith is now making will be the grandest, largest, most fantastic motion picture world anyone has ever created. Have you seen the walls going up at Sunset and Hollywood? They will be more than a hundred feet high, and so broad that chariots can ride on them! They are about to film the battle scenes this coming week, you know."

"Oh!" said Darleen, and her sincerity was like light shining through glass. "We would *love* to see those sets. Do you think we might? It would be such a delight! We have never had anything so grand constructed for any photoplay back in Fort Lee."

"But you have very nice cliffs, you know, along the Hudson River," said Lillian Gish generously. "There are lots of photogenic places right around Fort Lee." She had made films in New Jersey, too, before Mr. Griffith had moved their operations out to Hollywood—and also she was, like her mother, a kindhearted person, basically, despite being one of the most famous of photoplay actresses.

"But the ancient city of Babylon, re-created! That would be wonderful to see," said Victorine. "Do you think—"

"Yes, yes, why not?" laughed Lillian. "The head builder's little daughter wanders around the place there from time to time, so why not some other girls? How about this coming Wednesday? Does that work for you? There will be battle scenes being filmed on Wednesday—should be quite the show."

"Wonderful, wonderful!" they said, since Darleen's last day of filming for the orphan-and-lighthouse-keeper-or-sailor picture was, conveniently, Tuesday. In their beds that night, they whispered their excitement and their not-quite-thoroughly-baked plans back and forth, from bed to bed.

"This next bit is the hard part, though," said Victorine. "We have to convince that Mr. Smith that we are doing exactly what he is supposed to make sure we accomplish."

"Convince him!" said Darleen with a shudder. "Do you mean—"

"Yes, I'm afraid so," said Victorine. "We will have to speak to that awful man. I guess I'll try to do it right away tomorrow morning. If I think about it any longer than that, I'm pretty sure I'll lose all of my nerve."

"Just don't spend the whole night trying to write the perfect speech in your head," said Darleen. "It doesn't help words be calm and convincing, Vee, if you are exhausted when you speak them."

Victorine's heart swelled a little then: how well Darleen knew her! Victorine had lost so much over the last couple of years—her Grandmama, her childhood home, even (in almost all circumstances) the truth about her past and her own true name—but she had gained Darleen, a sister and a friend, and how can such a great gain not go far toward outweighing those other, older losses?

"I wish my Grandmama could have met you!" said Victorine. "I do think she would have said exactly the same thing. But it's hard to keep one's mind from fretting and worrying and rewriting words you will need in the future . . ."

"It's hard, but you'll give it your best try," said Darleen. "Won't you? And so will I!"

They did their best. Victorine used the old trick of remembering (in order) all the Mother Goose rhymes she had had in one particular large book from her childhood. She was asleep before Jack and Jill had even started *up the hill, to fetch a pail of water . . .*

The next morning they were nervous at breakfast, but tried hard not to show it. And then out they went into the world for the journey to Universal City for another day of filming (Darleen) or of watching and reading (Victorine).

They felt the presence of their watcher, of that awful Mr. Smith, before they actually saw him.

They waited until they were around a corner or two, well out of view of the Gishes' house. And then Victorine took a deep breath, stopped in her tracks, and turned around.

The burglar was about half a block behind them, lurking, as he liked to do, close to trees and fences.

"You, Mr. Smith!" said Victorine, and it took immense courage to say those three words.

The man was clearly taken aback. He stood still for a moment, and then probably asked himself why he should be afraid of two young girls.

Mr. Smith stepped a bit closer—but not too close. He hung back just slightly, as if worried these girls might throw a butterfly net over his head and trap him or something.

"What do you want?" he asked.

"Actually, I would like to make your job easier," said Victorine, trying to stand very tall (although neither girl was actually tall in any literal sense of the word). "Because it can't be easy for you, surely, having to shadow us all the time. So I'm thinking we should have a conversation, you know, about what that old woman wants from you."

"It's *you* who need to do the things," said Mr. Smith with a curled lip. "You heard her: I'm just the insurance it all gets done. You're to have that fellow agree to make that moving picture for her, right? And plant one of those old knobbly things in that old man's pretend city he's had built for the pictures. Hop to it, why don't you, so I can stop wasting my time with all of this!"

Victorine took a deep breath to steady herself.

"Well, what I wanted to tell you, you see, is that this coming Wednesday, we are going to visit that set of Old Babylon that Mr. Griffith is having built at the corner of Hollywood and Sunset. We can leave the cylinder seal on the set then. And that means we'll have done what that Miss Withering wants, and you can tell her so. And then leave us alone forever."

The burglar frowned. He was clearly turning Victorine's proposal over and over in his mind, trying to find the flaw in it. He wavered—he almost gave in—and then he deepened his frown and shook his head.

"No," he said.

"What do you mean by 'no'?" said Darleen.

"First off, that's not all of it," said Mr. Smith. "You heard her. She wants that picture made about her by that famous movie fellow."

"Well, but that's not *your* concern, now, is it?" said Victorine, aiming to sound as confident as humanly possible. "Think about it, Mr. Smith. We can ask Mr. Griffith about that motion picture, certainly, but then he'll simply go on to discuss the particulars with Miss Withering, won't he? So that's not for you to worry about. Just the cylinder going onto the Babylon set, that's all. And we'll be doing that Wednesday."

Mr. Smith scratched his head.

"How'll I know you've done it?" he said. "She'll be saying, 'Prove it to me. That they have done what they were supposed to do.' Won't count without proof.

Seems to me it's easier if you're hit by an automobile or something, isn't it? Easier if I say, they crawled off to the police, or was going to, and so I tossed them in front of a great big omnibus and made sure they were squashed flat."

Victorine felt Darleen shudder.

"Not really," said Victorine. "If we're squashed flat by an omnibus, we can't do what Miss Withering wants. She won't be at *all* pleased if we're squashed. And we'll get you your proof—I have a plan for that. You'll see. Come on now, Darleen."

And she turned her back on the burglar (which was again a small deed that took enormous courage) and, with Darleen's hand firmly in her grip, stalked away.

"Rude girls," said the really quite awful Mr. Smith, raising his voice at their backs. "Guess you'll deserve your unpleasant demise, when it comes to that!"

"Ugh," said Darleen.

"Ignore him," said Victorine to Darleen. They were walking very fast now. "It's almost your last day on that picture at Universal—after today, we have two days off, and then there's Monday and Tuesday, and that's all that's left in your lighthouse adventure. And then Wednesday we visit the Babylon set and leave a cylinder seal there. And then surely this Mr. Smith will back off."

"But Vee, you heard him—we have to *prove* it to him somehow, that we've planted that foolish rolling pin thing in Mr. Griffith's Babylon. Do you really have a plan for that?"

"Yes, I do," said Victorine. "Don't you worry for a moment. You just focus on making them all cry today in your little-lighthouse-girl picture, Darleen, and then, when work's done, I'll show you exactly what we're going to do about *proof*!"

# Chapter 33

# One Small Magical Box

*Make people see life as it is, without preaching.*
—How to Write for the "Movies"

After all, they were not the sort of girls to give up. When you have been kidnapped and have climbed down sides of buildings and chased villains on trains and so forth—in real life as well as in the photoplays—mere threats and hurdles are not going to keep you down for long.

Once Darleen's filming had ended that Friday afternoon—only two days of work left on that film, imagine!—Victorine's peripheral vision noted the presence of that rather bored-looking burglar outside the Universal City gates, and she said (loudly enough that the Mr. Smith could hear what she said, if he bothered to listen), "Brief detour for us this afternoon, Darleen!

We will be dropping in at the Rexall drugstore before we go back to the Gishes'."

Darleen said, "I can't even guess what you have in mind now, Vee! Yesterday the grocer's, today the drugstore—tomorrow will it be buying ourselves lengths of taffeta or new hats, I wonder?"

"No taffeta, I promise," said Victorine. "We must conserve our financial resources, after all."

But in the drugstore she surprised Darleen by insisting with great confidence that what she wanted was one of the Kodak Brownie cameras—"A Brownie 2A, please, with a roll of film and a carrying box."

"A present for your brother?" asked the man at the drugstore as he got everything together.

"No," said Victorine. "Can't girls be enthusiastic about photography?"

"Don't see why not," said the man. "That'll be four dollars."

"Four dollars!" said Darleen in a horrified whisper. "But Vee, I thought you said—*conserving our resources.*"

"And that's a bargain, miss," said the man. "The fanciest cameras could cost you eighty dollars, easy! Hard to imagine, isn't it? Nothing wrong with a Brownie, though. Even the kiddies can use it just fine. Comes with an instruction booklet, you know, and if you mail in the postcard, you'll get six months of *Kodakery*, free of charge. That's their photography magazine. Full of tips and helpful advice. You'll be taking great pictures soon as can be. Bring the film back here, and we'll make the photographs up for you."

"Thank you," said Victorine. Her second machine in a few days! And she wasn't sure which one she loved more, to be honest, the Underwood typewriter or the Brownie camera.

Mr. Smith was waiting for them (at a distance) when they emerged from the drugstore, as they had expected.

Victorine actually waved at him, which was a bit cheeky. And then she said to Dar, in a nice loud voice, "And now we have a camera! Aren't you going to ask me what we're going to do with it, Dar?"

"Oh, yes! Do tell me what we'll be doing with this *camera*!" said Darleen, also very loudly. It was rather fun, actually, overacting this way for the benefit of Mr. Smith.

"Well, we'll be documenting our placement of the 'story machine' for Miss Withering, of course," said Victorine with diction and drama. "Nothing like a *photograph* for *proof*, am I right, Darleen?"

Mr. Smith seemed to follow the gist of this little scene pretty well, and once he had heard about the camera and the photographs and "proof," he actually dropped back a few feet and gave the girls a little extra room, which was nice.

Talking about the Brownie wasn't all "acting," of course—and the camera wasn't just meant to appease

Miss Withering's distrust. Victorine was full of grander plans for this adorable little Brownie.

"And Dar, even after the Babylon thing, it will still be so awfully useful to have a camera, don't you think? We can practice framing images, you know, and all sorts of things that may even help us make better moving pictures in the future, not just photographs. Lots of work for us this weekend, getting to know our Brownie better!"

It was a wonderfully absorbing couple of days. Whenever they were not out looking for pretty trees to photograph—and reminding each other which little window to look through on the outside of that box to see what the camera would see (the windows were called "viewfinders," which is a very poetic sort of word, if you think about it, and there was one on one side of the box for horizontal pictures and another on the next side of the box for helping you take pictures in a vertical position)—Victorine was pounding away on the typewriter, becoming more and more confident about the location of all the letters as she worked to type up her very first effort as a photoplaywright: the entry for the *Vanishing of Victorine* contest.

It was astonishing to her how much progress she had made over the past couple of weeks. When she had stepped on that train in New York City, her little notebook had been almost empty. But she had worked faithfully and hard, had filled up those pages with notes and ideas, and then turned those scribbled words into something quite new: a glimpse of a fictional Victorine's fictional journey into a fictional future (which Victorine had finally decided to set in *Europe*, so as to put possible snoops well off the track of Hollywood). And all of this was written in true photoplay style, such as might even have satisfied her faithful teacher, Miss Louella Parsons. Of course, the thing was rather short: contest entries are not meant to be very long. But still, typing up the final product was a challenge. New skills always are.

But it could have been worse! All of those years spent practicing the piano had left her with strong and flexible fingers, quite capable, it turned out, of learning to dance across the keys of a typewriting machine.

"Look at that!" said Darleen, looking over Victorine's shoulder. "That really looks like an actual photoplay scenario, Vee! Are you sending that in?"

"I am," said Victorine, with some satisfaction. "I bought envelopes already. I'm sending one copy to Miss Weber, because she was curious, and one to the *Vanishing of Victorine* people."

She sighed, because various emotions were wrestling with each other in her chest. She had enjoyed sending off her Victorine Berryman to the shores of

Lake Geneva, where her fictional older self would live out her days in the luxurious rooms of the Montreux Palace Hotel, a place she had actually stayed as a child with her Grandmama, not that long after it had opened. Luxuries everywhere in that hotel, she remembered— hot and cold running water in all the rooms!

Writing it all out this way made her miss her Grandmama, of course. But she also realized, while flinging fingers firmly against the typewriter's metal keys, that she did not really envy the fictional Victorine her life of luxury. So much better, honestly, to be here in Hollywood, learning to use typewriters and cameras—becoming a person who could hope to support herself one day.

And then there was a third feeling, too: the thrill of having *made up* this fictional Victorine. She was frankly amazed that she had managed it. The truth was something very precious—she still felt that in every morsel of her being. But here's the strange thing she seemed to have learned, as she wrestled with note-books and ideas and typewriters: truth and fiction can speak to each other on occasion like good friends, and the dialogue between the two of them can then take on a power and beauty all of its own.

"Oh, Vee, you'll win that contest for sure," said Darleen. "Seven hundred and fifty dollars! Just think of it! We'll be rich!"

"Shh, shh," said Victorine. "Who knows how they

judge these things? My Grandmama never raised a single hen or rooster, but she did remind us frequently not to count chickens before they hatch!"

When it came to the little Brownie box camera, the girls were far ahead of most beginners: they had a photoplay studio's worth of understanding about lenses and apertures and advancing the film and exposure times and so on. After the larger cameras they were used to seeing on the moving picture sets, this little Brownie seemed to them a small gem: only three and a quarter inches by five inches by six inches!

"Off to Babylon tomorrow!" they reminded each other (and the lurking Mr. Smith) on Tuesday, and they made a point of waving that camera around where he could see it, just to remind him they had Miss Withering's odd quest well in mind.

They had been careful not to use up their film on pretty trees. There were twelve pictures on that roll, and by the time Wednesday morning dawned, they still had film for nine photographs left.

A car came to pick up Lillian very, very early, and the girls squeezed in beside her.

"What role are you playing in this picture, Miss Lillian?" asked Darleen.

Lillian laughed.

"I do think my main role has been to be the Everything Person," she said. "I have been helping with the research, with organizing things, with everything. But as far as the actual acting goes—just a few minutes' worth of me very symbolically rocking a cradle. That's it! And here we are . . ."

There were walls set up around the lot to protect the construction project from unwanted eyes, but you could still see scaffolding and large towers rising up beyond the barriers.

"Welcome to Babylon!" said Lillian. "Come right this way . . ."

There were a lot of horses and men in bits of strange-looking armor milling about.

"They'll be doing the last-minute preparations for the beginning of filming the great battle, you know," said Lillian. "The Persians attacking Babylon! No one has ever seen a scene like this one, I promise you. Today they're getting images of the horses on the walls, and some of the big shots of the battle. Might be rather tricky, because horses don't much care for balancing on tall, narrow walls, it turns out."

"Not so surprising, is it?" said Victorine, craning her head back to look at the walls. Her stomach did a bit of a wobble, just seeing how high those walls were. More than one hundred feet, Lillian Gish had said! Victorine shuddered.

"Goodness, no. Not surprising in the slightest," said Lillian.

"What fun this is!" said Darleen. Her eyes were

shining. Well, of course! Darleen was a person who really very much enjoyed dangerous, high places, hard as that always was for Victorine to understand or even imagine. "Miss Gish, do you think we could go up that wall? Just quickly, you know, right now, before the horses need to climb it? I would love to see what it's like up there!"

Lillian Gish laughed.

"Aren't you brave!" she said. "Too bad you're not a tall strapping fellow, Darleen—we are trying to talk the extras into being willing to leap off the walls for a little extra pay . . ."

"Oh, I'd do that," said Darleen.

"I'm sure you would," said Lillian, and then she checked her fancy watch. "I'm due in the office! Girls, it's in that building over there—do you see it? Go ahead and scamper up the walls if you want to take a peek—no interfering with anyone, naturally—but in ten minutes I'll expect you in the office building, meek and unharmed."

"Yes, Miss Gish," said Darleen. "And thank you so much!"

There was a long ramp that the horse-drawn chariots were going to take to get themselves up on the top of this complicated set, and Darleen and Victorine trotted up that slope now, quickly. There wasn't a minute to waste, was there?

They got up to the top. Victorine felt not just

peculiar, but awful. Thoroughly awful. Her head was spinning, and there was an unpleasant warm buzz in her legs and chest, as if her feet might really just give out and send her toppling to the ground, so many, many feet below.

"Look at that tower over there, Vee!" said Darleen as the wind blew her hair out behind her face. "It's so enormous, and look! It's on wheels!"

Victorine glanced in that direction and felt herself going green.

"Siege tower," she gasped out. She had seen drawings of such things in history books.

Darleen gave her a very sharp glance.

"Oh, dear," she said. "I don't think you're doing all that well, are you, Vee? Can you take a picture anyway? Get the Brownie ready—and hand me that lovely fake cylinder seal, won't you? We'll get this done very fast."

It helped, actually, to have a task to focus on. Victorine fetched the little fake cylinder out from one of her hidden pockets and handed it over to Darleen. Then she got the Brownie camera ready, and Darleen made a great show of holding the cylinder and then planting it in a crack in the wooden battlements of that enormous wall they stood on.

Victorine looked through the viewfinder, wound the film forward, and pressed the button to imprint a picture on the roll of film inside the Brownie camera.

Five or six times she repeated that series of actions—surely one of those photographs would come out clearly enough to convince Miss Withering that her nonsensical task had been safely accomplished.

"Now can we go back down to the office?" she then allowed herself to say, trying not to mind the wobble she heard in her voice.

"I suppose we must," said Darleen as she turned around to admire the view from up here (the very same view that Victorine was trying to ignore). "Look, there's the platform for the camera! Goodness! It's up even higher than we are!"

At that Victorine could only make a slightly horrified gurgling sound.

"Here," said Darleen. "Hang on to me, Vee. There. That's better, right? Can you look now?"

Victorine looked: to the right and ahead of them were more of these massive walls. Fake palm trees decorated the ground below—so very far below. Farther away from the wall was that massive tower on wheels. Farther away still—the ordinary, everyday buildings of Los Angeles. Behind the girls (yes, she even managed to turn and look the other way!) was that platform Darleen had noticed, with a large camera already perched on it, waiting for its cameraman.

"Very nice," said Victorine as bravely as she could. "Let's go back down."

Darleen laughed a little, but fondly, and they made

their way back down the ramp and to the plain little building that held the necessary offices for this enormous film set.

"Shall we knock?" whispered Darleen when they got to the door of the central office there.

"Of course," said Victorine. Office doors didn't frighten *her*! She knocked on the door—a voice called to them to "come on in"—and in they went—

Only to find themselves facing not just Lillian Gish, but also a tall, slender man who must be the eminent Mr. Griffith—and that was not all:

Ensconced in a big armchair—in a big chair now simply overwhelmed by lacy white skirts—was a familiar and very unwelcome face, belonging to someone apparently too impatient to wait quietly at home for news about the progress of her various schemes: none other than that wicked old Miss Withering herself!

# Chapter 34

# Battles, Large and Small

*Every great story, play, or photoplay must have suspense—*
*the intense moment, when the outcome is uncertain, when the unreal*
*plays upon our emotions with the strength of the real.*
—How to Write for the "Movies"

Darleen gasped. Victorine, trying to think very fast, squeezed Darleen's hand to keep her quiet. It is never wise to give anything away before you know as much as you can possibly figure out about your current circumstances.

It was bad enough to see that strange old woman with her staring, glittering eyes, but in that extra second of hush, Victorine saw, to her dismay, that standing right *behind* Miss Withering was none other than that really very terrible Mr. Smith.

Why were they here? And how had they gotten here?

Worse yet, Mr. Smith narrowed his eyes at

Victorine and Dar and then leaned and said something into Miss Withering's ear that the girls could not quite hear.

Victorine's heart was rabbiting away, and she could feel Darleen's pulse—equally speedy—in her hand.

"About time!" said Miss Withering, stretching out her hand toward Victorine. "I'm here for my photographs! Mr. Smith said you would have photographs for me."

Lillian Gish and Mr. Griffith stared at her in blank puzzlement.

"Photographs, Miss Withering?" said Lillian Gish.

"These girls! They're supposed to have photographs for me! Of my cylinder seal, seed of the cinema, planted here in Babylon!"

"Oh, dear," said Lillian Gish.

"I'm afraid you must be rather confused," said Mr. Griffith.

"Mr. Smith!" said Miss Withering in a commanding voice. "Tell them! Tell them!"

"Photographs!" barked Mr. Smith. "Wednesday! Babylon! Photographs! That's what they said."

And then he went back to glowering silently (which he really did very well).

"*That's* a camera, isn't it?" said Miss Withering, pointing right at the Brownie in Victorine's hands. "Isn't it?"

"Good heavens," said Lillian Gish, as if she had

just figured everything out. "You saw the girl's little camera, and that's what got you all muddled, Miss Withering?—Mr. Griffith, I'm so sorry. I had no idea Miss Withering could be so . . . *misled*."

"HA!" interrupted Miss Withering. (But then, everything she said had the pinch of an interruption.) "Slandering me, are you, Miss Gish? What a disappointment you are! And *you*, girl—"

That last phrase was directed at Victorine, and Miss Withering's voice was now so sharp it might as well have been a dart, an arrow, or a shard of glass.

"Tell me where my photographs are, then!" the old lady was saying.

Victorine gathered her courage. She told herself to stay calm. She said, as calmly and reasonably as she could manage, "But Miss Withering, you do know that photographs take time to develop? You can't take a photograph one minute and hand it over the next. It takes days if you're not doing the developing yourself—if you have to take the film back to the Rexall drugstore, you know, to be processed."

"The girl is quite correct," said Mr. Griffith, looking at Victorine with some curiosity. "And what's your name, little one?"

(Mr. Griffith was so tall that having him call her "little" didn't even bother Victorine.)

"But Mr. Griffith, these are the girls I've been telling you about!" said Lillian Gish quite brightly.

"The girls who are staying with my mother just now: Darleen Darling, you know, who has been in all those adventure serials Matchless makes, and her friend Bella Mae . . . Goodwin. (Have I got your name right, Bella Mae? Somehow it always does its best to escape my mind.) Out here from Fort Lee."

While Miss Withering sputtered icily on her side of the room, Dar and Victorine each had the chance to shake Mr. Griffith's long, thin hand. His forehead during this formal greeting was pleated with lines of worry and concern, however, as well it might be, considering the strange old woman muttering at him a few feet away, not to mention all the walls and towers and horses and battles that were about to go into action on the huge lot outside.

"Charmed, charmed, I'm sure," tall Mr. Griffith said, rubbing his narrow chin after the hand-shaking. "And you girls came out here to Hollywood on your *own*? I know we live in modern times, but that seems a bit—reckless, Lillian, doesn't it?"

"Oh, we didn't come here alone, Mr. Griffith!" said Darleen. "That is, we were with my Uncle Dan. But he got—delayed—in Ogden, and we had to come on ahead. Miss Weber wrote to Utah, though, so Uncle Dan will surely be here very soon. I'm sure he will— he's a cameraman," she added, loyally, at the end.

"He's a very good cameraman," said Victorine.

Mr. Griffith smiled slightly. "I'm sure he is," he said.

"Enough of this!" said Miss Withering rudely. "Before these girls barged in, we were talking about *my picture*, weren't we, Mr. Griffith?"

Mr. Griffith made a slightly strangled sound.

"*My picture*," said Miss Withering. "About *me*. To be made by *you*. Scenes from my glorious youth—my education at the knee of my eminent scholar father—our old home under the magnolia trees—coming to life on the screen. And in exchange, of course, I am willing to contribute financially to your artistic endeavors—to contribute immensely, I might add. There! *Song of a Southern Girlhood!* I have thought about it, and it will make a most wonderful photoplay."

She patted a small sack slung over her shoulder. "My helpful notes!" she said. "You, Mr. Griffith, will have the chance to bring all of my beautiful past *back to life!*"

Mr. Griffith looked rather put-upon. Also perplexed. As well he might!

"I'm afraid, Miss Withering, that I never make my pictures to satisfy other people's whims," he said.

Miss Withering made a ratcheting sound of displeasure.

"*Whims!*" she said. "Are you so careless, then, with the desires of your most fervent supporters? Because, Mr. Griffith, I assure you I have been perhaps the most fervent of all of your supporters—"

"I'm so sorry, Mr. Griffith," said Lillian Gish,

moving in between Miss Withering and Mr. Griffith, as if to protect him from her deluge of nonsensical words and thoughts. "I truly had no idea that this Miss Withering was so, so—"

"So *what*, young lady?" said Miss Withering. "Oh, now I'm growing quite displeased! Do you refuse, then, Mr. Griffith? Do you refuse my aid, my ample cash, my suggestions? Do you *refuse* to have your story machine devote itself to re-creating my radiant girlhood?"

"Use my cameras to make a picture of your youth? Yes, I certainly do refuse that," said Mr. Griffith. "I do refuse. Good day, Miss Withering. Miss Gish, please show our guest the door."

Lillian Gish, looking quite distressed by the way this meeting had gone so totally awry, moved toward the office door.

"You dare! You dare!" said Miss Withering. "Then I will bring it all down! I will destroy it all! I will explode your Babylon! Your pretty empire shall be undone!"

"Oh!" cried Darleen.

Because suddenly that awful Miss Withering was wielding an actual pistol (with a pretty pearl handle)—and she had that pistol pointed at Mr. Griffith himself!

Everyone froze. Miss Withering with a gun!

"Miss Withering," said Mr. Griffith, using his director's voice. "Please put that away directly."

"I most certainly will not," said Miss Withering. "You have all disappointed me most dreadfully. *This* Babylon is not worthy to house the ancient seed of the cinema! It is all a disgrace! I revoke my blessing! You girls! What have you done with my cylinder seal? I mistrust you and your lack of photographs! You must fetch me back my cylinder immediately!"

"What cylinder?" said Lillian Gish. "What do these girls have to do with any cylinder?"

But Miss Withering ignored her.

"I no longer care to honor my father by leaving real treasures in this fool's Babylon! Go and get me my cylinder! Or Mr. Smith will plant dynamite instead! Won't you, Mr. Smith? Show them what's in your pockets—"

Mr. Smith obligingly pulled another type of cylinder out of his pockets, and Darleen gasped.

"Vee, is that—"

"Yes," said Victorine. "I'm afraid it is. Stay very still, Darleen!"

It was a stick of dynamite.

"That's what you will have done, Mr. Griffith, with your stubbornness," said Miss Withering. "This Babylon will fall!"

All of them in that room held their breath, turned into statues for a moment by sheer surprise and alarm.

"Well, go!" said Miss Withering to Darleen and Victorine. "My cylinder! Fetch it back now! If you aren't back in ten minutes, or if you foolishly try to bring the police back with you, I'll shoot this ungrateful Mr. Griffith—I will. Perhaps Miss Gish, too, since she has disappointed me as well. Don't you doubt it."

"Girls, run," said Mr. Griffith, gesturing to the door. "Get them away from here, Lillian."

"Oh, not you!" said Miss Withering to Lillian Gish. "No. The other ones—go! Ten minutes!"

"Go!" said Mr. Griffith.

Victorine looked over at Darleen, who nodded grimly.

"Come on!"

Darleen was already pulling her toward the door.

"We will be back," said Victorine to the room already mostly at her back. "We'll be very quick. Don't do anything terrible, Miss Withering, *please* don't—"

And they were through that door and running, running like the wind—right into sunlight and all the confusion and noise of battle.

Because outside, the day's filming had begun: Babylon was under attack.

# Chapter 35

## The Fall of Babylon

*Directors do not like to produce a scenario that calls*
*for too elaborate sets, unless, of course, it is a big feature . . .*
—How to Write for the "Movies"

There were now people everywhere—cameramen in their high perches, horse handlers trying to keep their four-legged charges calm, and extras! Hundreds of extras, wearing strange helmets and fake bits of armor.

"We will stick out like sore thumbs in these dresses," said Victorine in frustration. "Sore, white, frilly thumbs."

Darleen was looking around.

"Over there, quick!" she said. There was a bin filled with nondescript cloaks—the sort of costume (or costume substitute) that might be fine on an extra far from the camera, or for a crew member trying not to look too modern, in case he actually ended up inside the frame.

The girls put on the smallest cloaks they could find, covering every last trace of their much-too-modern 1915 dresses, and then looked anxiously up the wall where they had hidden the fake Babylonian cylinder.

"Really, what's the point of fetching the fake one back?" said Darleen, with some doubt. So much was going on up on that wall now, and she had been trained since babyhood not to interrupt a performance, not to stumble onto the stage when other people were on it. "She'll want the real cylinder thingy, Vee. She won't settle for dough baked in the Gishes' kitchen."

"I have a plan," said Victorine, and somewhere deep inside herself she realized, almost to her own surprise, that she was telling the truth. She *did* have a plan—or at least the rough outlines of a plan. "You run up there, Darleen, and fetch that cylinder from where we hid it, and meanwhile I'll figure things out in my head. Just hurry, hurry, hurry, please."

Up at the top of that ramp there was a chariot moving along the walls, pulled by some very nervous horses. And extras waving their spears at the great tower that was being rolled forward by many other extras. In short, all was pretty much chaos, with instructions being shouted by men through bullhorns, while up on their perches, the cameramen cranked happily away.

"All right—time to do my best to be a Babylonian

soldier," said Darleen. "A short one. Well! Here I go! Wish me luck."

And she darted forward and up the ramp leading to the top of that wall.

She was so nimble, Darleen! And so strong! And so fearless when it came to heights!

"Go, go, go!" Victorine said—to herself, since Darleen was already too far up to hear any words from her.

She watched Darleen make her way up the ramp, being careful not to get in the way of the horses, and also being careful to pause from time to time to shake a fist in the direction of the "enemy" (the approaching siege tower), the way the other extras were doing. She was an actress, after all! She knew how to get her acting cues from the people around her.

She even cleverly paused from time to time, as if offering water or something to the "soldiers" on the walls.

Now Victorine had to crane her head back to see her friend way up on those walls.

The siege tower lumbered forward, pushed by lots of extras. The noise everywhere was deafening.

Although she didn't for a moment take her eyes away from Darleen's progress high atop the 150-foot wall, Victorine gave her head a slight shake, to clear it and to dislodge the distraction of that terrible din.

*I'll have the fake cylinder,* she thought. *And then—*

It was Miss Parsons's book that was coming to her rescue again: *How to Write for the "Movies."*

Because wasn't a "plan" really just a way of telling a story?

A story always has to have its audience in mind.

*Miss Withering,* thought Victorine. *A story for Miss Withering . . .*

And then, at that moment, just as the final bits and pieces of a story began to assemble themselves in Victorine's anxious brain, she blinked and saw that Darleen, way above her on the wall, had reached the place where they had placed the fake cylinder. Victorine saw her reach in and grab. She saw Darleen go to the edge of the wall again, to shake her acting fist at the approaching siege tower. She saw the extras on the siege tower throw their (hopefully not very dangerous) spears! And then she saw—

she saw Darleen—

on top of that tall, tall wall—

fling her hands in the air as if struck by something—

and JUMP!

Victorine screamed!

Nobody probably heard her scream—it was so busy on the set.

Had Darleen gotten so caught up in the thrill of acting that she had forgotten this was all make-believe?

"Darleen! Oh! *Darleen!*" cried Victorine, running forward and to the left side of the wall.

Victorine had been through many very, very hard times over the past couple of years, but these moments while she was recklessly running into the action on that set, dashing around the wall to see what had happened to Darleen—these were probably the worst ten seconds she had ever suffered in all her life.

She came around the end of the wall; she was breathless, sobbing for air, absolutely clobbered by dread—

And there was Darleen, gently bouncing up and down in a huge net that had been strung up below the wall. She was bouncing, bouncing, and grinning ear to ear.

"Did you see that, Vee? Did you?" And then, a moment later, as she scrambled to the edge of the net and caught sight of Victorine's expression. "Oh, Vee! What's wrong?"

"You fell off the wall!" said Victorine. "I thought—"

She had to put one hand on the wall itself, to steady herself now.

"I jumped into the net," said Darleen. "With our cylinder! How much time is left, Vee?"

Almost no time was left!

And the girls started running again, back to the office where the awful Miss Withering was waiting, with one eye on the clock and (oh, horror) one bony finger on the trigger.

# Chapter 36

## One Desperate Plan

*Your climax is the big scene where all the loose threads are*
*taken up and woven together into the big moment.*
—How to Write for the "Movies"

At the steps that led into the little office building, Victorine held out her hand to Darleen for the cylinder that they had created and baked up in the Gishes' kitchen so very recently.

"Here we go!" she said.

They nodded to each other—more like soldiers going into battle than any of those extras fighting off the invading forces on the movie set's great wall!—and Victorine, before fear could get in her way, opened the door.

She did remember to knock first, and then to open it quietly and calmly, because people can be very unpredictable when startled, especially when they are under stress and wielding a pearl-handled pistol.

"Miss Withering, you see we're back!" she said as they entered.

"Took you long enough," said the old lady. "Half a minute more, and—"

"We honestly went as fast as ever we could, Miss Withering," said Victorine. "And I have the cylinder seal here—just let me show you what I have—"

She was moving closer to Miss Withering as she opened her hand. She kept her feet moving smoothly and slowly; she kept her voice low and soothing. She used all the good manners that had been trained into her during her childhood in the "castle" on Fifth Avenue in New York City. She was perfectly, perfectly calm and polite—

After all, her Grandmama had always said that when confronting a tiger, remaining calm and polite was of the utmost importance. "You may yell at a bear, Victorine," her Grandmama had said, "but I would advise remaining very civil when facing a tiger."

And Miss Withering was definitely a tiger.

"What's that, you girl?" said Miss Withering, glancing at the little blobby "rolling pin" on Victorine's palm.

"Well, as you can see, Miss Withering," said Victorine. "It is a cylinder seal."

"Not *my* cylinder seal!" said Miss Withering. "What have you done with my valuable, ancient

Babylonian seed? That blobby thing there is a fake! And a very poor fake too. Ha! Look at it! What a mess. No one could mistake that thing for something real—"

Victorine tried not to take offense—she had been rather proud, to be honest, of her work on this cylinder seal made out of dough, but never mind that now. She forced herself to stay calm and calmer and even more calm.

"But do we always *know* what is real, Miss Withering?" she said. "I think a lot about the truth, you know. I do. I think about it all of the time. About what it means to be truthful in a world filled with movie sets and stories. Have you ever felt your name and past beginning to slip away from you, Miss Withering? Because I have felt that. And I used to think what I had to do to be truthful was to hold on very tightly—so tightly—to those things I was used to thinking of as true—"

All this while, Victorine was working so very hard to keep her voice as smooth as possible. There must not be the slightest hitch or hiccup in her words or in her movements as she politely, smoothly came closer to the old lady ensconced in her puff of a dress—and to that old lady's pearl-handled pistol.

"But sometimes one has to let go of old things, Miss Withering. Sometimes the world we belong to needs a different sort of object. A different story. And *this* cylinder seal, this one here, was meant for a moving picture set! What kind of artifact—what kind of truth—is most fitting for the world of the photoplay? Don't you see, Miss Withering: someone was thinking about that question very hard! Someone has taken the care to study your Babylonian cylinder seal so very carefully. Look, look, someone has made"—she was very close to Miss Withering now and spoke in as confiding a sort of voice as she could muster—"this lovely little seal, this handsome replica—something true to the spirit of the moving pictures. What sense does it make to ask it whether it's truly its original self when it is, in fact, a *prop*!"

And here, Victorine did something else she had learned from her Grandmama long ago. Without any warning, her own smooth, unhurried, calm right hand suddenly *slapped* right down on Miss Withering's wrist, and forced the pistol down and to one side.

Victorine might not be as strong as Darleen, but she had caught Miss Withering by surprise—along with everyone else in that room. There was a second of general shock, and then all chaos broke loose.

The burglar, Mr. Smith, seeing that the jig was up, suddenly sprinted forward, pushed Lillian to one side—still rude to the core!—and ran straight through that door and away.

Darleen jumped to Victorine's side, and the two of them carefully finished wresting that pistol right out of Miss Withering's hand.

Lillian Gish sprang over to the door, flung it open, and called for help.

Mr. Griffith (after failing to get a grip on the fleeing Mr. Smith) came over and helped restrain Miss Withering, who was absolutely shaking with surprise and rage, and was surprisingly strong for someone so tiny.

"But you should *thank* this brave girl, madam," he said to her sternly. "You should. She has saved you from committing a terrible crime."

"Fiddlesticks!" said Miss Withering in disgust. "Fiddlesticks! Fiddlesticks! Fiddlesticks! Thieves, these girls are! Thieves! *Where is my cylinder seal?*"

Soon enough the police arrived, gathered up and removed the raving Miss Withering, asked questions of everyone who had been in that room, and at the end of the interview shook the hand of "Bella Mae Goodwin" and said she had indeed been a very brave young lady.

That was when Victorine jumped a little and fetched another small cylinder out of a deeper, less obvious pocket.

"*This*, you'll find, is the actual antiquity—a real Babylonian cylinder seal," she said. "Miss Withering had it stolen to be hidden here, on the set of Babylon. But I wasn't going to hand it back to her!"

"Quite right," said the officer. "That's a valuable object, that is."

"It's a great relief to have it out of my hands," said Victorine, with complete and utter honesty.

"Now that everything's under control," said Mr. Griffith, perhaps ten minutes later, "I had better go attend to my battles out there. Good day, everyone—"

He was already turning to leave when Victorine took a step toward him and said, "Oh, Mr. Griffith!"

Mr. Griffith turned back. "Yes, my dear?"

Victorine steadied herself. What she was about to say was really the most like stepping out onto a 150-foot wall that any speaking up could possibly be.

"If the movies can change people's views of the world—if they can influence them for good or ill, then—"

"Goodness, child. Are you talking about that old lady there? She had simply lost her mind, that's all."

"But she thought *Birth of a Nation* was true history. She wanted more of what it showed her. That's why she wanted you to make a picture about her family. And *that's* why she ended up threatening you with a gun. And that's—that's—"

"You are clearly very upset," said Mr. Griffith, and he beckoned to Lillian Gish. "Do make sure these children are taken care of."

"But if moving pictures can change the world—" said Victorine more urgently, because she could feel the moment slipping past her; she could feel her own feet losing their purchase on this tall and flimsy wall of words. "If they can change things, doesn't that make us all terribly *responsible* for everything we do or make, all the time?"

It was no use, of course. Mr. Griffith tipped his head in a polite goodbye. He opened the door and walked out into the chaos of his imaginary battle—imaginary battles that could someday somehow change the shape of the real world. He left the girls behind.

"Oh, Vee," said Darleen, her arms strong around Victorine's shoulders. "Don't you cry! How brave you were, you know. You saved all of our lives! I guess *you* just changed a little bit of the world!"

*Not enough of it,* thought Victorine. So much harm being done by so many people in so many ways—didn't seem like anything any one person did to fix things would ever be enough.

And then she shook herself.

Despair (her Grandmama used to say) is giving up trying. It is important to *try to keep trying.* That is all a human being can do.

And anyway, Darleen was looking at her with fond and compassionate eyes.

"Have some butterscotch, maybe, Vee?"

Darleen knew her very well: Victorine always had a roll of restorative butterscotch candies in a pocket somewhere, ready to help out in moments of crisis.

Lillian Gish had moved over to a little burner

that was apparently kept in this hut for just such emergencies.

"And I'm making tea," she said. "This has been quite a day. That awful old Miss Withering—I feel terribly responsible. I quite mistook her for harmless, and look what came of that!"

"Perhaps you should also have a butterscotch, Miss Gish," said Darleen. "Hand over another, won't you, Vee?"

"Very kind, thank you," said Lillian Gish, accepting the offered candy. "But I've been wondering, girls. What does 'Vee' stand for?"

There was a moment of silence.

Then Victorine sighed. Every time we speak, we are making a choice, aren't we? We decide what the proper version of the truth is in this time and this place. And in a simpler universe, those versions would all be one and the same . . .

"Victo—" she started.

But Darleen interrupted: "VICTORIOUS! Vee is for Victorious! At least today."

"I'd say," said Lillian. "Have some more tea."

## Chapter 37

# Other Stories

*Touch their emotions, but leave them cleared*
*like the keen air after a refreshing rain.*
—How to Write for the "Movies"

As they walked away from the little office building, away from Old Babylon, Victorine looked back over her shoulder at the splendors of those walls—and stopped short in her tracks.

Quite far away, at the foot of those massive walls, a tall man dressed in full Babylonian soldier garb was having an earnest conversation with a young woman in neat and modern clothing—a familiar figure, now handing over to that Babylonian soldier a familiar book-shaped package.

"What is it, Vee?" said Darleen, and Miss Lillian Gish, who was a step or two ahead, turned around also.

"Why, that's Miss Waller!" said Victorine. "And

she's passing along that book her brother gave us—the one he thought would make an excellent photoplay. So that must be the man she said was interested in making moving pictures. He had a fine name—Mr. Noble Johnson! That's the name she mentioned."

"This is someone you know?" said Lillian Gish.

"Oh, dear, not at all! The man in the Babylonian costume, I mean. And I don't really know Miss Waller, either. I just ran into her at Universal while Darleen was making her lighthouse picture—I'm just so glad that book is being passed along. Maybe something will come of it someday!"

Lillian Gish looked amused.

"So you don't really know either of the people you are staring at, but you do know the *book*? Do you want to run back and give a warm greeting to that book you used to know?"

"No, no," said Victorine. "It looks like that would be bothering them, doesn't it?"

Not to mention that the book seemed now to be in perfectly good hands!

It was only quite late that night, after the girls had gone over the events of that day another few times together and were just about to lay their heads down on their pillows and trade in the real world for the peace of sleep, that Victorine was able to put her thoughts into some kind of words.

"It was such a reminder to me today, seeing Miss Waller and that book—"

"Oh?" said Darleen. "A reminder of what?"

"Of how many different stories there are out there, needing to be told. My own story is one—the real story, I mean, not the made-up version they've turned into that silly serial. Yours is another, of course. But just think how many other ones there are! And most of them not ours at all—but they may be so, so important to someone else! They may be truth itself for some other person. Anyway, that's what I was thinking: how we got a glimpse of that other story in the making, and I'm glad of it. Simply glad. That's all!"

"I'm glad you're glad," said Darleen. "But *I'm* mostly glad because Uncle Dan will be here tomorrow finally, huzzah!"

A telegram with that good news had come that very afternoon!

They were silent together for a few happy moments, and then Darleen clapped her hands in the dark.

"Oh, Vee! Too bad you already sent in your entry for that *Vanishing of Victorine*! It would have been so much more exciting with Miss Withering and her pistol!"

Victorine couldn't help laughing.

"No one would believe it," said Victorine.

"Oh, well," said Darleen. "At least *we'll* always know it's true."

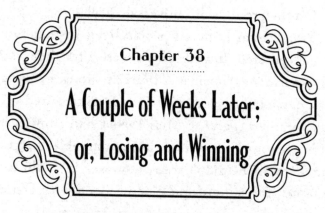

# Chapter 38

# A Couple of Weeks Later; or, Losing and Winning

*Once recognized, your path is much less thorny,*
*your way is clearer, and the chance to dispose of your other*
*photoplays looms in sight like a happy star of hope.*
—How to Write for the "Movies"

Letter for you, Bella Mae!" said Uncle Dan. And then he flipped through the little heap of mail and laughed. "And *another* letter for you. Oh, and a third! Not bad!"

Uncle Dan had finally arrived in Hollywood, after his unpleasant and extended delay in Ogden, Utah.

And then he got right to work, making up for lost time, as he said himself, echoing not only Victorine's Grandmama, but also Aunt Shirley, and really every determined and practical-minded person since that phrase was invented. He had, for instance, a long and productive consultation with Miss Lois Weber, and a few days later the visitors from Fort Lee found themselves all set up in their own little cottage—guess where?

On the grounds of Universal City!

Yes, several hundred people lived in that funny, movie-centered "town": there were little houses for those permanent residents lined up along a couple of very new streets, and with Dan Darling hired on as a cameraman (because Miss Weber had admired the skills that had gone into his remarkable anaglyph film, even if she didn't think now was the right time, quite yet, for stereoscopic cinema), and with Darleen Darling acting in one photoplay after another, and with Mr. Bill Darling, Darleen's father, probably going to join the laboratory crew here at Universal, the Darlings had been invited to inhabit not just one but *two* of those Universal City cottages.

That was going to save the Darlings quite a bit of money, and so Aunt Shirley had, from afar, approved the plan.

"At least while we're getting settled," she had said in a letter, "and until we find ourselves something more suitable. I'll be glad to get our Bill (who is much improved, thank heavens) to sunnier climes before winter sets in."

Darleen hadn't stopped smiling since that letter had arrived. Her Papa was much improved! Her Papa was coming! Her Papa was, in fact, practically on his way!

It was so nice to be reminded that she was actually somebody's child, and not always having to be responsible for everything all of the time.

Victorine, meanwhile, was also very glad for several reasons, and some of them were the same as Darleen's—and at least one was quite different:

Universal City had a *school*. And there students could learn, even while they were filming photoplays or doing whatever else needed to be done in a movie town.

It would be wonderful to start learning bookish things again. (Darleen was not sure she agreed. "But we will help each other when things get hard," said Victorine. "Ha ha!" said Darleen. "Nothing having to do with *school* will ever be difficult for you, Vee." "Oh, I hope it is!" said Victorine with all her heart. "Think how much more we'll be learning, if it's *difficult!*")

The first letter was from Miss Lois Weber, inviting Miss Bella Mae Goodwin to visit in her office a few days from now.

"I wonder what that's about," said Darleen.

"I suppose I'll find out soon enough," said Victorine, and then her face fell, because she had opened the second letter.

"Oh, well," she said.

"Oh, well, what?" said Darleen. "What is that? Let me see—oh!"

A brief but official letter, thanking "Miss Goodwin" for her entry in the official *Vanishing of Victorine* scenario contest: "Although your effort was not, in the end, our winner, the judges did feel it merited inclusion in the finalists' pool of ten."

"I'm only a *runner-up* in a contest about describing my own life!" said Victorine, and then she and Darleen caught each other's eye and laughed a little. Runner-up in your own life! What could you do, really, but laugh?

"Seven hundred and fifty dollars would have been nice, wouldn't it? But, anyway, silver linings!" said Darleen. "Because writing that thing certainly taught you how to use the typewriter, didn't it? Very useful skill. And how to tell stories. And at least no one's won that *other* contest, the one about figuring out where you actually are now. And that's probably the most important point of all, if you think about it. Now, quick, quick, open the last one. Where's it from? Oh!"

The last letter had come all the way from San Francisco!

It said:

> *Dear Miss Goodwin,*
> *As a sign of our gratitude for the part you played in the recent recuperation of precious Babylonian artifacts purloined from our exhibit—*

("Great goodness gracious," said Darleen. "Whoever wrote this was using the BIG dictionary, for sure! Sorry, keep reading—")

> *—we would like to offer you and two members of your family household a special visit to the*

*Panama-Pacific International Exposition, which is*
*now in its final weeks. We will provide train fare*
*from Los Angeles, lodging in San Francisco, and*
*three days' worth of admission at the Fair, including a*
*brief ceremony with the curators and administrators*
*of the Exposition, by way of expressing our gratitude*
*for your quick thinking and brave actions, and of*
*course souvenir Novagems for you and your guests.*
*Please respond to [such-and-such address] by [such-*
*and-such date]. We hope to meet you at the Fair!*

But by this point Darleen was drowning out the
words of the letter with her cheers and her jumping
and her clapping of hands!

"The fair!" she said. "San Francisco! The exposition! My dreamiest dream! Oh, Vee, you will let me be
part of your 'family household,' won't you?"

"Don't be silly!" said Victorine. "You are my truest
family—of course, you are coming to San Francisco! It
will be an adventure!"

Not quite as much of an adventure, perhaps, as
they had just had on the train, and in Ogden, Utah,
and here in Los Angeles and Hollywood—but still an
adventure.

"I hear there is a gigantic Underwood typewriter
on display there," said Victorine happily. "That will
be fun to see."

"And the electrical light beams at night! And

the Tower of Jewels! And EVERYTHING!" said Darleen. "You can be excited about the typewriter, Vee—I love that you are the sort of person who can be excited about typewriters—and I will be excited about EVERYTHING ELSE!"

And there was a fourth letter too. This one Victorine did not tell anyone about for some time, not even Darleen.

But one afternoon while Darleen was busy, Victorine took out the large envelope from her Grandmama, broke the seal, and carefully read through all the papers it contained.

Then she sat for quite a while with her head in her hands, thinking very hard, and filled with love for her Grandmama, and respect (deep, deep respect) for her Grandmama's fearless relationship with the truth.

Because there was a great deal of truth tucked into that envelope, and much of that truth was very hard.

"My darling Victorine," her Grandmama had written in that letter, "You are older now, and I hope you have been well cared for and happy! Now it is time for me to tell what I have learned over the past few years, and what bitter knowledge I must now pass on to you, for you to do with as you see best. My dear, I trust you absolutely! Whatever you decide to do, I know you will have chosen to do it because you feel in your heart it is what's right . . ."

All the papers in that envelope were about the Berryman fortune, that famous "railroad empire," and how it had been acquired. Victorine's Grandmama had begun, very late in her life, to wonder about such things, and once she started digging, she found ugly surprises everywhere. Perhaps this is true of every great fortune! How can so much money come into the hands of one family and not be trailing ugly stories, unfair trades, ruthlessness, and sorrow in its wake?

Her Grandmama had tried to rectify some of those crimes and omissions, she said in her letter, but she had begun looking into these things when she was already quite elderly, and no single person (she felt) could possibly live long enough to mend all the harm that the Berryman family seemed apparently to have caused in its transformation into a railroad empire.

Oh, this was a blow! This was many blows, all at once!

But Victorine read through all of it quietly and carefully, and not at all like someone who has just had a fancy brick castle tower tumble down on her head.

She realized she must have suspected, deep down, something like this. The past year and a half—of defending herself against those impostor relatives, of finding her way in an entirely different world (the world of photoplays), and of making a friend so dear she was almost a sister (Darleen!)—had all been a way of preparing herself to hear this news calmly, to think it over steadily, and to look up at the end of that hour with eyes and heart full to the brim with determination.

She would let it go, the Berryman name and the Berryman money. She would let it all go! Her Grandmama's will, as she knew very well, specified that if something happened to Victorine—or if she were somehow to vanish and stay vanished—then on her twenty-first birthday, the entire fortune would be turned over to the New York Public Library.

*I will let it go!* thought Victorine now. *I will let it go, and at least then thousands of children will have* books, *wonderful books, filled with all kinds of stories!*

And she would write stories herself, perhaps, too: the kind of stories that tell some part of the truth, and perhaps even tell it well enough to change some small corners of the world.

How she wished her Grandmama were alive and in that room with her right now, to put her arms around Victorine and murmur to her all of her love and faith and trust.

But the letters were that murmur, weren't they?

And perhaps Victorine's life (oh, she hoped!) would be a worthy answer to her Grandmama's murmured hope. Anyway, she would try!

"I promise to always try to keep trying, Grandmama dear," she whispered, and the pages of the letter rustled a little in her hands, as if they were trying to whisper back:

*I know you will, I know you will, my darling Victorine!*

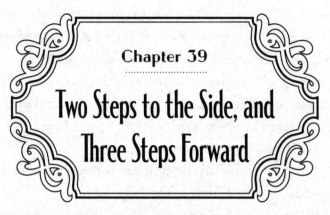

# Chapter 39

## Two Steps to the Side, and Three Steps Forward

*If I have been of any assistance to you in preparing your photoplay,*
*I shall feel amply repaid for the time and effort I have expended in*
*writing this text book for the ambitious playwright. Go to work, study*
*hard, and may good luck and success attend your efforts.*
—How to Write for the "Movies"

Later that week, Miss Lois Weber (she was not at home, so here she was not "Mrs. Smalley") smiled at Victorine over her desk in her formal office in the Universal administrative building.

"I did read your little screenplay, Miss Goodwin," she said. "Thank you for sharing it with me! I thought it was a remarkable effort for someone learning the trade. Really!"

"Thank you," said Victorine. She couldn't tell from either Miss Weber's words or her tone whether she was being praised or let down gently, so she kept her "thank you" as neutral and hopeful as possible.

"I have a question for you, you know," said Miss

Weber. "You said, when we first met, that you were worried you might not have much of an imagination. And yet this screenplay of yours, this ending for *The Vanishing of Victorine*, is as imaginative as can be. How did you manage it, dear Miss Goodwin, without an imagination of your own?"

Oh, her eyes were twinkling!

But Victorine had thought too seriously about this question to turn it into a joke.

"I figured out a process, Miss Weber," she said. "That's what I did. I found that if I took reality, you know, and then simply moved it, so to speak, two steps to the side and three steps forward, then it would seem very much like imagination had done the job, even though really it was, it was—"

"It was your remarkable brain," said Miss Weber, interrupting. "And so, my dear, it's pretty clear that you have as much imagination as anyone else around: you just know how to analyze its little cogs and gears and how they work, while the rest of us run around in the dark."

Oh! Victorine sat for a moment, quite thunderstruck. Here she had thought she was simply *pretending* to be creative, that all of this forging of "imagination" was just another way she was not being her authentic self (whoever that was), and now Miss Weber was suggesting that "pretending" and "being" might sometimes be overlapping conditions.

"In fact," said Miss Weber, "I would like to offer you and your remarkable brain a job. Would you be interested in joining our group of scenario and screenplay writers? As a sort of apprentice, I mean, of course, given your tender years."

"You want *me*? To be an apprentice? An apprentice photoplaywright?"

"You will be learning as you go, Miss Goodwin," said Miss Weber. "But this is a good moment, I think, for a young woman with an excellent mind and good writing and typewriting skills to get ahead in this business of ours."

"Oh, yes!" said Victorine, and then remembered: "But school!"

Miss Weber smiled.

"School, too, of course," she said. "School, above all! Your brain deserves all the fuel we can possibly provide. But when your schoolwork allows, come practice your scenario skills with the Universal writers."

Victorine found herself smiling so much that it was almost actually difficult to move the parts of her face and mouth that were necessary for speaking. But finally, she did manage.

"Thank you so much, Miss Weber," she said. "This is wonderful. This is so wonderful. And, oh! SUCH a responsibility!"

"Yes?" said Lois Weber.

"Because it turns out to be true, Miss Weber: motion pictures can change the world!"

That was what she had learned over the past few weeks:

stories change people,

and people change the world.

And sometimes those changes are wonderful and sometimes the opposite of wonderful, and it is up to us all to wield thoughtfully the words we choose: their magic, their power, their truth.

Walking through Universal City after her visit with Miss Lois Weber, through all the hubbub and bustle of movies being made, Victorine felt like someone floating in a cloud—a cloud made up of all the happy, serious, thoughtful thoughts filling her brain at that moment.

"Hello there, Vee!" called Darleen, waving down the road from the porch of their little cottage. The sun was shining—the air had the faintest hint of oranges in it.

"I'm coming home, Dar!" said Victorine, spreading her arms wide in joy.

"I guess you are!" said Darleen.

"No, I mean, really," said Victorine. "I've decided I'm ready to be my own self, with my own first name."

"Oh, Vee!" said Darleen. "Wonderful! But what about the Berryman part?"

"I'm leaving it behind," said Victorine. "Thoroughly and forever behind!"

Darleen came jumping off the porch to put her arms around her friend and almost-sister.

"Then how about you become one of us, another Darling?" she said. "You know my Papa would be so happy. We all love you, Vee, we really do!"

"Well, maybe I will," said Victorine. It was such a warm and tender thought—it was a thought that reminded her of the sweet smell of orange blossom.

And with it came another thought, powerful and true:

*I am myself,* thought Victorine.

At that moment she really, truly was.

Sometimes it is hard to know who we are, and sometimes, *sometimes,* clear as can be, *V is* (simply) *for Victorine!*

THE END

# Author's Note

Any movie set will be filled with a mixture of real things and make-believe: real people in fancy costume disguises, real chairs or tables or telephones in front of not-very-real walls or windows. Well, this book is like that too. My fictional characters travel to the Hollywood of 1915, where they have adventures that bring them into contact with some of the many real actors and filmmakers who were part of Hollywood's earliest history. Since it's always important to try to sort out what is true and what is made up in historical novels, let me start that sorting process here.

Lois Weber, for instance, was very much a real person. For some years in the 1910s, Lois Weber was the highest paid director at Universal, making films that tackled difficult issues with a great deal of technical flair. She was a person of many skills and talents, not only directing, but acting and writing scenarios too. She was even briefly mayor of Universal City, the film town! Lois Weber encouraged other women to consider careers in the movie industry, and during the years before 1920, women could be found holding many influential positions in and around Hollywood as actors, writers, journalists, and directors. These promising signs of progress faded away, unfortunately, in the years following the end of the First World War, when women were expected to return to more traditional domestic roles and when the major Hollywood studios consolidated creative power in the hands of a relatively few men.

When Darleen and Victorine visit Miss Weber in her bungalow on Santa Bonita, it is still 1915, however, and Miss Weber's encouragement of their dreams of having practical and independent careers in the cinema is very much in the spirit of those hopeful times. I recommend taking a look at Weber's short film *Suspense* (1913), which uses interesting camera angles and split-screen techniques to tell a scary story about a woman (played by Lois Weber herself) fighting off a burglar.

The Gishes—Lillian, Dorothy, and their mother— were also real people. You can see the sisters acting together in the early D. W. Griffith film *An Unseen Enemy* (1912), in which two girls (played by Lillian and Dorothy) defend themselves against burglars. (Notice a trend? The public loved scary burglar stories!) The Gishes had real-life experience with burglars, by the way, and I borrowed from the newspapers the story of Mrs. Gish frightening off an intruder by firing a pistol.

The director D. W. Griffith was at the height of his fame in 1915. Earlier in the year he had enormous box office success with his epic and disturbing *Birth of a Nation*, which depicted the rise of the Ku Klux Klan as something heroic and inspired a renewed surge of racism in the United States. In the fall of 1915 Griffith was filming scenes of the fall of Babylon for his next picture, *Intolerance*, which would come out the following year.

One of the Babylonian soldiers in Griffith's *Intolerance* was a man named Noble Johnson, whom we glimpse briefly in our story, and who had a really interesting and multifaceted career in the cinema. In the months after acting in *Intolerance*, Noble Johnson would form his own movie studio, the Lincoln Motion Picture Company, with the goal of making films that took African American actors and stories seriously, and he led that studio—first in Nebraska and then in Los Angeles—until 1920, after which he returned to acting.

In 1918 Noble Johnson's brother met with Oscar Micheaux, author of *The Conquest: The Story of a Negro*

*Pioneer* and *The Homesteader*, to try to talk the writer into letting the Lincoln Motion Picture Company make a film based on one of Micheaux's novels. Oscar Micheaux, who had worked as a Pullman porter and had farmed a homestead in South Dakota, was very interested indeed in the movie business— so much so that he ended up deciding to make films himself. His 1920 *Within Our Gates* was a powerful response to the racism of Griffith's *Birth of a Nation*. Oscar Micheaux would end up making more than forty films, although only a handful survived, and he worked into the sound era.

Two of my story's characters, Miss Ruth Waller and her brother, are fictional but inspired by two siblings who have left tantalizing traces of themselves in early film history. The historical Rudy and Fredy Walker (I changed the names in my book to mark the greater distance here between fiction and history) were children who became famous for their Cakewalk Dance in the early years of the twentieth century. They performed all over Europe, and in 1903 they appeared in a film made by Louis Lumière, *Le Cake-Walk au Nouveau Cirque*. But then a few years later the Walkers fade from the historical record. There are always so many stories left to be rediscovered and told!

And how about the machines and technological advances that pop up in *V Is for Victorine*: Underwood typewriters, Brownie cameras, pay telephones, and anaglyph film? All are drawn from real life. Although 1915 was a long time ago, people enjoyed their technological tools and toys just as we do today. And like us, the people of 1915 had to wrestle with big questions about the role of art in the world. If a story or a film can change even a corner of the world, then what responsibility do we artists have? That's really a question for all of us, no matter what century we happen to inhabit.